ROTHAKER

JENIFER RUFF

Chapter One

Brooke's new room for the next nine months resembled a big, ugly box. Four beige-colored walls with a bumpy texture attested to their cheap construction. A cracked sink separated wood veneer closets. Two phone jacks were destined to remain empty throughout each of the hundred dormitory rooms. At least the mattress was new. She left the thick plastic wrapping around it to deter bed bugs and dust mites.

It looked nothing like Brooke's charming room with the polished wood railings at Everett, the college she had recently attended as an undergraduate. Rothaker University was every ounce as prestigious, but its medical school dorm was the odd man out on campus and set away from the rest of the graduate schools. The five-story building sat alongside a highway ramp, adjacent to the Rothaker teaching hospital. Much of the medical school education took place in the hospital, whose ER saw three times more gunshot victims than any other teaching hospital. In part this was due to the dangerous communities that surrounded it, akin to Gotham city, making it an incredibly exciting place for an ER rotation, but a dangerous place to live near.

Brooke opened the screenless window to air out the room. It faced the backside of the dorm, an unattractive conglomeration of cinder block and dirty pavement, and provided a view of the hospital's multi-level parking garage. Directly below her window sat an enormous dumpster spotted with rust and overflowing with various-sized trash bags and random unpackaged rubbish. She could literally open her window and drop her trash down if she didn't want to carry it to the garbage chute in the hall.

That's actually pretty convenient.

As she was watching, a blue door opened near the dumpster and a large man wearing a stained white apron threw something over a metal railing and through the air. It landed and wobbled slightly, balancing precariously atop mounds of trash. Shifting her gaze higher afforded a more pleasing view of blue sky and, in the distance, the tops of several impressive structures on the Rothaker undergraduate campus. She turned away from the window, excited to get unpacked and established.

After placing her belongings in her desk, closet, and drawers, she changed into running clothes and headed outside towards the campus areas she had glimpsed beyond the parking structure. She ran at a comfortable pace for seventy minutes, covering about eight and a half miles of new territory. She returned to her dorm through the back entrance. It was temporarily blocked by a noisy garbage truck with a hydraulic arm that raised the dumpster up in the air and then unceremoniously tipped it over, spilling its contents into the back of the truck with a series of mechanical screeches and warning beeps. The light-weight backing from a sanitary napkin floated by her face as the dumpster remained suspended upside down. It fluttered to the ground to join other papers and trash that had become wet and faded over time and were now stuck to the pavement.

Where would the contents of the truck go next? A landfill? Deep into the ocean on one of those barges the length of four city blocks? Having considered it, she felt compelled to do the research, so she could be a more responsible citizen. Anyone who believed their trash magically disappeared once it was out of their house was both mistaken and arrogant. The managing of thousands of tons of trash suddenly became a curious mystery.

Brooke took her first shower in the coed bathroom on her hallway. The curtains didn't spread adequately from wall to wall, but she wasn't shy. She dressed, re-adjusted her pony-tail, and left her room at five twenty-five for dinner in the dorm's cafeteria. She would be eating three meals a day there from now until the end of May.

A neat young man exited the room two down from hers at the same time. He smiled. "Are you going down to dinner?"

"Yes. Are you?"

"I can't wait to see what we're going to be subjected to for the next year. I hope it's decent."

"I'm Brooke.

"And I'm Jeff. Just let me say that if you have loud sex in your room, I'm going to know you better than I'd like to." Jeff tossed his head to the side and laughed as he stuck out his hand to shake hers.

"That's an interesting way to make an introduction, and I don't think you'll need to worry about that." There was something unusual about Jeff, and Brooke liked him immediately.

"Sooo, Brooke . . . where are you from?" He walked alongside her, adjusting the collar of his shirt.

"Connecticut. And you?"

"Southern California, but I went to college at NYU, so I've already experienced four winters. Where did you do your undergrad?"

These questions were a dog's equivalent to territorial butt sniffing and would be repeated ad nauseam over the next few days until most everyone had judged everyone else's academic pedigree.

"Everett." It still filled Brooke with pride to say it and she was grateful to anyone who asked, although it was just one of many essential steps paving the pathway to her ultimate goal.

"Ohhh. Everett. Did you know Jessica Carroll? The girl who disappeared?"

Jessica's story had made national headlines not once, but twice—when she disappeared and when her body was found. It was currently one of the first things that came to mind when people thought of Everett.

"Yes, in fact, I did know her. She dated a guy who was best friends with one of my good friends."

"What do most people at Everett think happened to her?" Jeff tapped the button for the elevator.

"No one knows." *Except me.* "They have no idea. I guess it's destined to forever remain a mystery."

"Wow. I remember following the stories about her. Sounded like she was a mess."

"I suppose she was."

"Still . . . what a tragedy." The elevator doors opened, and Jeff gestured for Brooke to step out first.

The bare-bones cafeteria resembled a prison. The ones Brooke had seen on TV. She and Jeff grabbed orange trays and plastic yellow-grey plates that they pushed along a metal railing, selecting from pieces of fried chicken, burritos, and rice. Brooke skipped the cooked food and made her way to the salad bar, creating a gigantic salad with every available option except the jalapenos. She and Jeff sat on hard metal seats attached to a long metal table. Again, quite different from Everett, where every dorm had mahogany tables and its own unique china pattern. They joined two other first-years, Peter and Sundeep.

Sundeep and Peter chatted like old friends, although they had only met that afternoon. Their fathers graduated from Rothaker Medical School together, thirty years ago.

Julie, a pretty Asian girl with a chic blunt hairstyle, scanned the cafeteria for a place to sit. She spotted Brooke and Jeff, whose rooms were on either side of hers.

"May I join you?" She made minimal eye contact as she sat down.

The five students exchanged superficial background information, played the name game whenever someone went to a college where someone else had a friend ("Oh…did you know Martin Fulman by any chance? He went to my high school."), shared their initial feelings about the dorm ("so much worse than expected!"), and their first day of medical school tomorrow ("supposed to be harder than we can imagine"). Halfway through their meal, a petite young woman with her hair up in a bun sat down next to Brooke.

"Hi everyone. I'm Rachael. A first-year. Is everyone ready for tomorrow?"

Brooke nodded. "Absolutely."

"Well . . ." Rachael didn't continue speaking until everyone was looking at her. "I know exactly what they have in store for us. We're starting out in the lecture hall. We're supposed to spend the first fifteen minutes observing each other closely."

Brooke felt a surge of irritation as she listened to the confident know-it-all, but then Rachael leaned close to her plate. Brooke stifled a gasp and barely heard the rest of Rachael's words. A dark mole graced the back of Rachael's neck. It was difficult not to stare. Slightly raised and asymmetrical, a dysplastic nevus, which had a much greater chance of becoming a melanoma than a common mole. It screamed out to Brooke, tempting her to examine it more closely, and now that she was aware of its presence, she had to consciously resist the urge. She forced her attention back to the table, because she needed to try and make some normal social connections. She had promised herself to at least try. Her new classmates had more in common with her than most everyone she had ever met. They were passionate about medicine, motivated, chose Rothaker for medical school and most importantly, Rothaker chose them, which made them exceptional. Some of them wanted to be surgeons, just like her. Maybe not for the same reasons, but at least they were all in the same ball park even if they weren't exactly playing the same game.

***

When dinner was over, Brooke returned to her room alone, rolled out her yoga mat, and did some poses while she read the first chapter of her immunology and cell biology books.

Later that night, she lay in bed feeling wired, shifting her gaze between the pockmarked ceiling and the time listed on her phone. She was desperate to fall asleep, it was imperative to feel rested for the next day, but sleep eluded her. She went through several rounds of alternate nostril breathing, in through the left and out through the right, in through the right and out through the left. There was no place she would rather be than Rothaker. It was the top ranked medical school in the country, and she was so excited. But she also felt lost, like a fish out of water, because she didn't have a structured routine established yet, although she would soon. Her first demanding day of medical school was tomorrow. After that she would find a job teaching exercise classes somewhere. Every moment of her day would be full and busy, and then she would be okay. Very soon.

After finally drifting off to sleep, she was rudely awoken by an ambulance, sirens blaring, as it accelerated directly behind her dorm up the highway on ramp. As her hard found sleep was repeatedly interrupted, she formed an impression of just how many emergencies a big city hospital, particularly one in a dangerous city, received once the sun went down. And if it wasn't the sounds of an ambulance departing, every other driver seemed hell bent on flooring their gas pedal as they passed outside her window with their terrible music blasting out into the night. Nothing in the medical school brochures mentioned the proximity to the highway; the dorm was practically on top of the on-ramp. How would she ever get an adequate night's rest this year? One night had yet to pass, and she already had a huge issue to worry about.

Unable to sleep, Brooke used the time to contemplate the coming year. She made two promises to herself. One—try her best to be more flexible in all things, particularly with being open to social situations. And two—avoid any situations that might lead her into a dilemma with limited choices and force her to take compromising risks. *Yes, I'm smarter and more capable than everyone else, but I will not press my luck. Not this time.* She had come this far with all her dreams intact despite the people in her past who had threatened to ruin everything for her. They had learned their lessons the hard way. She promised herself things would be different this time, at this school, but the more she gained, and the closer she came to achieving her ultimate goals, the more she had to lose.

Chapter Two

Brooke was always early. She was highly organized and excelled at managing her time. It was almost impossible for her to be late to anything, even feeling as tired as she did. There was a bounce in her step as she entered the medical school building, its entrance a giant stone tower reminiscent of medieval times.

Inside, she quickly scanned the large lecture hall, the place where her mind would be pumped with the information necessary to become a physician, en route to becoming a cardiothoracic surgeon. Many of the seats were occupied, most likely by students who didn't know how long it would take to get to class and erred on the side of allowing too much time this first day. Brooke selected a chair front and center and sat down, back straight, abdominal muscles tight, and head held high—her normal posture.

She watched each person enter and take a cursory view of the group with whom they would be interacting for the next four years of their lives. Jeff appeared, dressed as if he was in-the-know on NYC fashion. She caught his eye and he waved, taking the seat next to her. Connor Reed and Xander Cross, who also lived on Brooke's floor, arrived together as the room quickly filled. Connor was a body builder who should have stopped lifting weights when he was ahead, forty or so pounds of muscle ago. He plopped into a seat while simultaneously drinking from a plastic half-liter container of milk as if it was a normal thing to do. Next to him, Xander was a perfect male specimen if there ever was one, solid, lean, clean cut, dressed in jeans and a dark plaid shirt. It seemed natural that Connor and Xander had developed a camaraderie, since the two of them virtually exuded testosterone. Jeff tapped Brooke's arm, shot his gaze over to Xander, and mouthed, "wow." Brooke didn't know what he meant but finding out would have to wait. A man in a suit and bowtie approached the podium and cleared his throat.

"Hello. I'm Dr. Ernest Sinclair, Dean of Rothaker Medical School." He coughed once and adjusted the microphone. "Welcome to the first day of your medical education. Look around at your fellow classmates. Take a good look at one another."

Everyone took a quick and polite look around. Dr. Sinclair waited silently, forcing them to look around again. First with shy glances but growing bolder when it became clear that the dean meant what he said, and he wasn't continuing until he was satisfied. Brooke and Jeff exchanged genuine smiles, after one day he was currently the person she knew and liked the best here.

Brooke stood out like a Ferrari amongst Volvos and Volkswagens. She was very attractive—long blonde hair, flawless skin, and a slim, toned body. Years of exercise, eating well, and good genetics were responsible. One of the few females in the room who wore no make-up, except for lip gloss to prevent chapped lips. She studied her medical school classmates with a critical eye, anxious to put aside these touchy-feely ice breaking activities and get on with the real learning. But at the same time, she was interested in checking out the students sitting around her. The competition. That's how she viewed everyone. All of them wanted to be physicians; many of them also wanted to be surgeons, and some of them might also have targeted one of the few cardiothoracic surgeon fellowship spots for their future. Was it possible there was someone here who was smarter than she? Someone who might be a more impressive first-year medical student? If so, Brooke had to differentiate herself from them by working even harder and standing out for her achievements. That was all it would take. She hoped.

It was impossible to tell much by simply looking at someone. Julie struggled to make eye contact, she appeared too shy and reserved to ever deliver a medical diagnosis. Connor, the bodybuilder, brought to mind a dumb jock, but it was impossible for him to sit amongst them if that were true. And perhaps someone thought that Brooke didn't belong there because of her outward appearance. Brooke was uniquely different, but not because of anything others could see. *How many of my fellow students have already killed three people?* Eventually they would all have death on their hands because of a mistake, a misdiagnosis perhaps. One slip of the hand during surgery could be the end of a completely innocent life. It was inevitable. If not, then why were physicians required to pay exorbitant insurance malpractice policy fees to treat patients? Did pathologists have to pay the same level of malpractice fees since their patients were already dead? Now she was curious and would have to find out.

As Dr. Sinclair wrapped up his "looking around" exercise, fulfilling Rachael's prediction, Brooke concluded that she was ahead of her classmates in attributable deaths. She harbored no guilt whatsoever as far as her past was concerned. She whole-heartedly believed everything she did was completely justifiable and necessary. And it had all worked out, hadn't it?

"First, let me congratulate you." Dr. Sinclair grasped the sides of the podium, reminding Brooke of her recent commencement speech where she sat on the stage as the valedictorian. "Four thousand and eighty-three people applied for the one hundred seats you occupy today."

I know. I've done my research.

"We have remarkable diversity. Seventeen percent of you are from outside the United States, coming from Bangladesh, India, China, Malaysia, Thailand, Ethiopia, Zimbabwe, Egypt, France, Russia, Canada, and the Ukraine. There are students from forty of the continental US states. Your accomplishments are truly humbling, and too many to list. But just to skim the surface, we have among us a former professional baseball player, winner of a national poetry contest, a cellist who plays at Carnegie Hall, several entrepreneurs, a veteran, and a world ranked Irish dancer. Many of you already hold advanced degrees, JDs, PhDs, MBAs, and master's in engineering. Your ages range from twenty to forty-two."

Brooke looked around again. *Who is twenty?*

Dr. Sinclair scanned his audience, his glasses resting halfway down his nose.

"Most of your class work will take place in the form of small group activities. At the end of four years you will know each other well, your strengths and weaknesses."

Oh great. I hate team work. Teamwork was inefficient and the only benefit she usually received was the reassurance that her intelligence and discipline were of a higher caliber than her peers, although she had done an adequate job of keeping her feelings on the matter hidden.

The dean held a finger in the air. "Hopefully you will form personal and professional relationships that will last a lifetime."

Brooke cringed at the thought of getting close to anyone, but then remembered her social connection pledge.

"Lastly, and this is important, and I know many of you will be grateful to hear this. If you are in the medical school dorm, as most of you are, let me assure you, you will get used to the noise. After a few nights of sporadic sleeping, you won't even notice it."

The room filled with laughter.

That better be true.

"I slept like a baby." Jeff whispered. "One of the benefits of spending the last four years in the heart of New York City. The city that never sleeps because it's too busy partying."

When they were dismissed, Brooke and Jeff walked together toward the gross anatomy lab.

"What was with your reaction when that tall guy came in?" Brooke asked Jeff.

"Because he's too good to be true. A nice Midwestern boy who played football in college, *and* he's going to be a doctor. Need I say more? You and he could be the Ken and Barbie of campus."

"The Ken and Barbie? What does that mean?"

"Let's just say that if he was hitting for the other team I would be the first one in line to bat, I can tell you that much."

"Oh, I see." Brooke smiled. "Were you the professional baseball player then?"

"Not a chance." Jeff raised his eyebrows. "I know I'm insanely fit, but there's not an athletic bone in my body. I was the last one picked for every team in elementary school. Thank God that's over. I'll have my revenge on the fourth-grade team captains one day in the future, when they come in for their prostate exams."

"Hah! I admire your confidence." Brooke could never expose her true self; many of her thoughts, ideas, and inspirations could not be shared. Some form of pretense would always be necessary, or she would be viewed as a complete social outcast, or worse. She had to be careful. Very careful.

Chapter Three

Five long tables were positioned around the room to greet the first-year gross anatomy students. On each table rested a cadaver, recently removed from refrigeration, covered with plastic and a white sheet. A handwritten tag poked out from under the covering, providing a scant bit of information. Between the tables, computers sat open to reference the anatomy textbooks. Students were assigned to the tables in groups of four and had received emails that morning listing the members in each group. One of their names had made Brooke groan with disappointment.

After changing into the required lab coat and shoe covers, Brooke found her table, tingling and a little breathless. In a matter of moments, she expected to see her cadaver for the first time. She had waited years to be a gross anatomy student—to learn via dissection and exploration that was finally, perfectly legitimate. She could poke, prod, dissect, and ask questions, all out in the open, with everyone watching, and it was all good. No one would try to stop her. No one would drag her off in handcuffs.

The first to arrive from her group, she licked her lips and surveyed the lab. She sighed when she noticed the security cameras in the upper corners of the room. They were an older type, the cameras in plain sight. Perhaps that was the point; the visibility of the cameras would deter anyone with half a brain from misbehaving. She had hoped to "borrow" some new dissecting tools, particularly a sharp new bone saw, but because of the cameras, that wasn't likely to happen now.

Anatomy class was a rite of passage for first-year medical students. Everyone arrived with nerves and excitement, confidence, and insecurities, wearing their new blue lab coats. Wired with anticipation,

Brooke could not have been readier. The groups were coming together, one by one fanning out around their tables. A young man named Rakesh introduced himself, followed by, unfortunately, Rachael Kline.

"I can't believe we are officially starting." Rachael's small frame swam inside her lab coat, giving her the appearance of a child playing dress up. "I went here as an undergraduate." She beamed at Rakesh. "I've been eyeing this building from afar for four years."

Show off. She's already informed everyone she graduated from Rothaker, and the only thing I'm eyeing is that mole on her neck.

Rakesh adjusted the collar of his lab coat. "Were undergrads able to take any classes here, at the medical school?"

Rachael shook her head. "No, it wasn't allowed. But I was fortunate enough to participate in three different medical internships at the hospital during the summers."

"What type of internships?"

"An internship at the HIV clinic, and I still work there, a summer internship in the Rothaker OBGYN department, not doing clinical work, just research, another joint project between the hospital and the medical school, a study measuring resource allocation for multiple admitting diagnoses. All of them were excellent."

Rachael's passion rivaled Brooke's, but Brooke did not feel she had met a kindred soul. Rachael had the opposite effect on her, as if the two of them were instant competitors.

Xander Cross entered last from their group.

"He looks like he should be an actor playing a doctor in a television show," murmured Rachael.

He had an easy, relaxed walk, intense brown eyes, and a presence that was difficult not to notice. He nodded at the other three group members, his eyes pausing for a split second longer on Brooke, whom Connor had designated as the "really hot blonde chick." Relaxing as they waited, he saw that the tag attached to their cadaver was only partially exposed. He reached forward for the edge of the sheet. "I'm just going to see what we've got here."

“Not yet,” Rachael snapped.

Xander stepped away from the table. Rachael smiled and dipped her chin.

In an instant, Brooke lifted the corner of the sheet and pulled the tag out.

Xander and Rakesh exchanged surprised glances. Rachael’s mouth hung open.

“Um . . . oh, my sister has those same earrings.” Xander pointed to Rachael’s ears, which had the effect of directing their attention away from the brief but odd action that just occurred. “She wears them all the time.”

“I do too.” Rachael was still eyeing Brooke with a frown as she spoke to Xander. “Every single day. They were a gift. They’re my favorites. It’s so nice that you noticed. Either you miss home or you’re a really sensitive guy.”

“Maybe both. I spent a few weeks with my family before I left for school. It had been awhile since we were all together. My sister came home to visit. She’s a nurse.”

“That’s sweet.” Rachael turned to face the front of the class. “Oh, this must be our professor.”

“Hello, first-year students. I’m Dr. Sarcough. I’ll be leading you through your gross anatomy dissections.” Dr. Sarcough had dark hair and thick dark glasses, both a remarkable contrast with his ghostly white skin.

Dr. Sarcough pressed a few buttons, and the gross anatomy curriculum instantly projected onto a large screen in front of the room. There was a lot of information to cover, and, in Brooke’s opinion, an inordinate amount of talking followed. Most of the information was already posted online. Hadn’t everyone read it prior to class? Brooke certainly had.

“In your History of Medicine class, you’ll be learning about the first use of cadavers for dissection and the former methods of cadaver procurement. It used to be far more difficult to obtain a human cadaver from which to learn. Medical professors had to be resourceful and creative, digging up freshly deceased bodies was just one of the criminal activities necessary to obtain cadavers so that they could teach their students. Fortunately, that all changed. Now it's just more expensive to learn. I won't subject you to later boredom by telling you something you're going to hear in another class, but there is one thing you need to know and be mindful of throughout the year." He waved his arm in a circular gesture. "These anonymous individuals donated their bodies for use in medical education. Your medical education. They did not receive financial compensation. Their bodies are gifts to be treated with the utmost respect and professionalism. They are your first patients. They are yours to study and learn from for the next two semesters, after which their remains will be cremated."

Then there were rules. Rules about the room. Rules about conduct. Rules about not working ahead of the assigned area. Dr. Sarcough ticked them off his list one by one as twenty-four students not yet accustomed to standing for long amounts of time shifted their weight from side to side.

"The doors and the windows to the room must remain closed at all times. This is for your own good; it allows the ventilation system to do its job and minimize our exposure to the preservation chemicals. No photographs. No videos. Nothing from your cadaver leaves this lab, which includes inorganic parts such as fillings, implants, pace-makers, you get the idea. No one other than the students enrolled in this course are to be in this room at any time. I won't tolerate any form of disrespectful behavior regarding the cadavers. Anyone who does not follow the rules will be dismissed from class."

"Don't joke about anything while we're studying our cadaver," Rachael whispered to her group. Rakesh and Xander nodded in agreement, but Brooke glared back at her. *Does Rachael truly perceive it necessary to convey that information? Who does she think she is? Does she believe the rest of us are children?*

Dr. Sarcough launched an overview of the dissection tools, the procedures for cadaver maintenance, and an explanation of the various buckets under the table, color coded to separate fluids, tissues, sharps, and trash. The cadavers lay still and silent, their shapes and forms barely discernible under the plastic and sheets, as if waiting patiently for their big moment of unveiling. Brooke felt like a child forced to sit in front of her presents at Christmas, unable to open them until she had read all the warranty information.

Dr. Sarcough cleared his throat and scratched his chin. "Okay, go ahead and lift the covers away."

Brooke lifted the sheet from one end while Rakesh took the corners of the opposite side. Rachael peeled down the plastic. They revealed a young Caucasian man with close-cut brown hair. The illusion of sleeping peacefully was destroyed by the greyish tinge of his skin and a half of a dark red Y-shaped incision mark stitched across his upper torso, as if a coroner had begun an autopsy and then changed his mind. The tag attached to his hand listed his age as thirty-three and his cause of death as cancer. The type of cancer was not specified. They would never know his name or where he came from, if he was a father or a brother, a banker, or an artist. He had selflessly made himself available for Brooke, Rakesh, Rachael, and Xander to study the systems that support life, and he would be getting nothing in return.

"Yes!" Brooke rose on to her toes and laughed. "We just struck the cadaver lottery. A young, lean guy who died of cancer. It doesn't get any better than that!"

Rachael watched Brooke and scowled. The look on her face might just as easily come from eating something that tasted terrible.

Brooke couldn't believe her luck. The probability of being assigned to an older individual with inches of waxy fat surrounding every organ and fiber was much higher. The fat layers had to be cut and scraped away in order to clearly identify structures. But she also didn't want to end up with a cadaver who had been healthy with insides that were normal until the moment he died instantly from say, a gunshot wound. That would not be half as interesting as one whose insides had been ravaged by the effects of both cancer and its treatments.

Rachael and Rakesh were watching Dr. Sarcough, still speaking from the front of the room. Unable to contain her satisfied smile, Brooke glanced at Xander to acknowledge their good fortune. His smooth and confident demeanor melted away. He seemed to recoil, but then leaned forward, one arm on the table as if to support himself, the other hand shooting up to cover his nose and mouth. His skin turned pale and beads of sweat sprouted across his face. He looked horribly ill.

You've got to be kidding me. If the sight of a cadaver makes him sick, he might as well pack up his bags and go back home right now.

But she kept her eyes on his pained expression. Her intuition suggested there was a more interesting explanation to the behavior she witnessed.

Chapter Four

Despite merit scholarships and financial aid, Brooke graduated from Everett College owing a huge amount of money. But attending Everett had been worth every penny she owed *and* everything that happened. It got her into Rothaker, her first-choice medical school program. It was all part of her master plan.

To pay for med school, she took out another whopping loan to cover her first year's expenses. After four years, her next task would be to complete a five-year general surgery residency, followed by a very competitive three-year cardiothoracic surgery fellowship, whose applicants had to be matched to a program. It sounded like a long journey when it was written out that way, but to Brooke, any other path was tantamount to failure. She wanted to be a surgeon more than anything else. She had known for many years without wavering in the slightest. There were no alternate paths.

A week had passed since Brooke last earned a paycheck. The daily exercise classes she taught all through college and in the summers covered necessities like her cell phone, school supplies, soap, shampoo, tampons, etc. It didn't make a dent in the actual costs to attend the school. The recent purchase of her books and school materials dropped her bank account to a new low. She needed to get a job fast so she could at least pay for a bottle of ibuprofen when she needed it. And, she missed the exhilarating high she got from teaching intense classes.

Only a mile and a half from her dorm was a gym and exercise studio called Performance Fit. A quick check of their website had shown a wide variety of class options were offered all day, seven days a week and she had the background to teach any one of them. She rode her bike there to apply for a teaching position, wearing cropped black workout pants and a tight-fitted yoga top, in case they wanted to see what she could do on the spot.

"Hi." Brooke flashed her winning smile to the young man working the check-in desk.

"Hi. Can I help you?" He glanced up for a quick second and had barely dropped his eyes again when his head jerked back up. He smiled.

"Yes. I'm Brooke. I'd like to talk to someone about teaching exercise classes here."

"Oh. Sure." He ran his hand through his hair. "You're in luck. Mike is in his office. He's the owner. Walk around the corner there and up the stairs. You'll see it, and he can help you out."

"Thanks. What's your name?"

"Oh. Sorry. I'm Nathan."

"Thanks for your help, Nathan. I hope to be working with you soon." Brooke could be exceptionally charming when she made a point of trying.

"Me too. Good luck." Then he muttered under his breath, "What a babe."

Brooke followed Nathan's directions around the corner, taking in the layout and equipment as she made her way to the office. It was a two-story facility. The décor was a little dated, the carpeting looked like it came out of the discothèque era, but the equipment was relatively new. The first floor had cardio machines on one side and weights on the other. The second floor had two exercise studios. The larger room had steps, stability balls, and hand-weights stacked across the back. The smaller room was for yoga and Pilates. Brooke stopped for a moment to watch a class in progress, before continuing to the office.

***

She poked her head in through the open doorway. "Hi. Are you Mike?"

"Yep, one second." Mike jotted down a few more figures while rubbing his temples and the top of his bald head. His busiest times were the first weeks of September, when Rothaker students returned to school, and then again in January when people who didn't like to exercise made their New Year's resolutions. Mike aimed to offer the widest variety of classes with excellent instructors to attract the Rothaker students, who had their own state of the art gym available on campus. He prided himself on keeping his gym a few steps above the Rothaker facilities, in the interest of his own livelihood. But he'd hired too many instructors and several of them were now bitching about not getting to teach enough classes.

He dropped his pen and looked up. One glance told him Brooke was not looking to get *in* shape. She was no exercise novice. Her fitted shirt hugged small but curvy hips and flat, defined abs. Probably a student. Clients like her were in it for the long haul and showed up regularly. "Can I help you? Are you looking to join the club?"

"Well, yes. I'd like to join your gym as an instructor. Do you need new instructors?"

"Uh . . . of course. I'm always looking for great talent. Tell me a little about yourself, your background and experience, what types of classes you teach." There was no denying that Brooke looked the part, but that didn't mean she was any good as a teacher.

"Sure." Brooke flashed a smile. "I just moved here this week. I'm starting my first year of medical school at Rothaker."

"Fantastic." In that one sentence she conveyed intelligence and responsibility. Everyone knew Rothaker students were smart and reliable. Her fitness would inspire people to attend her classes so that they could get a body like hers, even though most of her insane physique was probably due to genetics. Her face, her hair, her figure—all of it—guys would want to come to the gym to see her and be seen by her, which could lead to better membership maintenance. And the medical school part meant she could handle CPR and any minor health emergency that might occur during a class— an extra bonus.

Brooke stepped into his office. "I've been teaching for six years, generally five to ten classes a week. I have a resume with all of the places I've worked." She removed a one-page resume from her bag and handed it to Mike. "I've taught every type of class there is, but my favorite is a class I've developed over the past few years that mixes sculpt, Pilates, and yoga. It's intense, and it's very effective. There's almost no impact, so it appeals to all ages. It's a high calorie burner as well as a strength class."

Mike listened to Brooke while he scanned the resume. It detailed employment at a long list of fitness centers and described the revenue she had generated teaching classes of her own in rented facilities. She had also completed several summer internships at hospitals, both in research and direct patient care. A variety of other jobs made it look like the resume of a woman ten years older than her actual age. She kept busy. The education section of her resume stated that she had graduated from Everett College, summa cum laude. She had received highest honors on her senior thesis, Electrical Stimulation and Muscular Response.

"Wow! This is impressive! What certifications do you have?" He had to ask. His website and his recently printed marketing materials attested that all the instructors at Performance Fit held at least two certifications.

"I have several." Brooke smiled, and her eyes took in the room before she rattled off the names of three different organizations that certified fitness instructors. She frowned as Mike dropped his gaze and scribbled them down on her resume.

"Your resume is amazing. First thing, I'll have you teach a sample class. I'll get a few of our other instructors and maybe some of our regulars to take it. After that, if they think you're a good fit, we'll take care of the formalities, and get you rotated into the schedule."

"That sounds good. Thank you." She flipped her ponytail over her shoulder. "You have my number. I'm in school until three, so I can only teach in the late afternoons. Or any time on the weekend."

"We can work with that. If we hire you, and I hope we can, I'll need copies of your certificates to put in our files."

"Sure, no problem. I'll get them for you." She nodded. "Thank you so much for the opportunity."

***

Performance Fit had the newest stationary racing bikes, each equipped with the latest digital monitoring and a stand to hold her notebooks open.

After I finish teaching, I can ride those bikes for hours while I study.

Stopping to check out the women's locker room and finding stacks of fluffy white complimentary towels was the clincher.

This place is perfect and it's close to the medical school.

Thanks to a well-tuned knack for saying what people wanted to hear, she had nailed every interview she participated in for jobs, scholarships, and internships. But the certifications presented a small problem—she didn't have any and had no intention of acquiring any. The certifications cost money. She had taught hundreds of classes and couldn't imagine anyone possessed a greater understanding of anatomy and physiology and its application to fitness than she did.

They are going to hire me.

Chapter Five

Rachael Kline also maintained a packed schedule. A few days a week, between her last classes and dinner, she visited the outpatient clinics around the hospital. She made sure they were well stocked with informational pamphlets for Mercy Street, an out-reach program designed to help victims of domestic abuse, a program she helped build. She also wrote the pamphlets, which provided information on where and how to get help. She was adamant that the English and Spanish versions were always available and visible, in case someone who needed them came in for a clinic visit.

Rachael's volunteer work did not begin with the domestic abuse program. During her sophomore year of college, she started with an unpaid internship at an HIV clinic near the Rothaker teaching hospital. Rachael's main task had been to help write and produce their educational materials, but once a week she spent two hours at the free clinic with a physician assistant. The PA allowed her to observe patient visits, with their permission. Patients with the HIV virus and patients suffering from full blown AIDS presented with a wide variety of illnesses; it was a never-ending learning spree. HIV was no longer a life-threatening disease in the United States, if patients adhered to a strict regimen of medications, proper diet, and nutrition. But for some people it was more difficult to manage, particularly for those whose lives were unpredictable and filled with other challenges. During the first weeks of her internship, Rachael was surprised by the number of young women who had contracted HIV. Didn't everyone know how it was spread and therefore how to avoid contraction? She learned that protecting oneself was not that straightforward for everyone. Many of the women the clinic served were in abusive relationships with boyfriends and husbands who were HIV-positive addicts. The men didn't tell them or told them but refused to wear condoms anyway. The clinic could give away all the free condoms in the world, but they couldn't put a dent in contracting the disease if the free protection wasn't used. Many of the women she met didn't have the choice to protect themselves, not until they could break away from their boyfriend or husband, and by then it was usually too late. Poverty also created dependency that further limited their options.

Education alone was not enough to save the people most at risk in East Dalton, the residents of the impoverished and infamous Greenwood Circle housing projects near the clinic. She wanted to get to the root cause of their problems and help them before it was too late. With assistance from her mentor at the HIV clinic, she did an independent project during her junior year and started Mercy Street. It linked all the existing resources in the area and created new ones that helped women break free from the devastating cycle of physical and emotional abuse. Now the program had a full-time director who was paid with a grant from a Rothaker endowment and one from the city of East Dalton, thanks to Rachael's involvement.

Rachael still volunteered at the HIV clinic two hours a week. Her newest project was a mobile needle exchange program affiliated with the clinic. She had been involved for a month, but she still harbored mixed feelings about the endeavor.

In the evenings, when she was available, Rachael joined two salaried staffers and drove around the city in an older model, painted and refurbished ambulance with an office area inside. They traveled a route through East Dalton, particularly in the areas where drug users congregated, particularly the Greenwood Circle area, marked by neglected project housing, boarded up windows, unattended fire damage, and publicly discarded garbage. The mobile unit offered free clean hypodermic needles in exchange for used ones. This reduced the number of discarded syringes lying in the streets where children might come across them, and reduced the spread of HIV, as well as Hepatitis B and

C. Their clients were provided condoms, educational materials, and information and referrals for substance abuse treatment programs, support groups, and HIV testing.

Last weekend she had spent an hour in the needle exchange vehicle, emphasizing the outreach programs that were available. When they set out, an impending storm had further darkened an ominous gray sky, which was good. Those who needed their services were more likely to come forward in the dark. They stopped near a small run-down park with a ruined playground. Graffiti covered the broken slides and see-saws; it was a place no one would ever want their children to play.

Before they could help anyone, a man with wild gray hair and a fisherman's wizened skin approached their vehicle as if he had been waiting. He began yelling, passionately, while still yards away from them.

"What kind of message does this send!" His voice cracked, but his words were clear. "You're saying—do all the drugs you want, and here are free needles to help you! It's illegal and you're condoning it! Whatever money you're using should be spent on providing food and shelter for those in need! Pay for their methadone treatment for God's sake! Don't help them be drug addicts!"

"That's our signal to go." Rachael's companion started the engine.

Rachael was about to speak but froze when the elderly man pointed his finger at her. "You, that's right, I'm looking right atcha. You, young lady, should be ashamed. God will punish you. You're an enabler."

Chills ran down her back as they drove away, leaving the old man alone beside a broken swing set frame, his gaze locked on Rachael, his finger still pointing accusingly.

The driver sighed. "That guy comes out and yells at us at least once a week. His son's family was murdered by a heroin addict needing money for his next fix. All of them killed just a few miles from here, for whatever cash they had in the house."

Rachael squeezed her hands together. "No wonder he's so upset."

"He's threatened us a few times, but I think it's just scare tactics.

He's harmless. Probably. We don't wait around to find out."

Afterwards, Rachael popped in and out of a few clinics, distributing the pamphlets from her bag, the older man's bitter words stuck in her head, particularly now because she understood his motivation. She returned to the dorm for a late dinner, deeply contemplating the moral implications of the needle exchange program. She dropped off her purse, locked her door, and went to see if anyone else on her floor was around. After two years as the coxswain on Rothaker's crew team, it was in her nature to round everyone up and keep them together. She usually knocked on doors on her way to dinner so whoever was willing could sit and eat together. It was a habit. She believed dining should never be a solitary activity.

Peter opened his door as she was poised to knock.

"Oh. Hey." He poked the bridge of his glasses. "What's up?"

"Ready for dinner?"

"Sure. I'm more than ready." He closed the door behind him. "I'm starving."

"I had a really unsettling experience today. Really got me thinking about some of the volunteer work I do."

"What happened?"

As they headed to the cafeteria, Rachael told him about the needle exchange program, her interaction with the man who had lost his family, and her reasons for regularly distributing pamphlets to the clinics. Their conversation continued through dinner.

"Sex with an IV drug user is the number one reason people contract HIV in East Dalton. The victims can multiply quickly, so many of them are innocent women. Drug use is one of the main reasons that the Greenwood Circle hospital area is economically depressed," she explained. "Handing out clean needles prevents the spread of HIV and Hepatitis C, and it isn't going to make IV drug use more prevalent. If addicts don't have clean needles they use their dirty ones."

Peter set his elbows on the cafeteria table and leaned forward. "But at the same time, it is contributing to an activity that is both illegal and has catastrophic repercussions to the lives of those around them."

"Agreed." Rachael set down her silverware. "Addiction is a terrible problem, a menace to society, a contributor to violent activities. And I do have great respect for the law. That's why I'm ambivalent, despite my passion, especially after today."

"It's an ethical dilemma."

"And you're a great listener." Rachael offered a giant smile.

Xander strolled over and sat down next to Peter. "I've already eaten, but I'd kinda like to procrastinate some more. It's going to be a long night studying no matter when I start."

"Same." Connor straddled the seat next to Rachael, guzzling from a water bottle. Peter shared a bit of their discussion on the needle exchange program.

Connor laughed. "Is that for real? You ride around in something like an ice cream cart? Ringing a bell and yelling, free needles! Get your free needles!"

"It's nothing like that." Rachael's face was stern although it was very much like that.

"In my neighborhood we called the ice cream truck the ding-dong cart. Except ours played a distinctively annoying melody, and your drug mobile probably plays 'they tried to make me go to rehab I say no, no, no' by Amy Winehouse." Connor had an excellent and smooth singing voice and he wasn't shy about sharing it. After a few days in the dorm, everyone knew he could sing as well as he could pump iron.

"No. It would be, 'I've become comfortably numb.'" Xander sang the refrain.

"Who's that?" Connor tilted his head.

"Pink Floyd."

"I don't know him."

"Seriously?" Xander raised his eyebrows. "No way. It's a classic."

"Once you've lured them over with the promise of new paraphernalia, why don't you just arrest them instead and take them to jail?" Connor put his elbows on the table and rested his chin in his hands.

"Last I heard, shooting up heroin was illegal."

"It's not our job to arrest people. That's not what this is about." Rachael shook her head.

"I respect what you're doing. It's also dangerous. Drug addicts can be desperate and violent. It's surprising that you're not afraid. You have to be careful," Xander said, becoming more serious.

"I assure you I'm not in any danger."

"Just watch your back when you're out there at night." Peter held Rachael's gaze for longer than normal.

"Joking aside, I truly admire your altruism." Connor crushed the plastic bottle in his hands. "You must encounter a lot of very troubled people. Do you get a chance to really talk to them?"

"For one thing, HIV doesn't discriminate, but most of the people I try to help are struggling to sink or swim in a sea of problems that most Rothaker students have never encountered. Most of them have had some terrible, bad luck, have seen and experienced things that you and I cannot even imagine. Many are good people who have simply made some terrible decisions."

"Yeah," Xander murmured under his breath. "I can relate to that." His brows furrowed, and he turned away from his new friends.

Chapter Six

Gasping for breath, Xander's eyes flew open at two in the morning. Wide awake, eyes darting around, he tore off his shirt, damp with a hot sweat, and listened. He got out of bed and grabbed a bottle of cold water from his refrigerator. His eyes adjusted to the darkness as he paced the floor, needing to stare at each object: his desk and chair, the sink and refrigerator, each wall, each corner, and out the window to confirm that he was in his new room, at his new school, thousands of miles away from the thick smoke, sharp stench of fear, and the screams. In his sleep, he had revisited, with disturbing clarity, one of the most horrific events he ever experienced.

An ambulance siren screeched before fading into the distance. After a few minutes, his racing heart had returned to normal.

I'm at school. I was just dreaming.

Sitting on his bed, back pressed against the wall, he drank from the cold bottle while his breathing calmed, and his mind rooted in the present. He sank to the floor and did push-ups and sit-ups until his muscles ached. He stretched and walked through the silent hallway to use the restroom. Returning to bed, he resumed a restless sleep.

He shot up straight, heart pounding and fists curled tight. Horrific visions had again plagued his sleep. Repressed scenes from his past had intruded into his brain as if he were reliving them. The evil mocking grin of a small Afghani guy he had never seen before, and, most disturbing of all, a vivid picture of himself, something he didn't remember happening—an image of him snarling, trembling with rage, and soaked in blood.

He stood up, sweaty but chilled, and focused on everything that connected him to the present to escape the panic sweeping over him.

I'm at school. This is not happening. I'm just dreaming.

His alarm wasn't set to go off for over an hour. It was too early to wake up but being tired was preferable to going back to sleep and continuing to have nightmares. With a shaking hand, he opened his laptop to get a head-start on his school work for the day. It was imperative to be fully functional to survive the insane work load expected of the medical students. He had been out of college for over two years. His study skills were a little rusty. The heavy first-year work load involved memorizing massive amounts of material, challenging for him even under the best of circumstances. At this point, his circumstances were jeopardizing his success.

Xander earned a free ride through college on a football scholarship. Football was a full-time job, and the cost of tuition was his salary. It had taken him five-and-a-half years to graduate with the classes and credits he needed to apply to medical school. He had to drop physics twice because games kept him from being able to participate in the labs. But he kept on signing up and going to summer school. Slow and steady had always been his internal motto, although he was anything but slow outrunning defenders on the football field. When he was almost finished with college, he applied to medical school. He planned to stay at the University of Nebraska. It had been good to him thus far. His college advisor convinced him to pick one other school "because he should." He couldn't imagine himself anywhere except Nebraska, so almost in jest, he chose Rothaker, the most renowned medical school in the country. He did not expect to get in and at one point he even felt foolish about wasting the application fee. His response from Rothaker arrived in the mail slim and weighing less than a quarter of an ounce. He almost didn't open it because it seemed so likely and evident that it was a rejection letter but was surprised to find an offer for admission instead. Apparently, Rothaker was impressed with a man who could play Division I football and still manage to get mostly A's in his classes, even if it took longer and even if his MCATs were very good but certainly not the best.

Xander wrote back to Rothaker requesting to defer his enrollment for two more years. He was in for a second surprise. He imagined they might say something like "no, there are plenty of other better people who might apply in two years," but instead they said "absolutely," and from that moment on they proceeded to treat him like a saint, going above and beyond, in his opinion, to communicate with him in the interim. Not for the first time or the last, he felt lucky, like someone was looking out for him.

But now, his medical school experience was marred by panic, anxiety, and despair. First, the incident in the anatomy lab. He was shocked when they unveiled the cadaver. He saw a corpse with manifestations of grotesque mutilation, a gaping abdominal wound, and intestines torn out and stretched up and around the neck. His nostrils filled with the stench of thick smoke, dust, and fresh blood, replacing the cloying smell of formaldehyde ever present in the lab. His muscles tensed, his heart raced, and nausea rose up from his stomach. His reaction was powerful and unexpected. He struggled to compose himself on the outside, for the sake of the impression he would leave the group he needed to work with for the rest of the year. Suddenly sweating where he was cool only moments ago, he battled to push through panic and pull himself back into the moment. His fear had been very real.

What the hell had happened?

Now, for the second night in a row, his nightmares confirmed that whatever was happening to him was no isolated occurrence. His inability to keep his unwanted memories locked away terrified him. He had been mentally and physically strong until recently, aside from his recurring back issues, but they came with the territory of playing college football. But now he had a new problem, far more disturbing than his bad back.

Not now.

He lowered himself to his knees and prayed it would stop.

Chapter Seven

When his phone rang, Robert Mending, a recent graduate of Everett College, was trying to find a parking spot not too far from his new Beacon Hill condo.

"Hey Robert. It's Tripp." The voice of his boarding school friend held its familiar mischievous tone.

"Tripp. Hey." Robert switched his phone to his car's speaker, so he could parallel park, something he was proficient at from growing up in Boston. "How long has it been?"

"When was that party where the shots had live goldfish?"

Robert chuckled. "Oh, God . . . two years ago?" He remembered vomiting in a well-lit area, disturbing because the fish were completely intact and looking like they could be plopped back into the bowl. All part of the fun.

Tripp was a good guy, a lot of fun, and someone destined to be successful since birth for too many reasons to list.

"What have you been up to, Robert?"

"I'm working for my father right now." Robert disliked saying it. He hadn't been able to secure a job that he wanted, solely because he wasn't sure what it was he wanted, and his father was happy for him to be involved in managing the family's philanthropic organization. "How about you?"

Robert instantly felt guarded, and hoped Tripp wasn't calling because he was looking for a job. That had been happening too often lately as his fellow graduates became more desperate, and it made Robert uncomfortable.

"I'm in law school."

"Law school, that's right, I remember hearing that. Where?"

"Rothaker."

Robert's attention leapt to a new level. Since summer ended, Rothaker often crept into his thoughts because of a certain female currently enrolled there.

"That's why I called you. I saw someone who made me think of you. Remember that hot girl who dated your friend, Ethan? I think I saw her running outside, around the law school. Do you remember her?"

Did he remember her? That was an understatement. Robert had never come close to forgetting Brooke. She occupied many of his thoughts, even while he was living it up in Boston. He had been trying to figure out how to see her. Tripp had just given him an excuse. It was time. Finally, it was his turn.

Robert's best friend Ethan had "dated" Brooke for two years at Everett. Robert hesitated to call it dating, only because it was a different sort of relationship than most. Brooke was a unique individual. Ethan had been in love with Brooke from the moment he set eyes on her in the library during their junior year and for most of that time she had treated him like nothing more than a close friend and her best study companion. She seemed willing to spend hours with him, if they were studying. Ethan was used to having young ladies practically throw themselves at him, he couldn't figure out what he was doing wrong. Robert listened to Ethan's confused thoughts on the matter, pretended to commiserate, and felt terribly guilty. Despite his best efforts to quell his feelings, Robert was also hopelessly in love with Brooke. No one knew about it except his mother, who had listened to him explain his awkward dilemma. Stabs of envy shot through him on the rare occasions where he had witnessed Brooke showing signs of physical affection towards Ethan. Brooke was perfect, and his mother, without having met her, tended to agree based on everything Robert had shared about her: smart, independent, passionate about being a physician, and unpretentious. He wasn't sure if he had ever mentioned that she was beautiful.

After graduation, his friend Ethan had secured an incredible job with a consulting firm on the West Coast. He would have willingly flown out to see Brooke on a regular basis, but she ended things, saying it would be too much of a distraction for them to try and maintain something long distance when they were both so busy on opposite coasts. That their relationship could no longer work had been obvious to Brooke. Ethan did not feel the same.

Four months had passed since Brooke ended things with Ethan. Robert had waited long enough. Not that Ethan had gotten over her. He was still crushed, even though he was dating plenty of women. Whenever Robert and Ethan spoke, Ethan said something along the lines of how no one else compared to Brooke. Robert quickly changed the subject because he didn't want to hear it. It filled him with guilt and made him feel like there would never be time sufficient enough for him to make his move without negatively impacting his friendship with Ethan.

Robert locked his car and strode toward his condo. "Most likely that was Brooke you saw. She's a medical student. And she's a dedicated runner."

"I thought so. Hard to forget her."

"Any good parties there?" The wheels in Robert's head turned rapidly.

"I don't know. There are dinner clubs. We're supposed to sign up to host dinners with the other grad students, get to know each other." Tripp snorted. "I'm not sure I'm ready for dinner clubs yet. I've been to the city—New York—for the past few weekends, a blast, but it's also a hassle to drive there. I need to take responsibility for the grad school party scene here."

"All the drinks for your first bash are on me."

Robert proceeded to invite himself down to Rothaker for that very weekend. He couldn't wait to see Brooke. But first he had to make sure she would be there. It was going to take some courage to make that first phone call, only because he needed it to go well.

Robert's last two years at Everett proved difficult, not academically, but emotionally. Keeping silent about being in love with his best friend's "girlfriend" might have otherwise been a huge deal, but it was relatively easy to handle compared to what happened to his own girlfriend, the now infamous Jessica Caroll. Robert and Jessica were together for over a year, which included the Hamptons in the summer. But half way through their junior year, as Robert became more enamored with Brooke, he finally became exhausted with Jessica's snobbery. Ironically, one of the people she was most fond of criticizing was Brooke.

Robert decided to break up with Jessica right before he left for Christmas break. He was on the verge of telling her, but she was acting so emotionally crazy at the time, freaking out and throwing things because he hadn't invited her to Aruba with his family for the holidays, that he put it off to avoid stirring up further drama. At some point, just hours after he drove away from campus to go home for winter break, she disappeared from the school. Disappeared without a trace. It was incredible. Robert was never a real suspect, because fortunately for him Jessica was still on campus causing a stir when he was half way home to Boston. There never were any real suspects. But he was interviewed constantly by the police, and private detectives. Hounded by the media. His parents' attorneys helped protect him, but their wealth also sensationalized his part in the story. And he was certain people looked at him differently because someone had to be responsible and the boyfriend/husband/jealous lover is almost always the guy.

Months after Jessica's disappearance, when the deep mounds of New Hampshire snow finally melted, her body was discovered by a biology professor who studied birds. It was the same woman who stumbled upon Jessica's car a few months earlier, stolen, vandalized, and left along the same back country roads in a separate, unexplainable incident. Talk about bad luck. She found Jessica under a bridge located miles away from campus where her body had been buried under the snow since December. The media and the detectives were back with a vengeance, and the whole ordeal began again for Robert. Because her case remained a mystery, Robert didn't think he would ever be completely free from the trouble it caused, but leaving Everett had helped somewhat. He was more than ready to move on with his life and begin pursuing what he desired. He had wanted Brooke just as long as Ethan had, from the first day they both met her in the library. And he had been so patient since then. This was his chance.

Chapter Eight

Brooke lay on her bed with one leg stretched over her head, using the fifteen minutes she had before dinner to study pictures of cells, understanding and memorizing their normal and pathological appearances. The plastic covering her mattress pad crunched as she shifted her weight, and she considered removing it when she had more time. The now familiar and intrusive screech of the garbage truck lifting the dumpster broke through her thoughts. Thank goodness that truck came as frequently as it did. On more than one occasion, the dumpster had been close to overflowing. She was certain people were throwing away items that should have been recycled. And that was *not* okay.

A week ago, she had opened her window and startled two black vultures from picking through the trash. One peered up at her suspiciously, as if it was she who didn't belong.

"Oh!" She sat up straight. "I don't hear the ambulances anymore!"

She had slept soundly through the previous night. In fact, now that she thought about it, she couldn't recall hearing a single ambulance in two days. The ambulance departures were no less frequent, she had simply become immune to the sounds. It was true, eventually a person can get used to anything.

Her phone rang, interrupting her thoughts. A number she didn't recognize appeared, and she debated picking it up. She wasn't quite finished with her review of the cell sections, but she took the call anyway.

"Hello?"

"Hi. It's Robert. Brooke?"

She forwarded to the next image. "Yes?"

"It's Robert Mending."

"Oh. Hi. Robert." *Why is he calling?*

"How is medical school treating you?"

"Good." She couldn't imagine what his call was about. All her previous interactions with Robert had been in some way related to Ethan.

"I'm visiting a friend at Rothaker this weekend. He's at the law school. I was hoping you and I could get together while I was down there. Any chance you're available Saturday night?"

"Umm." *Why does he want to see me? I'm busy this weekend, really busy. I have to do that interview class at Performance Fit and maybe they'll have me start teaching right away. I have to study. I have to eat in the cafeteria in the dorm. I have to do laundry. I have to buy a hand soap pump.*

As she ran through excuses in her mind, she realized how lame they were. She was supposed to be trying to be more social. It was critical to make an effort to have fun, occasionally, doing something that didn't involve exercising and studying. Perhaps it was a good time to get out, before her workload got even heavier, before she added exercise classes to her almost full schedule.

She flipped to the next cell picture. *Normal and abnormal are almost impossible to differentiate.* "I guess I'm available. What were you thinking?"

"How about dinner on Saturday, then maybe we can tour the campus and go to a party with my friend afterwards."

"Okay, maybe the dinner. I'm not familiar with the campus yet, other than the medical school. I run around it, but I don't really know my way or what's what. I don't think I could give you a tour."

"Then I'll give you the tour. How about seven on Saturday? Early dinner so we can walk around later."

Dinner at seven isn't an 'early dinner!' Seven is too late! I'm hungry at five-thirty. I can't wait until seven.

She took a deep breath and exhaled to keep from getting too worked up and upset. *Be flexible.* She sighed. "How about six-fifteen?"

"Sure. Six-fifteen is even better. Are you in the medical school dorm?"

"Yes."

"I know where it is. I'll pick you up in front at six-fifteen? You have my number now in case you need to get in touch before then."

"Okay. See you then."

She felt trapped. The upcoming dinner now loomed ominously in her future, something she had to grin and bear until it was over. And she forgot to ask where they were going. She would be wearing the same outfit regardless. It wasn't like she had many options, but it would be nice to know.

Should I just call him back and see if he'll meet in the dorm for a salad? No. Robert wouldn't want to eat in the prison-like cafeteria. He'd want to go somewhere nice, the kind of place where one salad costs more than the cost of the ingredients to make a salad every day for an entire week.

She took a deep breath.

I can do this.

Chapter Nine

On Saturday morning Brooke ran to Performance Fit to teach her "test class" so she could be officially hired. When she arrived, her audience of judges consisted of three female instructors and three of the gym's members, all of whom appeared to believe they were something special. While it was a letdown to have a small group instead of a packed room, it was fantastic to have an audience who could handle one of her toughest workouts. She let them have it. She felt great about the class; it was as good as any she had taught, maybe better because there were no slackers to distract her. After being thanked and praised by the participants, she mounted a stationary bike to do her cardio and study, regretting that she agreed to waste most of the evening with Robert.

***

Mike busied himself with paperwork, more anxious than usual for the verdict to come in on Brooke's class. He wanted her to work for him as much as she wanted to work there. The three members he assembled to take her class, along with two other instructors, were a group of his most demanding members. They loved to screen new instructors. Partly it was a power trip, but they also wanted to ensure there were no "weak" instructors. At the last minute, Rosalie, his most hard-core and challenging cross-fit instructor, had shown up to work out on her own and volunteered to take the class with the others. Rosalie was hard to please. Mike would ignore her opinion if she didn't think Brooke was good enough. He planned to bring Brooke on board if her class was marginally above okay. Maybe even "okay" would be good enough this time. He had only been able to watch her for a few minutes before he had to leave, reluctantly, to speak with someone. She appeared professional and confident. And God almighty, he had never seen anyone look so incredible in workout clothes, and that was saying a lot considering he saw people in workout clothes all day, every day for over fifteen years.

Rosalie rushed into his office and slapped his desk. "Wow! That was awesome." Her eyes were beaming.

"And that means what?"

"That. Was. A. Very. Good. Class. Mike! You know how hard I have to work to get a good work out, right? She got it done, Mike! She knows her stuff, talking about all the muscles and how they're interacting. Build here. Elongate there. And it was different. Great find, Mike! I loved it!"

Rosalie raving about someone's class, other than her own, was highly unusual. So Brooke's class had turned out to be better than Mike expected or even hoped. Rosalie's sentiments were echoed with similar feedback from the other four participants. The verdict was unanimous. The members insisted he give her prime-time slots if possible. They were already naming the instructors he could bump to accommodate Brooke. His current instructors, especially the ones who were already begging for more classes, would not be pleased.

Mike planned to call and give her the good news later. It would be nice to see her around the gym on a regular basis, in her workout clothes. But when he passed the stationary bike area an hour later, he discovered she was still there.

"I've got good news." She raised her head from a notebook. "Your class was very well received."

"That's wonderful." Her legs kept spinning the pedals around at a remarkable speed.

"So, if you can come into my office, we can start getting you on the schedule."

"Okay, I'm almost done." She dabbed at her forehead with a towel. "Can I meet you there in a few minutes?"

"Of course. Any chance you have copies of your certifications with you?”

She dropped her head back to face the ceiling for a second. “No, sorry. Ughh. I forgot. I’ll bring them next time. Don’t worry.”

Chapter Ten

In the shadows cast by the Medical School Tower, Brooke paced around outside, waiting for Robert. She was dressed simply in expensive tan slacks and a silky blouse, past gifts from Ethan. They fit perfectly, yet she was uncomfortable wearing them. She checked her phone. Six-twenty. Robert was already five minutes late.

She took deep breaths to quell the persistent hum of her increasing agitation. Regardless of the situation, it infuriated her when people were late. It was disrespectful.

I'm never late and I'm a very busy person. What if everyone was late for everything? What a mess the world would be. What is wrong with people that they agree on a time and can't manage to stick to it?

Once, she witnessed an accident while riding her bike to an appointment. She had to wait for the police to arrive to provide her account of the situation. Immediately, she called the office where she had been headed to let them know she was delayed. She apologized profusely, even though the situation was in no way her fault. She provided a revised arrival time and called again with an update when she was almost there. *That* is what one did if they weren't going to arrive on time, if circumstances truly were beyond their control.

On the surface, Brooke appeared composed, but inside she was getting worked into a frenzy.

I'll wait one more minute and then I'm done. I can go inside, take off these clothes and study.

Robert pulled up against the curb, waving, at six-twenty-four.

Nine whole minutes late.

She was expecting a forest green BMW, the car he drove in college.

Instead he emerged from a silver Audi convertible, its hazard lights blinking madly. He was dressed just as she remembered him, an understated preppy style consisting of khakis, expensive loafers, a leather belt and a tailored but soft and well-worn dress shirt, sleeves rolled up. Had he arrived in jeans and t-shirt, she would have been amused, if she'd been in a better mood.

He rushed over and surprised her with an embrace, unusual because they had never done that before.

Brooke glared. "You're late."

Robert ran his hand through his hair. "I know. I'm so sorry. I texted you to let you know."

"Oh." Brooke took her phone out of her purse. Sure enough, there was a text from Robert. *"On my way, took wrong turn in traffic jam. Sorry!"* and another that said, *"Almost there."*

Brooke's anger dissipated as she walked to his car. She had always considered Ethan lucky to have a loyal friend like Robert. And now Robert was proving to be considerate of her time as well. She did her best to smile. "How do you know your way around at all?"

Robert held open the passenger door for her. The top of his car was down, it was a warm day for early October, and Brooke was glad her hair was back in its usual ponytail, so it wouldn't blow in her face.

"My grandfather went here."

"When was that?" Brooke sat down, drawing her long legs together.

"Forty-something years ago." Robert lingered next to her before shutting the door. "He used to bring my sister and me here when we were younger. Often. He loves this place like you can't imagine." He got in and draped one arm over the steering wheel, facing Brooke while starting the car. "It's been a while since I was last here. I forgot more than I remembered and took a wrong turn. But I can give you a pretty decent tour of the undergraduate campus after dinner."

Ughh. How long will that take? Dinner better be quick. "Sure. And I won't know if you mess up or not. You can get away with telling me the chemistry building is the conservatory and I won't know the difference.

At least not today."

Robert laughed. "I have a dinner reservation for us at The Shale."

"That's the member's only dinner club, right?"

"The one and only."

"Okay. Let's do it."

Now that she was out of her dorm room and her workout clothes, she felt more civilized and saw the whole evening as one more challenge at which to excel.

Robert parked his car a half block from The Shale. He left the top down and opened his trunk to remove a coat and tie. In a few smooth, practiced gestures, he slipped into both. Once inside, they were seated in a dark wood paneled room lined with framed autographed photos of powerful and famous Rothaker alumni. Silver sailing trophies and ribbons were spread across a ledge lining the top of the wall. Every surface appeared old and polished. Most of the other women in the restaurant wore cute cocktail dresses.

I do have one black dress that looks amazing on me, but how was I supposed to know the appropriate attire when he didn't say where we were going? He's lucky I'm not wearing jeans or something with a Nike label.

"Do you know the history of this place?" Robert signaled for a waiter.

"I don't. Well, I know that it was only for men until a few years ago."

Robert nodded. "That's right. It's been about ten years since they allowed women to join. I'm embarrassed to say that my grandfather wrote letters to prevent women from joining. When my mother found out, we weren't allowed to talk to him for weeks, to teach him a lesson. Not that she wanted to come here, just because of his stance in general. He was outvoted anyway, fortunately, for the sake of social progress."

After Robert ordered an entrée and Brooke a salad, he drank his beer and she sipped her water while Rothaker's a cappella group, the Palapazoos, sang two songs in their tuxedos. Brooke made a mental note to tell Connor about them, since he was also a talented singer. While she listened to their renditions of Havana and Brown Eyed Girl, she absentmindedly traced her fingers across the names and initials that had been etched into their table over the past century. Her fingernails were short and in need of attention, but she didn't care.

When the Palapazoos moved on to the next room, Brooke asked, "Have you seen Ethan lately?" because she felt she should. Even though they hadn't talked in months, Ethan had been her closest friend in college, and he had considered her to be more than a friend. He had been exceedingly kind and generous. She only had good things to say about him. But she didn't miss him or think about him at all.

"He's fine." Robert took another swallow of beer. "He's doing well. Loves his job."

"Good." Brooke meant it. She wished nothing but the best for Ethan. She just wasn't good at maintaining relationships and keeping in touch with people because it wasn't on her priority list.

After dinner Robert guided her through the undergraduate campus, pointing out the library, the dormitories, fraternities, sororities, and everything else they passed. The campus reminded her of Everett in many ways, the ornate stone buildings, the carved towers and arches, everything looking centuries old and everlasting. But Everett was surrounded by rural country side, and there were large expanses of grassy landscape between almost every building. In contrast, the Rothaker campus was packed together inside a city that had seen better days, with just enough strategically-placed foliage here and there.

They walked through the library and an art museum that was open for a special event. Most everything else was locked, including the undergraduate dormitories, which was disappointing because, according to Robert, they were exceptionally special and mired in unique tradition.

"What's that?" Brooke pointed to the side of one of the newest looking buildings, a massive stone structure with ornate carvings. "It's pretty darn fancy."

Robert seemed to ignore her question. He placed his hands on her shoulders and physically turned her halfway around on the path. "Look—I'm pretty sure that's the gym."

After walking for almost an hour, they got in the car and drove at a snail's pace around the outskirts of campus, pointing out the athletic fields, stadiums, and the other graduate schools, most of which she had passed on her runs, although she didn't know which fields of study they housed. It had grown too cold to keep the Audi's top down, but it was still a beautiful moon-lit evening and Brooke appreciated the spectacular campus.

Robert glanced toward Brooke and smiled. "Tell me about medical school."

Brooke's face lit up. "I love it. It's fantastic. But I wish we could get to the real meat of the program faster. During first year we mostly learn about the anatomy, chemistry, and biology of the body, but also medical ethics and history. Starting next year, we'll focus more on diseases, and we'll start working directly with patients."

"Great. I expected you to say it's hard or it's tough, some complaint along those lines."

"It's demanding, but as long as you stay on top of everything and don't let things get in your way, it's not hard."

"I should have known it wouldn't be a challenge for you."

Brooke nodded to acknowledge his compliment. But that was the past. She still had the future to conquer.

"So what type of work are you doing now?" She asked to make polite conversation.

"I'm working in Boston, managing funds."

Brooke imagined Robert working with people who made huge amounts of money manipulating stocks and bonds, mortgages, and commodities. She pictured men just like Robert in beautiful suits with fancy desks increasing their own wealth and that of those who already had plenty, without adding any value to the rest of the world.

If there was ever a catastrophic event like a nuclear war or Armageddon, hedge-fund skills won't be very useful. All the intangible numbers on the stock exchange will become meaningless. But real merit will always exist in the ability to resection a thoraco-abdominal aneurysm, re-vascularize an acute myocardial infarction, or transplant a heart and lung.

That was how she saw it, but if Robert wanted to finagle with a bunch of numbers so that the insanely rich could have even more money, that was his prerogative. People valued different things. She wouldn't hold it against him. Robert didn't elaborate on the details of his work, and she didn't ask.

"I'm going to Europe next week, for six weeks," he said, sounding disappointed about it.

"For your job?"

"No, it's like . . . it's like a vacation."

"A six-week vacation?" She raised her eyebrows. "What about your job? How can you leave for so long?"

He tapped the steering wheel. "Oh . . . I planned this before I started working. It will be fine."

"Oh." *Clearly whatever he's doing isn't very important if he can be away for that length of time.*

Robert pointed ahead. "Here's my friend's place."

Tripp sat on the porch drinking a beer with his housemate. He stood to greet his guests when they got out of the car. Robert introduced Brooke.

"Let me get you a beer," Tripp offered.

"No, thank you, I'm fine. I have to get back."

"No. You just got here! Come to the party with us tonight. We deserve a night out." Tripp grinned. "Too much work, too little play, you know what that does to someone, don't you?"

"No," Brooke tilted her head and met his gaze, "what does it do?"

"Didn't you see *The Shining*?" Tripp laughed. "It makes you nuts! We don't want any beautiful psychos running around Rothaker do we?"

"No. That would be awful," Brooke allowed a devious grin to take over. "But what are the chances of that really?"

"Let's not find out. I'll get you a beer and we'll celebrate Robert's visit."

"Thank you, Tripp, but I have to get back. It was nice meeting you."

Robert apologized over his shoulder. "I'll be back later."

Robert took her back to her dorm, driving below the speed limit and following the longest possible route.

"Now that I've had a comprehensive tour, I believe my dorm is not only the most unattractive building on campus, it's the *only* unattractive building on campus."

Robert slowed to a stop when a light turned yellow. "It looked okay from the outside. But it doesn't fit in, does it?"

"The front reminds me of a movie set façade because the back is like one big, shady back alley, and I mean 'shady' as in sinister, not as in trees providing shade. It's all concrete. The inside is like those temporary trailer classrooms you have at school when the rooms get overfilled. Oh. You might not know what I'm referring to there. They probably didn't use those at Deerfield." She grinned. "Anyway, it's not attractive. It's the poor unfortunate step-sister on campus. And I'm not overly particular about my accommodations. If I've taken note, there are some students who are probably distraught about it." Brooke laughed.

Robert insisted on walking her inside to make sure she arrived safely back to her room. Brooke told him several times that it wasn't necessary, particularly because it was taking a while to find a nearby parking spot. Finally, he maneuvered into a tight spot and they walked to her dorm together.

Robert fidgeted with his hands and wiped them on his pants more than once. He was nervous, and Brooke didn't like the feeling it gave her, like something unexpected might happen.

Just as Robert opened the front door for Brooke, Rachael stepped out.

"Hi, Brooke. And who is your friend?"

"I'm Robert Mending." He stepped forward and extended his hand.

Rachael clasped his hand between hers. "Robert Mending? Like the fabulous new science building on campus? Any relation?"

Robert coughed, covered his mouth, and muttered, "maybe."

Rachael batted her eyes, still holding his hand. "I'm Rachael Kline, one of Brooke's lab partners. It's nice to meet you. Doing anything interesting tonight?"

"We had dinner, and a tour of the whole campus," said Brooke. "I'm heading back in to study."

Rachael chuckled. "That might be hard to do in your room right now, maybe all weekend from what I understand."

Brooke frowned. "What are you talking about?"

"Jeff was hiding out in my room earlier…" Rachael laughed again. "I'll let you find out for yourself. It was sooo nice to meet you, Robert Mending. I hope I see you around."

Robert nodded at Rachael and walked inside with Brooke. "Do you know what she was talking about?"

"No. I have no idea."

"I'm intrigued. And I'm glad I got to meet one of your friends."

"Oh, well to be honest, I would not call her a friend exactly. She's probably the most annoying, bossiest person I've ever met."

"She seemed nice."

They climbed the stairs to the third floor and as soon as they exited the stairwell, they were assaulted by loud and amorous sounds. They froze at the end of the hallway. It was coming from Julie's room.

Robert grinned. "I think I know what Rachael was referring to."

"Her boyfriend's visiting," Brooke explained, her face turning red. She glanced back at the door to the stairwell, unsure of what to do.

They basically ran to Brooke's room, where she hurriedly unlocked it, rushed inside, and shut the door. But with just a thin wall separating their rooms, the ardent noises were even louder from inside. The moaning grew increasingly more urgent, virtually impossible to ignore. A deep voice murmured, "Come on, baby, yea, yea, oh yea, that's it." Heat rushed to Brooke's face and Robert put a hand over his mouth to contain his laughter. There was no chance of conversation because what was obviously happening just inches away from them was beyond distracting.

"I feel sorry for you now." Robert laughed.

Brooke couldn't make eye contact.

"Are you sure, now, in light of your home situation that you don't want to go out with Tripp and I?"

"No, I can't. I have lots of work to do. I'll go to the library—fast as I can."

"I hate to say it, but you weren't exaggerating about your dorm."

"I know, right? And now I've just learned that the walls are paper thin!" She walked toward her door, essentially escorting Robert out.

"I'd like to see you again soon, if that's okay."

"Okay."

Robert hugged her and gave her a quick kiss on the cheek.

She waved goodbye as he strolled backward down the hall, laughing, hands over his ears.

Brooke couldn't get out of her room quickly enough. She dashed out of her clothes, into a t-shirt and jeans. She couldn't believe she agreed to see Robert again, but what else was she supposed to say? And it wasn't that she didn't like him. She just didn't want to squander away her time seeing anyone other than the people she absolutely did *have* to see. She was grabbing her laptop when she heard a light knock on her door.

She opened it, expecting to find Robert had returned. When she saw Jeff, they both burst out laughing.

Eyes wide, he gripped her arm. "We need to get out of here!"

"I can *not* believe that is Julie. How long has this been going on?"

"Way too long! Let's go!"

Brooke was annoyed that she was essentially being driven from her room, her sanctuary, but the erotic sounds they were hearing—ridiculously, comically loud—made it hard to keep from laughing.

"Do you think she knows we can hear?"

"God. I hope not. I think she would die if she knew we could hear her. She would totally die."

"You have to tell her." Brooke's eyes pleaded with Jeff as they fled the hallway and Julie's persistent sighs. "Tell her tomorrow. Please! He is here for the whole weekend!"

Jeff jammed his finger on the elevator button. "I'm not going to tell her. I don't want her to know I know!"

They piled into the elevator and slumped against the back wall as the door rolled shut. Tears of laughter slid down Jeff's face.

Brooke shook her head, her mouth hanging open. "I can't believe this! I had a friend here with me. A male friend! I couldn't even look at him. It was beyond awkward!" She laughed so hard that her stomach ached, and she gasped for breath. She couldn't remember the last time she enjoyed such all-consuming laughter.

The elevator door opened, and Brooke stepped out. "Okay. Here's the plan. We'll have a really loud conversation tomorrow in the cafeteria about how thin the walls are and maybe she'll get the hint."

Jeff wiped a tear from his face. "And to think, I was worried about *you* entertaining gentlemen in your room, not shy, quiet, little Julie. It turns out you're the one who studies twenty-four seven and might as well have a sign on your forehead that reads 'I'm just not interested.' That will teach me to judge a book by its cover. So trite but true!"

Chapter Eleven

"How many of you want to be family doctors?" Dr. Harriet Lipsett, PhD., professor of medical ethics, scanned the auditorium as a very small number of hands were raised.

"How many of you want to be dermatologists?"

Three hands. One of them went half way up and then down again. Undecided.

"How many want to be surgeons?"

Dozens of hands flew up with confidence.

"And therein lays the inherent problem between what this country needs and what we have. Break into your groups, just use your anatomy groups for now so we can do this quickly. Find out why each of you wants to pursue a career in medicine and what avenues of medicine interest you. We're going to spend fifteen minutes on this."

Oh, come on! I don't care why anyone else wants to be a doctor or what kind of doctor they want to be.

Brooke hated the touchy-feely stuff Dr. Lipsett was determined to have them discuss daily. It was all supposedly part of building compassion and relationships. Brooke didn't need it. But then she remembered a piece of information from a previous class. The physicians deemed to have the best communication skills also had the least number of malpractice suits, meaning the best listeners, not necessarily the most proficient physicians, were sued the least. She would have extraordinary medical skills, she was confident about that, so she would receive the most complicated cases.

I won't have my name in a database of malpractice suits just because I'm not the queen of empathy. Empathy is overrated. It can't repair a blocked aorta. Still, I better put some effort into learning what contributes to the perception of a stellar bedside manner. Otherwise I could end up being unfairly treated by my future patients.

Brooke drummed her fingers against her arm rest yet appeared to listen as Rachael shared her grand story about wanting to save the world.

"There's nothing more rewarding than earning a patient's trust and helping them through their most vulnerable time. I want the knowledge to help people when they're sick and at their most needy. . ."

Blah, blah, blah.

". . . and it's a team effort, working together with the patient and other doctors to achieve the best results."

Brooke rolled her eyes.

Rachael continued: "I'm considering immunology, because I volunteer at the HIV clinic at Rothaker. I've done that for the past few years, as you all know, learning about the ramifications of a compromised immune system and treatments. I also completed a summer internship doing research for the OBGYN department, and everything I learned there was fascinating, so rewarding."

Brooke crossed and uncrossed her legs. *When is she going to shut up? We all know about her internships.*

"I'm also considering internal medicine. I love how it's broad based and allows for seeing a large spectrum of issues. Every day might be completely different from the last. I'm looking forward to our clinical rotations, so I can get a better idea of where I would be best suited. Hmm, let's see, oh, I'm also interested in dermatology due to the growing need for that specialty and with few emergencies it might be ideal because someday, when I have my own family, I could work part time. And that's important because . . ."

Rachael finally caught Brooke's attention when she mentioned dermatology, reminding Brooke of the mole on Rachael's neck.

Why doesn't she have it removed? It's so distracting.

Aside from that, Brooke barely listened, bouncing her leg while she ticked off the items she needed to do for the rest of the day—teach her first official sculpt class at Performance Fit, get in at least an hour of cardio, study for the cell biology test. She glanced at the group to her right that included Jeff and Julie, and her mouth crept into a smile. Julie kept glimpsing down at her notebook as she spoke, as if she was too shy to maintain eye contact with her classmates for extended periods. It was hard to believe she was the same person who had unknowingly forced Jeff and Brooke, and probably others, to flee from the dorm. She seemed possessed by a porn star when that boyfriend came to visit. Julie had good reason to be embarrassed now, at least amongst the dorm's third-floor residents, but she appeared blissfully ignorant of the disruption she caused.

Xander was up next. His story was simple and all-American, just as Jeff would have predicted.

"I've wanted to be a doctor since I was in elementary school. My sister contracted meningitis when she was ten. Wait." He held up his hand, a smile on his face. "Before you ask or assume that my parents have religious beliefs that prohibit medical intervention, she *was* vaccinated. But she contracted a form of bacterial meningitis anyway."

Rakesh spoke up. "Meningitis is an inflammation of the membranes surrounding the brain and spinal cord. Meningococcal disease is the most common cause of bacterial meningitis for children. Much more dangerous than viral meningitis."

"Yeah, that's right." Xander nodded. "You're a walking medical dictionary. Anyway, she was hospitalized for weeks, on an antibiotic course. She had a pediatrician, an infectious disease specialist, and a critical care specialist taking care of her every day. I got to know them all. Her follow up care was at home with a primary care doctor. He was young, and he played basketball at the YMCA at night with my dad. I admired him. He made an impression on me."

"Statistically speaking, the doctors with the best bedside manners know the least," Brooke said in a deadpan voice. She knew someone, most likely Rachael, would take the bait and respond.

"That is not true." Rachael frowned. "That's not at all what we learned, Brooke. You've confused things. We learned that the doctors with the best bedside manners get sued the least. There is no correlation between bedside manners, excellent or poor, and clinical expertise."

"I know that, Rachael." Brooke sneered. "It was a joke."

"Really?" Rachael tilted her head. "It didn't seem funny."

"Anyway," said Xander, "he came to our house a few nights a week. I don't know if that's even still done."

"Maybe he was having an affair with your mother." Brooke tossed her head back and laughed.

Xander frowned. Rachael made a face to show her disapproval.

Did I say that aloud? I'm becoming too relaxed about saying what I'm thinking, and its mostly Rachael's fault. Something about her rubs me the wrong way.

Xander continued, "I've always been attracted to rewards, I think I stole that word from you, Rachael . . . rewards that come from hard work, and any career that takes this long must be rewarding. So, I think I want to be a primary care doctor, or a pediatrician. It remains to be determined. There's a lot I don't know."

Rachael nodded, reminding Brooke of a mother hen. She lifted a hand, about to make a point. But it was Brooke's turn next, and she wanted to be done with the entire exercise. She wasn't paying Rothaker thousands of dollars to learn why her group wanted to be doctors, not during class time, so she started speaking and continued as if she hadn't noticed Rachael's half open mouth.

"I find anatomy and physiology fascinating. I always have. I want to understand all there is to know about medicine and then figure out the rest. I'm going to be a cardiothoracic surgeon."

She didn't need to impress them, they weren't admissions officers. That was all they were going to get from her. She had already produced an account of why she wanted to be a surgeon in her medical school application essay and then again during the interviews. She had done a phenomenal job fabricating a story the admissions board loved hearing.

As soon as Brooke finished speaking, Rachael asked Xander a

question, as if Brooke had never uttered a word. "Xander, I was going to ask you, was that the same sister that became a nurse, the one with the same earrings as me?"

"Same one, I guess the whole ordeal made an impression on her as well."

Rakesh went last and said he was interested in becoming a neurosurgeon or a vascular surgeon like his father. Then they broke out of their small groups and returned to the forward-facing chairs and Dr. Lipsett continued her lecture.

"In the United States we have a shortage of physicians that is expected to increase rapidly, even though medical school enrollment is up. The population is also increasing, and we are heavily concentrated with the aging. In addition to shrinking supply, we have a distribution problem, by geographic location as well as specialties. Yesterday you learned about the impact health care policies and government regulations have had on supply, but now let's talk about misallocation of specialties."

A click of Dr. Lipsett's computer and a slew of geographically arranged statistics appeared on the large screen to support her point.

"There are not enough family care practitioners. It costs approximately half a million dollars to become a doctor in the U.S., almost twice what it costs in most countries. This, no doubt, encourages you to specialize in one of the higher paying areas of medicine, forces many of you, to be accurate. If there were no medical school debt I can guarantee more hands would have gone up when I asked who wanted to be a general practitioner. And, if all the areas of medicine were paid equally, we would also see a different allocation."

The next slide graphed the average debt incurred by a medical student in different countries.

"You will earn millions of dollars more over a lifetime as a specialist than as a primary care doctor. A radiologist will earn twice as much, on average, as a primary care doctor. What is a strategically-thinking young medical student in the United States going to decide?"

The professor opened her water bottle and took a sip. "In India general practitioners and specialists make similar salaries. Same in the United Kingdom and across Europe." She turned to face the projected images. "Here are some of the policies being discussed to remedy the situation. It's essential for you to hear about them now, as they might influence this important choice of specialty, a choice each of you will make in the near future."

Brooke took notes and struggled to pay attention as Dr. Lipsett explained the different proposals and opinions of health care policy makers. She could see how the information would be useful for students who didn't know what type of medicine they would practice, but she had no doubt, and it had absolutely nothing to do with the salary she would eventually make as a cardiothoracic surgeon. It was simply her destiny.

The professor cleared her throat. "Rothaker has three scholarship opportunities available to each class of medical students, our small, but nonetheless well-intentioned, attempt to remedy the misallocation of specialists, based on the needs of the population. There's one for family practice; it requires you to work in an underserved inner-city area for two years, one for dermatology and one for surgery, each with its own requirements. You can apply for them online."

Brooke's hand shot up, but Dr. Lipsett ignored her and said, "You can look up the details on the school website under scholarships."

Brooke quickly located the details of the surgical scholarship on her laptop, reading that it took into consideration clinical excellence, academic achievements, and leadership. She had received an award at Everett that had similar criteria, minus the clinical part. It was a great honor. She had been nominated and selected by her professors; she didn't even have to apply. If she could get selected for something similar once, then certainly she could do it again, particularly if she knew it existed and went after it. As she continued reading, she saw that the surgical scholarship was only awarded to a fourth-year student and that the award would pay for the final year of tuition *and* all outstanding loans.

Excellent.

Adding one more goal to her list offered a tingling rush of exhilaration. She lifted herself up a little straighter, pushed her shoulders back, and smiled. *Everyone else in the room who wants to be a surgeon, too bad for you.*

Chapter Twelve

A bouquet of flowers sat on the floor outside Brooke's room. She picked them up and Jeff popped his head out of his open door.

"Who are they from? Everyone's dying to know. Are they from Xander?"

"Excuse me? Jeff, why would Xander send me flowers?"

"Because you're perfect for each other. Physically."

Brooke scrunched up her face. "Maybe I should ask Xander which team he's on, just to make sure. Since you're so interested." She sounded unusually playful as she picked the card out of the bouquet's center. "I don't know who they're from."

Jeff hovered next to her. "Open the card."

She opened the envelope and read the note aloud. "It says: 'You were right. It's not the nicest dorm by a long shot. Maybe these will help. See you when I get back from traveling the world. From Robert.'" Brooke snorted. "They're from a friend. A friend from Everett. I saw him on Saturday. When Julie was, you know . . ."

"Friends send flowers when you're sick and when you die. He's not a friend, sweetie."

"Hmmf." Brooke entered her room and tossed the flowers in her sink.

Great. Just what I needed.

Chapter Thirteen

Xander's door was part-way open. Jeff's voice carried down the hallway and into his room. "Are those from Xander?"

He heard Brooke's response, "Why would Xander send me flowers?"

The questions didn't make sense. Xander's own troubles were weighing on him, despite his attempt to ignore them until they went away. He certainly hadn't been in the mindset to send flowers to anyone.

His laptop lay open to a description that perfectly summed up his condition:

Feeling detached from others and emotionally numb, experiencing sleeplessness, difficulty concentrating, depression, anger, irritability—

Xander closed the web page mid-sentence with a sharp click, before the power of suggestion made his symptoms worse. If only he could get control over what was happening to him. Why here? Why now of all times? Well, he thought he knew why, and it just sucked. He grabbed a Gatorade from his fridge, laced up his running shoes, stuck his room key in his pocket, and headed outside to run himself to the ground. This was how he would fix his problems and it was much healthier than getting wasted. He would run through drills he remembered from his toughest college football workouts. If that didn't wear him out enough to sleep through the night, he didn't know if anything would.

Xander exited through the back door to the dark and dumpy backside of the dormitory. He jogged across the road that led to the highway, past the parking garage, a Subway sandwich shop, and a donut store toward the undergraduate campus and its athletic fields. The late afternoon air was crisp and cool, a quintessential fall day. There were people of all ages running laps on the track when he arrived. He waited until a large space was open before entering between a girl with a bouncing brown braid and an older male runner with short shorts. He switched on his music and started to pick up the pace, immediately passing the girl. After a quarter mile he began to sprint on the long sides and pull back to catch his breath on the short sides, making a note of each lap when he passed Rothaker's mascot, the clever white fox staring up at him from the track. He pounded away on the rubber, arms pumping, all his muscles fully engaged. Rivulets of sweat coursed down his forehead and stung his eyes. He pushed himself to the edge of being sick, and then let up just enough to continue.

***

Brooke finished her timed interval workout on the track and slowed to a jog. Xander's solid, well-muscled figure dashed past. He wore loose athletic shorts and a University of Nebraska t-shirt. The edge of a tattoo peeked out from under one shirt-sleeve. Brooke studied his form from the back, continuing to observe him while she stepped off the track and performed a graceful cool down routine of yoga poses and stretches alongside the bleachers. His shoes pounded the ground, his muscles strained. It was easy to imagine crowds cheering for him at a football game, how they would be impressed with his intensity and stamina.

Xander continued to push himself. He appeared to be motivated by a need deeper than the desire to be fit, fast, and have ripped abdominals. He slowed, his expression set in a determined grimace. Close to where she stood, he came to an abrupt stop and bent over as if he was going to be sick. He didn't seem to be aware of anyone else as he closed his eyes briefly, pressed his lips together, and straightened up again. After a few unsteady steps he returned to running, back to a sprint within seconds, as if someone or something sinister was chasing him.

Brooke recognized the relentless urge in his eyes. She didn't know what type of force was driving Xander Cross, but she could relate.

Chapter Fourteen

Robert believed his date with Brooke had gone well. In his mind, he replayed every minute he could remember. At the time, he was agonizingly aware of how long he had waited to have a chance with her. Once they were finally alone, he did not want the night to end. He longed to take her hand, he wanted to hold her, kiss her, hear her say that she always had a thing for him . . . but as much as he wanted it, he didn't sense that she felt the same at all, and the moment needed to be right.

The night ended with a brief embrace, a chaste kiss on the cheek and Brooke saying she needed to study. Robert wasn't offended. She was unusually driven and studied an inordinate amount of time. He was only disappointed that none of the scenarios he fantasized about for the past two years were going to become reality, at least not yet. He reminded himself of how Ethan must have felt, month after month of incredible frustration, and that steeled his own determination. The will to pursue something with perseverance was the difference between wanting it and having it.

Brooke sent a text to thank him for the flowers. She didn't know that Robert agonized as much over those four sentences as he did writing an entire chapter of his senior thesis on comparative political theory. "See you when I get back," had been "Hope to see you when I get back," "Would like to see you when I get back," and "Can't wait to see you when I get back." At one point the message was a poem expressing his interest in seeing her when he returned, but fortunately in hindsight, that effort was totally scrapped. Even his closing had taken a dozen different forms, all carefully analyzed before he finally gave up and settled on "From Robert."

He followed her text with a phone call and was interested to hear about the gym where she would be teaching and the radiographic anatomy lesson she had that day. She sounded polite and, unfortunately, in a rush to get off the phone.

Brooke stayed incredibly busy with her studies, and not because she required more time than others. She was just the most disciplined of perfectionists when it came to her school work. As an undergraduate, she won the very prestigious Peak of Everett award during her junior year. He imagined there were people who would kill for that type of incredible honor. Well, not literally.

Money could buy almost anything, even people. That wasn't how he wanted to shape his relationship with Brooke, but it was also frustrating to know that she was one of the few people who were not impressed with his family's wealth, merely because, he assumed, he hadn't played a direct role in earning it. It was both a positive thing and a difficult one to swallow. For two long years now, he had wanted her, but on his own merit.

How can I get more involved in Brooke's life?

She didn't drink or party. She didn't do much aside from studying and exercising, as Jessica had pointed out to him many a time, but when she did go out she was charming and sweet, and despite an abundance of confidence, there was something a little quirky and innocent about her that he found extremely endearing. He was willing to travel to Rothaker every weekend and take her to lunch and dinner, every day even, he could buy a condo nearby . . . she had to eat, didn't she? Perhaps she would want to catch a movie or a play? Hopefully a relationship would evolve from there.

But they weren't there yet.

He needed a reason to come back to campus often, as soon as he returned from Europe.

He planned his six-week trip weeks ago, with a friend who had not found gainful employment four months post-graduation and wasn't overly concerned about it either. It was meant to be a free-spirited tour around Europe, like many students did during college or after graduation. Except he and his friend would be staying in five-star hotels instead of youth hostels. Although they had committed to using actual backpacks, part of the experience, everything they bought would be mailed directly home. And since they could purchase anything they needed, they were going to be relatively unencumbered. It was an adventure he looked forward to, until now. The chance to build a relationship with Brooke, now that Ethan was out of the picture, changed everything.

I don't want to be so far from her.

He needed to see her again as soon as possible. And, to add insult to injury, the once essential, unstructured tour of Europe now made him feel like a spoiled child.

With a deep sigh, he sat behind the modern desk in his favorite office in the family home and logged into his computer. Before leaving, he intended to accomplish some of the work for which he got paid. He was in charge of researching and narrowing down recipients for his grandfather's philanthropic organization, the Mending Foundation for Charitable Works and Social Improvements, simply called the Mending Foundation, or the Foundation for short. His research involved a great deal of travel, if he deemed it necessary to find out more about an organization. Every other month, he and others would make their recommendations to the board, (all members of his family) who cast a vote and then dinner was served with an exquisite wine. He was also responsible for presenting the checks, or endowments, whatever it turned out to be, with vastly different amounts of fanfare depending on the situation, after the details had been worked out by their financial and legal experts.

With his loafers up on the desk, he read correspondence from a slew of organizations that wrote to the Foundation in hope of receiving aid, but he couldn't focus because he couldn't stop thinking about Brooke Walton. He needed to build on his recent visit, to hurry back to that awful dorm of hers. He scrunched his face until a great idea popped into his head.

It makes perfect sense. Or is it too obvious? Only one way to find out.

He picked up his phone and called his Grandfather.

"Hey, Grandad. It's Robert."

"Oh." His grandfather grumbled, and it sounded to Robert like he dropped the phone and picked it up again. "Robert?"

"Yeah. Hi, Grandad."

"How are you?"

"Doing well. And you?"

"I'm not going to complain today because I know it's all downhill from here." His grandfather had been using that same line for as long as Robert could remember.

"I visited Rothaker last weekend, so I was thinking of you. I have two good friends there, one from Deerfield at the law school and a friend from Everett at the medical school."

"Who is your friend from Everett? Is it that Jewish boy? He was a fine young man."

"Ethan? No, it's not Ethan. Her name is Brooke; she's a woman." He deliberately mentioned her gender because his grandfather's expected response usually proved entertaining.

"A woman? That's right, they're letting women do anything they want there now, aren't they? They have special criteria for admitting them, don't they? It's called affirmative action. That's what it's called."

"Women have been attending medical school for almost a century, Granddad. And I don't believe they benefit from affirmative action anymore." How did his sister tolerate these comments? His mother could not. "The female surgeon who removed your gallbladder last year was pretty competent."

His grandfather huffed. "That was an emergency and I had no choice. There was no male doctor available . . ."

His grandfather didn't seem any less outraged about it six months later, despite the best expected outcome. Robert shook his head, chuckling to himself. He had better change the subject or he would be listening to the injustice of being operated on by a female physician for the rest of the call.

"I called to run something by you, about Rothaker."

"Why didn't you go to Rothaker, Robert?"

"Because I wanted to go to Everett." Robert laughed. They had this conversation almost every time the words "college" or "university" arose. At least now that he had finished college, his grandfather could only ask him why he hadn't gone to Rothaker instead of "when are you going to transfer to Rothaker? I'm sure they'll still take you. I can have a word with them."

"Deerfield and Rothaker, those are the best schools for a fine young man like you, Robert."

"I got one right then. Anyway, I was working, identifying targets for the Foundation, and I was thinking about the medical school dormitory at Rothaker. I was there this weekend and it's a disaster. I think it needs help. It's not on par with any of the other buildings or dorms. They have students coming from all over the world to study there, and the dorm reminds me of temporary construction at a community college. What do you think?"

"I would rather have the money go to a new academic building or the sports facilities, but I would be in favor of helping Rothaker with whatever it is they need. I love that school. You should have gone there, Robert. What's the matter with you and your father?"

"Great! Thanks, Granddad. Gotta go." Robert loved his family and he wanted to keep it that way. He could only tolerate his grandfather in small doses.

Chapter Fifteen

On the way to anatomy, Brooke reviewed the name, attachment, and main action for every muscle in the back and upper limbs. She repeated each five times, like a mantra, before switching to the next one, pulling the information from where she had already compartmentalized it in her brain. When she arrived, Rakesh and Rachael emerged from the walk-in refrigerator, maneuvering their cadaver table between them.

"Oh, Rakesh. I almost forgot," Rachael said. "This morning I saw the information for the scholarships Dr. Lipsett mentioned. I'm considering the dermatology one, but I reviewed the surgical one too. It's very generous. I wanted to make sure you saw it. If you know you want to be a surgeon, there's no reason not to apply."

"Thanks, Rachael. I'll look at it later today."

Rachael glanced at Brooke, who was now assisting them. "It helps to review the criteria now, so you have the next few years to position yourself as the best candidate, should you decide to apply."

Brooke glared at Rachael. *She knows I'm going into surgery.* "His dad is a surgeon, Rachael. Do you think he needs a scholarship? I know it's an honor, but shouldn't it be reserved for the people who don't already have a free ride from their parents?"

"How much one's parents make has nothing to do with scholarships." Rachael wagged her finger.

Xander held up a hand. "Calm down, everyone."

"Surgery in India is much respected," said Rakesh, "but it is not highly paid like surgery in America. Can we—"

"Well, it doesn't matter anyway." Brooke shrugged. *That scholarship is mine.*

She hadn't minded accruing a mountain of debt to become a surgeon. The cost of her dream had a price tag. But now that she knew about the surgical scholarship, why should someone else less deserving achieve their dream for free when her dream cost hundreds of thousands of dollars plus interest?

Rachael and Rakesh went to get the tools. Xander stood next to the table, fidgeting with his hands, his expression grim. When Brooke pulled back the plastic and the sheet, a moan escaped his lips. Xander staggered sideways and braced himself against the wall. His chest heaved, and he was instantly shaking and sweating.

Brooke watched it happen. *That's the third time I've witnessed his strange behavior.*

He struggled to right himself. His face contorted, and he stumbled from the room.

Rachael didn't appear to notice anything unusual. She turned to Brooke. "Where's Xander going?"

Brooke shrugged.

"Okay. Whatever." Rachael watched him leave. "I'm going to assume he's coming back. Let me figure out who gets to make the first dissections today."

Dr. Sarcough began his overview of the material they would be covering during class. By the time Xander returned fifteen minutes later, he had missed the entire lesson instructing the technique for inserting a central line as well as his turn practicing on the cadaver.

"Are you okay?" Brooke whispered, leaning close.

"Yeah. I'm okay. I just had to take care of something." Xander focused on the enlarged lymph node pictures Dr. Sarcough projected on the screen. Perspiration covered his brow even though the room was always cool.

Brooke nudged Rakesh. "What type of cancer do you think our guy has?"

Rakesh tapped his finger against the edge of the steel table. "He's young and otherwise looks healthy. We can narrow his cancer down to one of the most aggressive forms of cancer that has no cure. Or he would not be here."

Brooke nodded. "Power of elimination. That's good, Rakesh."

"I'm guessing leukemia." Rakesh held a scalpel in his gloved hand, poised to make an incision. "We're supposed to dissect the axillary lymph node first."

"Okay." Xander's voice sounded weak and shaky.

"Our first sign of disease." Rakesh beamed.

"What do you see?" Brooke stepped closer. "In the lymph node?"

"Scarring, a slightly unusual color and texture. Don't you think?"

Xander leaned forward against the table. "I'm not sure."

"I see it," said Rachael, leaning closer and blocking the area from Brooke.

Xander rubbed his chin. "How is the scarring related to the cancer?"

Brooke edged into Rachael's space, forcing her to move to the side. "It's a result of treatment to the site."

"So, a cancer in the lymph nodes?" Xander stared at the back of Rakesh's head.

"Lymphoma?" Rachael peeled off a glove and consulted the computer.

"Non-Hodgkin's lymphoma is more aggressive." Brooke's voice rose. "We need to prepare a section for the microscope."

"That's one of the most common cancers," said Rakesh. "If it is non-Hodgkin's lymphoma we should see atrophy in the thyroid gland, lungs, the GI tract, the liver, the kidneys…"

"It can spread to any tissue I think. Most of our findings will be histological. And we're speculating," said Rachael. "We haven't even learned about these diseases yet."

"We're brainstorming." Xander wiped a single drop of sweat from his temple.

Brooke leaned in close to Rakesh. "Are your hands cramping yet? Do you need me to relieve you of that scalpel?"

"My hands are just fine."

"This is exciting," said Brooke, "finding our first abnormal discovery."

Rachael frowned. "We should try not to be so excited about finding this man's cancer. I doubt he was happy about it."

Brooke huffed. "He wanted us to be excited about the opportunity to find it and learn from it. That's why he's here on this table."

"Still. I feel sad for Charlie," said Rachael.

Brooke shook her head. "We're not supposed to name the cadavers."

"Charlie was the name of the first patient I befriended at the HIV clinic. He was about the same age as our cadaver when he died from rare sarcomas."

While her classmates took turns enthusiastically examining the axillary lymph node, Rachael dutifully sprayed the cadaver's exposed body with the wetting agent to keep it moist. And Xander did his best to keep most of it covered.

Chapter Sixteen

"I'm Xander Cross. I have an appointment with Dr. Chavez."

The office manager smiled up at him. "Are you a new patient?"

"Yes."

"Do you have your insurance card with you?"

Xander removed his wallet and handed his student ID over the desk. The manager typed on her keyboard and handed it back.

"Please have a seat, Mr. Cross, and fill out these forms while you wait. Dr. Chavez will see you next."

After filling out the required paperwork, Xander thumbed through a Sports Illustrated magazine. It was the first time in weeks that he had picked up any piece of reading material not related to his school work. He stared at pictures of Alabama's offensive line, but found himself unable to focus on the articles, he was too anxious. He had become increasingly desperate to see a psychiatrist since he made the appointment and now that he was there, hearing his name called couldn't come fast enough.

The last few weeks had been hell, and he wasn't getting better. Until recently, his mind had always been dependable and trustworthy, he'd always been in control of his memories and reactions. Before his recurrent nightmares started, the last nightmare he could remember was over a decade ago, back in elementary school.

"Xander Cross." Dr. Chavez offered a neutral smile and held the door to his office open while Xander rose and crossed the room. The doctor wore horn-rimmed glasses and a tweed blazer over his lightweight cashmere sweater. Wiry black hair protruded from his head and from eyebrows that needed a trim.

“Come in, please.”

“Thanks. This is my first time visiting a psychiatrist.”

The room lacked the chaise lounge that was ever present in the movies. It appeared like all the other professor’s offices, but with only a few books neatly stacked on shelves and minus any mess. Dr. Chavez motioned to a leather wingback chair and sat down in an identical chair across from Xander.

“Hello. Mr. Cross. May I call you Xander?”

“Yes, sir. Of course.”

“Please tell me a little about yourself and why you’re here today.”

“Okay.” Xander crossed his leg over his knee without realizing it because Dr. Chavez did the same. Where to start? He considered what information he should provide to enable his doctor to efficiently return him to his old dependable self. “I’m a first-year medical student here, at Rothaker.”

“Excellent,” said Dr. Chavez in the same neutral tone one would use to say, “this is a pencil.” No judgements. At least, not yet.

“I’m from Nebraska. I went to college on a football scholarship. I was thirty pounds heavier then.” Xander let out a short, nervous laugh and uncrossed his leg. “I applied to medical school, didn’t expect to get in to Rothaker; was surprised when I did. Once I received my acceptance, I requested to defer my enrollment for two years, so I could enlist in the army.”

“What made you decide to defer medical school for the army?”

“I wanted to serve my country, but I didn’t want to make a career of it. My father, grandfather, and two of my uncles were in the military. The two-years as an infantry soldier guaranteed me some money for med school. I have six years in the reserves, and I can graduate almost debt free.”

“Sounds like a good plan.”

“After a year, my unit was deployed to Afghanistan. I have to say, there were hours and days and weeks in Afghanistan when I was incredibly bored and hot, or incredibly bored and cold, and the prospect of going to medical school to learn to save lives in one of the most respected institutions in the country seemed like the product of a hallucination."

Dr. Chavez chuckled.

"Most of what I did there involved the same routine day after day, nothing complicated." Xander looked down at his tightly clasped hands. "But . . . there were a few experiences that I wish I had missed."

Dr. Chavez nodded.

"Five months have passed since I returned, and I've been fine. The transition was strange at times, common places and activities seemed almost surreal on certain days, but mostly I was grateful to be home with my family and friends. In fact, I appreciated them like never before. And they treated me like a hero, even though I didn't deserve it."

Xander pressed his lips together and shifted his gaze to the doctor's bookshelf. "The time between Afghanistan and here was relaxing. It flew by. I earned some extra money doing construction for the same people I'd worked for every summer during high school. I was looking forward to medical school the whole time. I had no problem coping and I was in control of my thoughts and my memories. I felt normal. And healthy."

"Which brings us to an important question then. The reason for your appointment today?" The doctor uncrossed his leg, shifted in his seat, and crossed the other on top.

"So, yeah, the reason I'm here. On the first day of school, I was in gross anatomy, and everything was still good. Then we unveiled our cadaver. It was a young guy and as soon as I saw him, I had my first flashback. Like I was back in Afghanistan. I could even smell the place. It smells bad in some parts of the city, a dirty smoky smell that hangs in the air and gets under your skin and into everything. When I saw the cadaver for the first time, that smell was so real again, all around me. It was the first time I've smelled it over six months. And then, what I saw . . . I saw a different body on the table. I guess I had a panic attack or something, but it was so real, what I was seeing and smelling."

The Doctor wrote on his tablet.

"Since then I've been having flashbacks and nightmares and I'm just not myself. I've had three incidents in the anatomy lab. If our cadaver stays mostly covered I'm usually fine, but I never know if I'm going to be okay or not. I'm anxious, nervous, and depressed and that is *not* me. I can't focus like I usually can. Whatever is happening to me is disrupting everything. I need help."

"Is there one event in particular that you keep re-experiencing?"

"Yeah, there is." Xander squeezed his eyes shut for a second. "It's been difficult. I feel like I'm stuck. I feel like I'm losing it." *Particularly when I keep watching myself charging forward at full speed, angry, covered in blood, and I don't know why.*

Xander curled his hands into fists then splayed his fingers wide.

"Have you discussed those incidents with anyone else since they occurred?"

"We were debriefed for a few days, answering the same questions repeatedly. But outside of the debriefings, no, I haven't talked about anything specific."

"So, you have not discussed what you saw?"

"Yes. I mean no. I was debriefed. I wouldn't say I discussed what I saw."

"Have you discussed how you felt with anyone yet?"

"No."

"Okay. I just needed to know where we were starting in this process. I'm sure you have a good idea that you're suffering from post-traumatic stress disorder."

"Yeah. I figured. I did all the research I could on it and it makes sense and I know I need help. Because it's been a few weeks now and I'm not getting better and it's not going away."

"After a traumatic experience your mind can be in shock. It usually manifests three months to a year after witnessing a traumatic event, so it happening at this time is not surprising." Dr. Chavez took a deep breath. "Cognitive-behavioral therapy would involve careful and gradual exposure to the situations that remind you of the trauma. But in your case, it sounds like the cadaver you saw was a rude re-exposure that triggered your post-traumatic stress disorder symptoms."

"So, can you help me?"

"Yes, there are a few things we can do that should help, but one thing I might suggest is that you consider taking a leave of absence until you've recovered before continuing your studies. Medical school is a stressful time, I remember that part well, and that stress can exacerbate the emotions you're experiencing. Treatment could take months to be effective."

"There's no way I'm doing that. I can't take a month off, or even a few weeks off, you know that. I'd have to defer another year. No way."

"I understand. Well, on the one hand, you will have access to support close by and on a regular basis while you're at Rothaker, and that will help. However, if you're going to continue with your studies while you receive treatment, I'm going to recommend you take a serotonin reuptake inhibitor, which can help minimize the anxiety you're feeling."

"Okay. Fine."

"Exercise can also help."

"Okay. Good."

"And it can be helpful to share what you're feeling with others, particularly other veterans that may have experienced something similar, or with any family or friends that you feel close to."

"Okay."

"Do you have family you can talk to?"

"My family would listen in a heartbeat, but I wouldn't feel right calling to tell them my problems. It would be difficult for them because they're so far away. I know they would want to help me and it would put pressure on them. My mother would worry."

"A friend or another veteran? Someone going through a similar situation?"

Xander rubbed his palms on his pant legs. "I'll figure something out, I can do that."

"I'd also like you to keep a journal where you jot down any depressing thoughts, unwanted emotions, and disturbing memories. It will make it easier for us to access them in future sessions."

"Okay."

"Will you tell me if you feel like you're a danger to yourself or anyone else?"

"Yes, sir. Of course."

"Schedule another appointment on your way out and we'll work through this."

Xander bowed his head. "Thank you, sir."

Chapter Seventeen

Brooke taught back-to-back classes at Performance Fit the next day.

"Please grab a small ball and light weights," she told the class, "and let's get started. Take a deep breath in, lift your sternum, exhale, and let your rib cage drop down and relax. At the same time, contract your abdominals in and up, find that core connection, and gently draw your sitz bones together. It's subtle but that's your neutral position, it's how you want to sit, stand, and move, so try to maintain that position throughout and breathe."

They began with an arm series, working biceps, triceps, deltoids, and traps to the point of fatigue while activating the stabilizing muscles around the spine. Brooke kept her eyes peeled for improper form, which she promptly corrected.

She spotted Mike waiting outside the studio doorway when she finished. *Darn it!*

"Great class," he said, "that's what I'm hearing all around."

"Thanks. This is a great gym, a great place to teach."

"Hey, um, any chance you have copies of those certifications with you?" He sounded almost apologetic.

"I'm so sorry. It turns out I don't even have them at school with me. I left them at home. But I've asked my mother to mail them. I should have them shortly. Don't worry."

"Okay, no problem." He ran his hand over his scalp and smiled.

She took a quick shower and stole two of the gym's complimentary sparkling white towels, depositing them into her bag to add to her growing collection. On her way out, a woman who had just been in the front row of her yoga class stopped her.

"I heard you were a medical student." The woman smiled. "I'm a fourth-year. Jan. Do you live in the dorm?"

Brooke nodded.

"Did you drive here?"

"I don't have a car."

"That's what I figured. I live off campus, but I drive by the dorm." She twirled her keys. "I'll give you a ride."

"Oh, thanks. I appreciate it."

"No problem. I liked your class. I came to de-stress, but it was challenging. I feel like I have more energy now."

"Glad it worked for you."

They walked beside each other to the parking garage. "Here it is." Jan laughed and opened the door to a beat-up, older model Honda. "No need to lock it."

Brooke opened the door and settled onto the stained fabric seat. "What type of medicine are you going into?"

"General Surgery."

"Oh!" Brooke's face lit up. "I want to be a surgeon also."

Jan snorted. "I don't *want* to be a surgeon."

"Really? Then why?"

"I wanted to be a pediatrician, but after eight years of schooling I owe too much money to ever pay it back on that salary. Especially now, with all the insurance and government limitations on payment. So, to pay back my loans and not be poor into my late forties, I had to do four more years to specialize. I'm just saying, it's different for a lot of women, different than it is for men. If you ever have kids, you won't have the option to stay home with them. You can't decide you want to stay home and raise your kids when you owe a few hundred grand. Unless you marry a surgeon. I should have been a nurse. I could be a nurse practitioner with a few years of experience under my belt by now. Think it through. That's what I'm saying."

Dr. Lipsett's recent lecture on the misallocation of physician specialties came to mind. Jan could have shared her story there, to illustrate Dr. Lipsett's point. But for Brooke, surgery was the only clear choice.

"I've wanted to be a surgeon forever. A cardiothoracic surgeon. I won't be happy doing anything else."

"Good. Because you have to give up a lot. A bunch of my friends are getting married now, buying houses, having children. I bought my younger brother's piece of crap car to get from my pathetic apartment to school every day." She smacked the dashboard. Broken plastic knobs ran down the center and the symbols on the unbroken ones were faded beyond recognition.

"I'm not really interested in having children." *And I can handle not having a nice car or a starter home. I'll be fine, especially since I'm getting the surgical scholarship.*

"Which side is your room on?" Jan glanced toward the dorm.

"The back side."

"Oh no! I was too. You get used to the ambulances yet? They come flying out the hospital bay and they turn their sirens on right behind the dorm. They do it on purpose. They think the medical students are prima donnas. They get off on keeping them awake at night. I remember that first week. I'll never forget it. I almost moved out. I should have. I should have quit while I was ahead. Maybe if I hadn't gotten used to the ambulances . . ." She laughed as Brooke got out of the car.

"Thanks for the ride."

"Good luck."

Brooke considered Jan's comments as she walked to her room. She never had money available for anything beyond the basic necessities, but her growing mountain of loans kept her moving forward. She had to be a surgeon, but she also wanted choices. If she didn't owe hundreds of thousands of dollars, maybe she could work as a surgeon in a third world country where she could do a little more experimenting without anyone watching over her shoulder. The surgical scholarship allowed some freedom. She needed that scholarship.

Chapter Eighteen

After much thought, he called Brooke. “Hi. It’s Robert.”

“I know.” Brooke exhaled loudly. “I have your number in my phone now. Hi.”

“Visiting you gave me an idea.”

“What sort of idea?”

This was the challenge. What to disclose? When she asked about his job, he told her only that he managed funds. She hadn’t asked who he worked for, so he didn’t explain that the hundreds of millions of dollars he managed was his family’s own philanthropic trust and that his main responsibility was to help figure out where to donate chunks of that money. The whole point of making another donation to Rothaker was so he would have an excuse to visit with Brooke. But how could he visit with her and not tell her what he was doing there? Other women would be impressed and interested if they knew. Those were the type of women he needed to avoid. There were plenty of people around who liked him because of his money. Brooke, on the other hand, was all about hard work and perseverance. He worried she would be turned off when she discovered he was working for his family, as if it didn’t count as work.

He fiddled with the bronze paperweight on his desk. “The funds that I manage are part of a philanthropic organization. My job is to help find places that can use donations. Universities, hospitals, museums, places like that. We’ve given gifts to Rothaker before, earmarked to fulfill specific needs. So, I was thinking, that dorm of yours isn’t exactly up to par with the rest of the buildings on campus, despite being associated with one of the top medical schools in the country. I was thinking it should be remodeled.”

"What? That doesn't make any sense."

That was not the response he was expecting. "So, it would fit in with the rest of the university."

"But it's already built. I know I said it was ugly, but it's perfectly functional. The medical dorm needs to be near the medical campus, and the medical campus needs to be near the teaching hospital, which happens to be surrounded by some really depressed neighborhoods. If your company has money to give away, aren't there more important places for it to go? Cancer research? Starving children?"

"Yes, but that's not really the type of donations we provide." He wasn't sure what to say, she had definitely burst his bubble. "I thought you said—"

"And Rothaker? I mean, seriously, of all places? Surely there are more deserving organizations that don't already have huge multi-million-dollar endowments. Does your company just do building improvements? Maybe the Foundation should help spruce up the neighborhoods surrounding the hospital instead. Like I said, there are some pitiful areas nearby. Dilapidated. It's sad to imagine people living there. The homes look abandoned, but they're not."

Robert chewed on his fingernails. "Well, um. I guess I figured—"

"Look, if that's what they want to do, fine. I'm just always surprised when large amounts of money are spent making things look fancy when it's not necessary, but I'm not an architect, or a decorator. I'm sure it will be appreciated if it's done, and why not have it look more like the rest of the buildings on campus, like you said."

"Yes, it's because, you see—"

"Just for the record, no one is going to turn down an offer of acceptance from the best medical school in the country because of the dormitory. And if it really bothered anyone, they could always move out and live off campus. How can there be money freely available for something like that when there are so many more important things that need financial attention? And why would any organization pay to make a building look better, a building that wasn't even their own when they could help people and organizations that didn't have enough to survive? It just doesn't make sense!"

Robert had previously witnessed Brooke's passion regarding various issues— recycling, for one. Brooke had seen beer bottles in Ethan's trash can once, and sort of freaked out about it. He wasn't sure how to proceed.

"I didn't mean to stomp on your company's plans, Robert. I apologize." Pages shuffled on her end of the phone.

Robert took a deep breath and tugged at a tuft of hair. "Even if you're not fully on board with the idea, I was hoping I could get some ideas from you, since you're living there, about improvements. I wouldn't specify how it needs to be done, but I do make certain stipulations about what needs to be addressed as conditions of accepting the donation."

"Okay." She sighed. "I can ask a few classmates to think about it and come up with some ideas to send you."

"Like your friend Rachael?" he joked, remembering Brooke's comment about not liking her.

"I told you, I'm not fond of Rachael and I wouldn't call her a friend, but she would be perfect. I'm sure she'll have a lot to say. She has a lot to say about everything. She'll probably draw up a blueprint for you."

Robert laughed.

"Just let me know when you need the ideas. When do you think you'll be here next?"

He could be there tomorrow, he could be there in two hours, but Brooke would be busy with classes and studying. It would have to wait until he returned from Europe. By the time he got back, seven weeks would have passed.

"As soon as I get back from my trip, I'll start working on it."

I hope Brooke keeps her head in her books while I'm gone and no one else notices how wonderful she is.

"Okay."

"So, I'll see you when I get back then."

"Have a good time." Brooke hung up the phone as Robert was saying goodbye.

Chapter Nineteen

Xander climbed out of bed and stretched. Thanks to the many beers he consumed the previous night, while Connor stuck to seltzer waters, he'd slept more soundly than he had in weeks. After brushing his teeth, he heard a knock. He stuck his toothbrush in the stand, spit, and yelled, "Yeah?"

"It's Brooke."

"Hold on a second." He pulled on athletic shorts before opening the door, baring a well-developed chest and an inquisitive grin, but puffy eyes.

Brooke leaned against his doorframe. "Would you like to go for a run with me?"

"Uhh. Sure? That's random."

"I saw you running on the track last week. Pretty intense." She grinned. "I believe you'll prove to be a good running partner."

Xander raised his brows. "Okay. What time?"

"How about nine-thirty? Or I could wait until nine forty-five"

"Nine forty-five it is. Oh . . . and Brooke?"

"Yes?"

"Next time, ask me the night before so I can maybe not drink so much." He chuckled. "Although this might be the best thing for me, to sweat it out." He smiled at Brooke's backside. He didn't have much choice, she had walked away while he was still talking.

There was something strange about Brooke. Maybe a touch of Asperger's? She was smart as a whip, but it was her single-mindedness that might cross the fine line of normality. Her social skills were slightly off, possibly. Most people didn't notice because she was gorgeous. It was hard to see past her looks, which were also intimidating. Not that he was one to judge anyone, particularly these past few weeks— talk about being slightly off one's game. But while he couldn't put his finger on it exactly, he was pretty sure there was something different about Brooke, something with a precise diagnostic code. It would be interesting to spend time alone with her. He didn't know what to expect.

***

It was cool outside, typical weather for early October, perfect for running.

Brooke bent over to stretch. "What sort of pace?"

"You can set the pace." Xander didn't mind a slow jog. He could end with some sprints later if he still needed a workout, although today would probably not be the day to push it. Not after last night.

They started running. Faster than Xander expected. At a pace that might induce yesterday's Coronas to make a second appearance. *I really underestimated her.*

"So where did you go to school?" Xander was one of the few people in their class who had not asked everyone where they went to college. He only knew that Connor had attended another Big Ten school, Northwestern, and could talk football details with him.

"Everett. I transferred there my junior year from Cedarhurst College."

"I know Everett, but not Cedarhurst."

"No one does. My father works there. He teaches history. It's a good, small school. I got lots of attention."

"Why did you leave?"

"Oh, you know," Brooke smirked. "I just wanted to expand my horizons."

"Fair enough."

After a mile, Brooke removed her light hoodie and tied it around her waist. Xander couldn't keep from staring at her fantastic body. He averted his eyes and instead thought about how nice it was to have slept peacefully for a change. Then he tried to clear his mind until he heard nothing but comforting white noise forming a rhythm between his breath and their strides.

Xander studied the perfectly manicured athletic field to their right. It reminded him of old times. “Friday and Saturday nights seem like the only times that any of us stray from the usual grind. What did you do last night?”

“Studied. I guess I didn’t stray.”

“You didn’t go out?”

“I went out to dinner last Saturday. That was my going out for the month.” Brooke laughed, even though it was pretty much true. “How about you? Oh yes, you already said. You did some impressive beer drinking.”

“I was with a bunch of the first-years. It was an impromptu outing. I’m sure you would have been more than welcome.” Why hadn’t Brooke been included? Connor of all people would have wanted her along, he always said how lucky Xander was to have her as one of his lab partners. At least Connor didn’t call her “the really hot chick” anymore; he definitely respected Brooke.

“Don’t worry about me. Connor invited me. I told him I had to study.”

Xander laughed. “That sounds like telling someone you can’t go out because you need to wash your hair.”

“It was the truth.”

“I know. I believe you. That’s why it’s funny.” After several weeks as classmates, he knew that she was beyond serious about school, even compared to the other medical students.

They kept up a demanding pace, following the same route Brooke drove in Robert’s convertible. They passed the modern business school and ran through a giant tunnel of contemporary art, before Brooke finally broke the silence.

“Would you mind if I asked you something personal?”

He raised his eyebrows. “Fire away.”

“What is going on with you? Do you have a particular medical condition?"

Xander turned his head to study her. "Huh?"

"You had a reaction or an episode in anatomy lab. Three different times."

His mouth dropped open. "I was trying to hide it, apparently not well enough." This was the first time he acknowledged one of his episodes to anyone besides his psychiatrist. He'd almost told Connor last night, but the opportunity to have a serious conversation never arose. He had no reason to be embarrassed. It wasn't his fault and it wasn't uncommon. And Dr. Chavez said sharing might help him.

Brooke jumped over debris on the path like it was a small hurdle. "Do you mind talking about it?"

"Why not." He sighed, more like a huff since they were running. "I'm supposed to be talking about it with someone."

Brooke nodded, waiting.

"After college I enrolled in the military. Afghanistan. Front lines."

"I can't believe I didn't figure it out. I knew you were a veteran. You're experiencing post-traumatic stress disorder! Flashbacks?"

"Yes."

"That makes perfect sense. I can't believe I didn't think of that. That first time, we had just unveiled the cadaver, and it appeared you were going to be sick. I thought you were seriously squeamish. I couldn't believe it."

"In that case, I'm glad you know the truth now. I don't want anyone thinking I faint at the first sight of a dead body. What kind of doctor would that make me?"

"Um, one who keeps their patients alive?" Brooke grinned and Xander chuckled.

"The next time you reacted, I thought you might be having a diabetic episode. I figured you left the room to administer insulin. But I wasn't sure. What is it you're experiencing?"

They ran around a group of slower joggers, three girls who were giggling and unknowingly blocking the entire path. "I saw some harsh things there. I hate to share this with anyone, but it's true, there are some sick people in the world, capable of doing some unbelievable things. I tried to forget the worst shit I saw, but now I can't stop remembering."

Brooke studied him, eyes riveted.

"The first episode I ever had was when we initially uncovered the cadaver. I was fine until that moment. The timeline I'm experiencing is typical for PTSD symptoms. Seeing naked dead bodies and pictures of internal organs seems to trigger the flashbacks. I've learned the hard way that first-year medical school images are not the best for people returning from a war with atrocities."

"That's why you're so intent on keeping our cadaver covered. I imagined you were overly concerned about hydration."

"I seem to be okay when it's mostly covered."

"Good to know."

"I'm seeing a psychiatrist, here on campus. His name is Dr. Chavez."

"Glad you told me. You can talk about it with me, you know. I don't mind hearing the details, even the atrocities. I'm happy to listen."

Xander murmured, "thanks." They ran on silently for two blocks, their strides and breath in sync.

"Are you going to tell the rest of the group?" Brooke asked.

"I don't think so. Rachael would ask lots of questions, out of concern. I'd rather try and pretend it's not happening, if I can. At least for now."

"Sure. You're right about Rachael. Don't tell her."

Her response reminded Xander that Brooke and Rachael didn't always see eye to eye.

"I'm glad someone will understand what I'm going through in case I freak out in anatomy class again, but I'm hoping there won't be a next time, now that I'm getting treatment."

"I hope so too."

"I'd appreciate if you didn't mention it to anyone."

"I won't."

"Let's change the subject."

"Yeah . . . okay. If you want to. But like I said, you can talk to me anytime."

Chapter Twenty

The majority of Dr. Chavez's patients were depressed and anxious. They tended to suffer from stress brought on by the discrepancy between their expectations and the reality of their everyday lives, or the real and perceived sufferings of their childhoods. Eating disorders were also plentiful, which was not surprising in an academic environment plagued by perfectionism. He had to be particularly alert for signs of suicide and impending nervous breakdowns amongst the highest achievers. But many of his patients simply complained to him for a full hour. Xander Cross presented something new to work with.

***

"Good afternoon, Xander." Dr. Chavez dipped his head and swept his arm for Xander to enter. He wore a different cashmere sweater under the same tweed coat. His eyebrows were even longer than before.

"Hi, and thanks for seeing me again."

"How have you been since our last visit?"

"Pretty much the same. I've had a few good days and some bad days. Part of the problem is not knowing when I'm going to be okay and when I'm going to experience something that yanks me out of reality, so I'm always nervous. When I have the flashbacks it's like I'm truly back in Kandahar. My heart rate increases, I'm sweating, I'm afraid, and I can't control it."

Dr. Chavez nodded. "Are you sleeping well?"

"No. The nightmares are destroying my sleep. I didn't always get a full night's rest when I was overseas, but it was because I was uncomfortable, or someone was being a jackass and waking everyone up, but never because my mind was screwing with me."

"Let's try and get right to the incidents that you believe were most traumatic, so we can begin to process and make sense of them. Is that okay?"

"Yes, sir."

"You might uncover something else along the way, but we'll start with what you remember."

"Okay."

"Begin by sharing your most distressing memories, the ones that you're experiencing in your flashbacks and nightmares."

"There are just a few that I can think of."

"We're going to talk about those memories. My goal is to make sure you're remembering them correctly and to try to remove any fear or guilt or shame associated with them. When severe trauma remains unresolved it can overwhelm normal cognitive functioning."

"Okay. Where do I start?

"You decide what you think is important, so we can understand the specific experiences that are upsetting you."

"Okay." Xander rubbed his arms. "That would be . . .," he took a deep breath and exhaled slowly, "the worst experience was near the end of my deployment."

Xander spoke in a matter of fact manner. As long as he was grounded in the chair at the psychiatrist's office he had no problem recounting the tale, at least he had no problem with the background leading up to it. Telling the story was manageable. The flashbacks were different, because he wasn't merely remembering, he was reliving. His body reacted to his visions as if he was there.

Dr. Chavez nodded calmly for Xander to continue. His tablet sat untouched, balanced on his lap.

"I had been in Afghanistan for four months in the Army's 1st Battalion 20th infantry regiment. Three times a week we escorted John, a civil engineer, to a small village in the southern province of Kandahar. John was a good guy. Kind. Generous. He had three daughters. He knew I was going to medical school when we got home. His younger brother was a doctor, he talked about him to me all the time. He and I hit it off. We had loads of time to talk on the way to the village and back every week. John was working on a critical infrastructure plan for their citizens, improvements that would make a huge difference for them." Xander intertwined his fingers, together and apart, together and apart. "We'd been doing this for months, escorting John to where he would meet with the governor and the minister and a bunch of other guys who ran the area. There were always at least ten of us. Each mission could be different depending on what happened. Sometimes we had extra stops to drop something off or pick something up. We might check out reports of roadside bombs on the way. But mostly the trips were the same. While John met with the leaders for a few hours we were supposed to move around to patrol and talk to people, make sure nothing was brewing. For the most part there were just regular people going about their everyday business and we would walk around like we were browsing, pretending it's normal for us to be walking around in full military gear, thirty pounds of gun and ammo slung around our shoulders. After a few weeks it did seem normal. It became a routine and we knew what and who we would see on the way and when we got there. We always bought fresh fruit at the same stand from a boy and his mother. She never spoke to us, but he was always excited to try." Xander smiled sadly, remembering the broken English— *Here soldier. For You. You buy and like these grape.*

With his head lowered, Xander peered up at the psychiatrist. "I guess we got comfortable. You know how you can get comfortable when something becomes routine?"

Dr. Chavez nodded. He hadn't taken any notes yet.

"I liked the routine of the military. And of school and sports. I do well having a routine. And I like rules. Without rules just about anything goes. Rules are important."

Dr. Chavez nodded again and scribbled two words on his tablet.

"It rained that morning. It's so dry there. I hadn't seen a drop of rain in months. We were so psyched. The whole battalion went running outside, tipping our faces up, opening our mouths like we were kids catching snowflakes. I'll always remember that."

Xander crossed his arms in front of his abdomen, leaned forward.

"So, when we went to the village, two guys would stay behind in the MRAP to monitor a wider range. We rotated."

"What's an MRAP?"

"Sorry. It's an armored car, like a tank, built to withstand attacks and explosions. It stands for mine-resistant ambush protected vehicle. There's a telescopic camera on top. It's the safest place to be when you're out in the middle of a valley and there's gunfire."

Xander swept his gaze around the room noticing the perfectly arranged but mostly empty bookshelves and the tidy desk. His eyes settled on Dr. Chavez's feet. He wore running shoes. "All the officials in Kandahar wore running shoes. They were a sign of prestige, the equivalent of fancy Italian custom shoes here."

Xander stared, unseeing, at a spot over his doctor's head. Dr. Chavez switched the cross of his legs and waited silently.

"Sometimes we heard gunshots in the distance while we were on those trips. We had to wander the mountains trying to locate the source. Since we never found anyone we sort of stopped worrying. We didn't stop being prepared, but we probably stopped worrying." Xander shook his head. "I don't know." He struggled to pick and choose which pieces of information were relevant and necessary to describe a world that was as different from here as Mars. And yet Kandahar had become more mundane than anyplace at home because of the repetitive nature of his job there.

"That's okay. This is good. Keep going."

"Eight of us were spread out around the village, always in groups of twos. I was with Charlie, he was my age from Texas. We bought some fruit from a stand and were hanging out there. If something went wrong we were supposed to get John, the civil engineer, and get out of there. Those were our orders. Charlie and I were the farthest away from the office where the meetings took place, when the guys in the MRAP got a tip from an Afghani. They told all of us to move toward the office, and to be prepared for a probable ambush."

Xander pressed his lips together. Up until that point in his story there was a logical order to the day. Once chaos ensued, it was difficult to recollect how events had transpired.

"Before we reached the offices, we heard gunshots, rapid fire gunshots. An evacuation alarm shrieked, warning civilians to clear out. The gunfire continued, joined by explosions, thick, dark smoke, people screaming . . . and then our commanding officer was shouting for us to get back to the MRAPs. He said we needed to retreat and return with reinforcements. The villagers were scattering like pinballs, yelling words in Pashto or Urdu that didn't mean anything to us, the alarm kept sounding. It was so peaceful one minute, I was eating apricots for Christ's sake, and then it was chaos."

He had provided his account of the ambush to countless officers after the event, but that was months ago and most of what he had said had been prompted by informed questions. Repeating it today was frustrating because Dr. Chavez had not been in Afghanistan to experience any of it, and Xander didn't have the oratory skills to paint a true picture of the fear and the adrenaline and the horrifying sounds that surged and spiraled out of control, beyond imagination.

"I had a few MRIs of my back for a football injury during college. That's what I thought the situation sounded like while it was happening. Have you ever had an MRI?"

"Yes. I think I know what you mean."

"The whole area was like being inside an MRI but one hundred times louder, deafening. An assault of noises, constant and intermittent, from all around. It was overwhelming." Xander coughed and attempted to clear his throat.

Dr. Chavez stood up and took a bottled water out of a small refrigerator in the bookcase. He offered it to Xander, who opened it and drank like he was parched.

Xander set the bottle on the hardwood floor. He covered his mouth with his hands for a few seconds. Sweat formed over his brows. "So, we received the command to abandon our original directives and return to the vehicles immediately, until we had reinforcements. Six of us returned, including Charlie and I. Dan's arm was shot and spurting blood like a sieve. And Juan, one side of his face and neck were badly burned. Dan and Juan told us that John and the other two men were dead. I was almost to the office when we got the command to return, but I followed orders. I was the last one to return to the vehicle, just behind Charlie." Xander nodded. His heart pounded and his mind reached for something just out of his grasp. He wasn't sure what it was.

"I think we all panicked, at first, but we pulled it together. I applied a tourniquet to Dan's arm. He was going in to shock and in a world of hurt. I administered a shot of morphine and he stopped moaning. You know, you think if something like that happens to someone an ambulance is going to be there in minutes and ER docs are going to start ordering tests and taking care of you. But it wasn't like that. We were out in the middle of nowhere, there was surface to air fire from anti-aircraft artillery, shoulder launched rockets, and we were told to drive as far away as we could to meet a medevac. Dan and Juan both needed an OR. Thank God for morphine shots or the ride would have seemed so much longer."

Dr. Chavez leaned forward. "So, you had to witness two of your friends in terrible pain, and the rest of you weren't immediately able to give them the help they needed?"

"Yes."

"Helplessness is a very taxing, stressful condition."

"Yes. It was stressful. The guys were tough. Brave. Don't forget, most of these guys were young."

"As you are still young."

"I don't feel like it. My back doesn't feel like it. I know I'll look back in ten years and think that I was. That's how it works right? But I don't feel like it now."

"How did it feel when you had to retreat, leaving some of your company behind?"

"Oh, God. I don't know. Terrible? Sick? Like a massive failure? We believed they were dead, but still. Those were our orders, retreat and return shortly with reinforcements, so I didn't spend a lot of time questioning the decision, it wasn't mine to make. We had two guys who needed immediate medical attention. I was helping them stay calm, that's what I did. It's important to follow orders in the military. Following the chain of command is paramount, even when you don't agree. Otherwise there's no order, anything can happen. The military doesn't need rogue guys thinking they're super-heroes."

Dr. Chavez waited to see if Xander had more to add. "So, is that the scene that you keep revisiting?"

"No." He exhaled slowly. "I haven't gotten to the bad part yet."

Chapter Twenty-One

Brooke waved hello to Mike as she passed his office at Performance Fit. The exercise studio was packed with people waiting on her, all of them early to get a spot before the room filled. She had only been teaching there for four weeks and word had spread.

Mike smiled and waved. "Hi, Brooke. Did you have a chance to get your certifications mailed?"

"Hi, Mike. I'm so sorry. I just called my mother on the way here to make sure she sent them, and wouldn't you know it—she forgot. I think she just hates going to the post office."

Mike sighed, watching Brooke walk away. He considered looking up the certifications online and printing out copies, so he wouldn't have to pester Brooke.

I should have done that in the first place. I wrote the names on her resume when we met.

It took longer than he expected to search, figure out passwords, and make several phone calls, insisting his employee should be listed in their databases. When it was all said and done, so far as he could tell, Brooke wasn't registered as having certifications with any of the organizations she mentioned.

Perhaps I made a mistake in writing them down. Many of these places have similar names.

He popped out of his office to have a quick conversation with Brooke before her class started, but he was too late. He stood outside the studio, observing her as she alternated between demonstrating her moves and traveling around the unusually packed room adjusting postures and offering encouragement. He trudged back to his office but kept an eye on the time, so he could catch Brooke when her class ended. At the end of the hour he walked back to the studio and waited in the doorway again. Inside, Brooke answered questions and graciously accepted thanks until the next instructor cranked the volume of her music, a sure sign she wanted everyone from the last class to disappear.

"Hi, Mike," Brooke said, slipping her arms into her jacket.

"Looks like your class went well."

"Yes, it did."

"Before you leave, can you just give me the names of your professional certifications again? I must have misplaced them."

"Sure. Let's see . . . "Brooke answered with different organizations than the ones he had previously written down.

He returned to his computer and checked for her name in their databases. Nothing. Two of them didn't seem to exist at all. He debated calling the only one that was indeed real . . . *Just face the obvious. She's lying.* He dropped his head into his hands.

"You okay, Mike?" One of his regular exercise class attendees stood inside his door.

"I'm fine. How can I help you?"

"I just took Brooke's class. She's my new favorite. Please could you try and give her as many evening classes as possible? Can you just sort of boot Cindy and replace her with Brooke?"

"I'll take a look at the schedule. Thanks for letting me know." He was one of the first to hear when anyone was unhappy with a class, but it was more unusual to get feedback from happy customers. Brooke was doing a great job and he was receiving multiple requests to give her additional classes. He sighed and shook his head as he picked up his phone and called the guy who managed his website.

"Hi, Phil. It's Mike. I need you to make a change to the website. That bit about all the instructors being certified. I need you to remove that reference from the site completely. Not sure how many times it's in there, but please make sure you find them all and take them out. Thanks."

***

After class, Brooke took a shower and neatly folded another of Performance Fit's clean, complimentary towels into her duffel bag. At this rate she would soon have an entire set. It really was a good place to work.

Chapter Twenty-Two

Xander pressed his back against the chair and contracted his abdominal muscles, preparing his back as his physical therapist instructed so he could sit for the next hour.

Dr. Chavez cleared his throat. "At your last appointment you told me about the ambush in the Kandahar village. You got to the point in your story where you and five other members of your company were heading back toward your base. Two of them gravely wounded. Did I get that right?"

"Yes, sir. That's right."

"Would you like to continue from there?"

"Yes, sir." Xander bit on his bottom lip. "The injured men were taken away in a helicopter and other battalions joined us to return to the village. It had cleared out quickly. The booths were down, the animals gone. We approached in our formations. We had a plan to get directly to the office to retrieve our men."

"How did you feel about going back?"

Xander tipped his head up and stared at the ceiling, then back to the psychiatrist. "Scared. Maybe from seeing what had happened to Dan and Juan, scared thinking that's what we were in for. But my adrenaline was on steroids, I was so ready. It's almost like that before an important football game, the pressure, and the excitement, but this was different, because of the fear. We were determined to get our guys back."

"What did you expect to find?"

"We expected to find John and the two other men, and they would be dead. But the whole way there I devised different scenarios where they would be knocked out but still alive or hurt but not fatally injured."

"What else were you thinking?"

He curled his hands into tight fists. "I wanted to find the people responsible for the ambush."

"Why?"

"Because what they did . . . it was awful. How can I . . . how can they live with themselves?"

"Okay, let's back up a bit. Are you talking about what you found when you returned to the city? Is that what upset you the most?"

"I think so. I think it was when we returned." Xander twisted the hem of his t-shirt, crushing it between his fingers. *I'm not positive of when events occurred. Why don't I know for sure?*

He exhaled slowly and continued, sharing the story that for the past many months, he believed was the truth. "The first guy I saw was John." Xander grimaced. He lowered his head, rested his forehead against his palm. His shoulders tightened with tension, his heart rate rose, and anger brewed just below the surface. He could scarcely believe that he wasn't positive of what had happened, particularly his role in it.

"The guys from my company were dead. It wasn't like they had secret intel . . . there was no reason . . . they were just soldiers. Their main purpose was to keep peace in the city. It was awful, but John . . . What happened to him was unbelievable."

Suddenly, the air was hot and dense, heavy with the fresh smell of death. Xander saw the man from his nightmares, staring with mocking eyes. He also saw himself—soaked in blood, trembling with rage, feeling like a wild predator just escaped from its cage. Sitting in his chair, he shook his head, clasped his hands, and fought to stay in the present. A wave of nausea took over his stomach.

"I think I'm having a flashback," he whispered, grateful he could tell Dr. Chavez as it happened instead of struggling to hide it. Just as quickly as they arrived, the sensations passed. He swallowed hard and caught his breath.

With his hands on his head, he continued. "It was messed up. I know we were there to kill if necessary, but it wasn't necessary, and even then, there's still a line you don't cross." He rubbed a hand down one side of his face. "Like in football, you don't tackle someone and then repeatedly bash their head into the ground after they're down."

Xander had skipped crucial bits of information by not mentioning what happened to John that had him so disturbed, but the psychiatrist let him continue on, in case he was approaching the heart of his issues.

"I think all of us need to identify those lines that we don't ever cross. Otherwise you shouldn't be allowed to wear the uniform, or go on the field." Xander sat perched on the edge of his seat, his muscles tense, his voice rising. "Our coach at Nebraska, he made sure we knew what it felt like to be fired up. That's half the game, getting psyched up in your head, feeling unstoppable, feeling like you want to destroy the other team, but you know how to use that energy and where it gets capped. You don't beat the crap out of asshole guys in bars because you can. There are lines that you don't cross!"

Dr. Chavez maintained a calm composure even though his new patient, a former college football player and ex-military, was a formidable man, powerful and strong, and on the verge of exploding out of his seat. He could pose a real physical threat. The psychiatrist sat up straight and crossed his arms. But just as suddenly, across the room, Xander relaxed, dropping his head and slumping his shoulders.

Dr. Chavez scribbled furiously on his tablet. "Keep going, if you can. You've hit upon an area of conflict between what you experienced and how you feel things should be or should have been. Very important. Any issue producing this much passion and distress can continue to fuel the intensity of your flashbacks, if not dealt with." He stared directly at Xander. "You're starting to flush out some complex feelings dealing with expectations and trust."

"Trust? Yeah. I believed they wanted our help and we were helping them. And it wasn't just one way. We learned from them. Simplicity, humbleness. I don't know. There are rules. And things just went out of control." Xander's body drooped forward. He had been talking as if to himself, his words spewing out fast and furious, and had lost his train of thought.

“We have what we need to start moving forward.”

“Sorry.” Xander shook his head. “I’m all over the place with what I’m saying.”

“This has been a great session. We’ve uncovered critical themes that we can explore next time. When you feel ready, I’ll need you to tell me what you saw when you returned to the city with your enforcements. Not because I need to hear it, but because you need to be able to say it. I believe that will be an important piece of your recovery.”

“I went off on a rant, didn’t I?”

“Don’t apologize to me. That’s not going to help you. I think you’ve gone through enough recounting for the day. But that’s where we’ll start next time.”

Xander rose from his chair.

“Remember that talking to family and friends about how you’re feeling is an important part of recovering.”

The color drained from Xander’s face, but he nodded.

I’m not sure that I even know what happened anymore.

Chapter Twenty-Three

Two more hours until sunrise. A familiar ache gripped Xander's forehead: it happened whenever he didn't get enough sleep. His last nightmare was so intense that he felt physically and emotionally depleted by his body's reaction. If he went back to bed and his nightmares returned, he would be worse off than if he lost a few hours of sleep, so he got up long before his alarm was set to ring.

He spent a solid hour reviewing basic tissue and cell section pictures on his laptop, the most tedious and uninteresting aspect of the semester so far. He took an online self-test and bombed it. He would need to start the review again from the beginning. At least the virtual slides didn't remind him of anything except the boring cells they were.

How could he escape from his own mind? He wanted to leave a part of it behind. According to his research and Dr. Chavez, his disturbing memories had been inadequately processed and stored in an isolated network in his brain. There were the initial memories he tried to forget, and now there were disturbing bits of new ones, even worse than the first ones he remembered.

He was using so much of his mental energy turning inwards, worrying and analyzing in hope of working through his issues so he could go back to being the way he was before his PTSD. He didn't want to identify with this man whose terrifyingly real flashbacks led Brooke to believe he couldn't handle the sight of a dead body.

Some doctor I'll make at this rate.

Thank God they didn't have clinical rotations yet. What if treating a burn victim reminded him of Juan and generated a flashback? He couldn't start hyperventilating in front of a patient. And if a patient presented with gunshot wounds to the arm like Dan? Would it trigger a memory that caused him to pass out? Or, much worse, would his own strength and powerful combat skills betray him with a violent response?

He didn't have the time to deal with his psychological issues. He needed to finish his section of the gross anatomy project today. After that he would revisit the cell and tissue slides and retake the quiz until he could identify most of them correctly. He had to write an essay for ethics and had over a hundred pages of textbook to memorize. With so many important and time-sensitive tasks racing through his brain, his next train of thought caught him by surprise.

Brooke Walton.

I wonder what she's doing.

Chapter Twenty-Four

"Where is Rakesh?" Brooke stood inside the second-floor study lounge, hands on her hips, scanning the hallway. "I don't have time to waste like this."

Rachael, already wearing her flannel pajama bottoms, sat on one of the red chenille covered chairs with a mug of hot chocolate cupped between her hands "Chill out. It's just supposed to be a quick review to make sure all our pieces line up before we hand in the project tomorrow."

Group projects were stressful. A portion of Brooke's grade was dependent on someone else's effort. Would anyone else's work meet her standards? They were also a huge, inefficient inconvenience, starting with figuring out a time that worked for all of them to get together, and now this—waiting around for Rakesh. And she hated leaving loose ends until the night before; it was not her style.

According to her professor, group projects were important because they helped facilitate empathy and teamwork, critical components of quality health care. But unless Brooke was completely calling the shots, she preferred to work alone. Not everyone was cut out to be a team player. Knowing that Rachael enjoyed working in groups made her dislike it more.

The anatomy report was similar to autopsy reports compiled by a pathologist, except more thorough. It was not their final report; that would be delivered at the end of the year and would detail everything they had discovered throughout the entire body. This interim report covered only the areas they had studied so far, the back and thorax. Any variations from normal had to be documented and explained. Brooke had taken the histology section because she felt it was the most complicated and she didn't trust the others to scrutinize the tissue specimens as she would, exhausting every possible avenue for analysis and discovery.

Xander slumped in an orange chair, one leg slung over the arm, eating cereal out of a box. Brooke paced, breathing audibly through her nose. "Rakesh is fifteen minutes late."

The rest of the group had exchanged their work and reviewed it for any edits and changes they might suggest. Brooke had several already, conclusions she would have presented differently, findings she would have explained in more detail, but they needed to see what Rakesh had written before she could start making changes.

Connor burst into the study lounge, his bulk filling the space like a bull in a port-a-john.

"Hey. Who wants to see my hemorrhoid?" He had a huge smile across his face.

"Get out and grow up," Rachael told him, but she was trying to suppress a laugh.

"And I'll have you know this baby is not from constipation. I'm as regular as the sun rising and setting; two dumps a day like clockwork."

"Get out, Connor!" Rachael frowned, but Xander was laughing.

"It's what you get when you squat 450 pounds! Yeah, baby!" Connor stuck out his palm to collect a high five from Xander. "Can't sit down for a few days now. It's like a bummer battle scar." He waved as he backed out the doorway.

"Wait! Connor!" Brooke called. "Have you seen Rakesh?"

"Have not seen Rakesh." Connor's voice trailed off as he headed away.

"Good thing Rakesh wasn't here." Xander sat up and grabbed another handful of cereal. "You know he would feel compelled to provide us with a detailed account of hemorrhoids, and I don't want that picture stuck in my head."

"It's true. He would." Rachael laughed and sipped her cocoa, her legs curled up underneath her. "I really don't want to picture it! Change the subject . . . please!"

Normally, I would have thoroughly enjoyed studying Connor's hemorrhoid. Especially if it was thrombosed. I could have sliced it open, removed the blood clots, and viewed them under a microscope in tomorrow's histology class. But tonight . . .

She was too upset regarding the whereabouts of Rakesh and the unknown future of her anatomy grade, which was partly dependent on his contribution.

Brooke threw up her hands. "I'm going to look for him."

"You've already knocked on his door, and I texted and called him. I'm sure he'll be here any minute." Rachael took another sip of her cocoa, appearing calm and relaxed.

Brooke marched directly to Sundeep's room on the second floor because she knew he and Rakesh were close friends. Sundeep opened his door and said hello, stroking his newly grown goatee.

"Do you know where Rakesh might be? He's late for a study session."

"Yes. He's probably over the Atlantic right now on his way to India."

"What!"

"He got a call this morning. His father was in a bad car accident. Rakesh was told to get the first flight out there as fast as he could."

"Really?" Thoughts flew through Brooke's mind and, luckily, she remembered to filter them, taking the time needed to formulate an appropriate response. "So, his father is in bad shape?"

"I don't know the details. But I would imagine so. Rakesh was told to drop everything and get out there. That usually means so you have a chance to say goodbye, or to see him before he dies."

"Right, of course." Brooke chose her words with care. "This is terrible for him."

Sundeep nodded.

"By any chance, did he give you something before he left? Like papers or a flash drive?"

"No. Why would he?"

"We need his portion of the anatomy project. The radiology section."

"Maybe he emailed it to someone in your group. I'm sure he'll get an extension for the project. Don't worry about it. And . . . I'm not from there, you know."

"What?"

"From India. I'm not from India. I was born in Chicago and I've never even been there."

"Oh." She shrugged. "I never said you were." She turned away, took a step and turned back. "I'm not a dumb blonde, in case you were wondering."

Brooke stormed back to the study lounge and informed the rest of the group what she learned about Rakesh.

"Oh, man." Xander folded his hands in his lap and shook his head. The cereal box fell on the floor.

"Check your emails and see if he sent his piece." Brooke scrolled through her own.

"Poor Rakesh." Rachael stared down at the tile floor. "I feel so sorry for him."

Brooke spoke through clenched teeth. "Could you please just check your email."

No one had received anything from Rakesh.

"What are we supposed to do about the project?" Brooke's hands curled into fists, her frustration reaching a new high with regard to teamwork.

"We can hand in our sections, and I'm sure Rakesh will get extra time for his." Rachael echoed Sundeep's comment on the extension.

"I don't know." Xander shook his head. "It will be tough for him to catch up if he doesn't get back soon."

"Well we shouldn't wish for his father to die quickly." Rachael threw up her hand.

"What I was thinking is that I hope his dad recovers quickly so he can get back here before he misses too much," Xander explained.

"But how can we hand in our pieces without knowing what he wrote?" Brooke circled the room. "We won't know if we have everything covered." *No one but me seems to get that. They don't seem concerned about the report at all. Am I the only one who cares?*

"You need to calm down, you're being ridiculous." Rachael closed her laptop. "He had the assignment. I'm sure he did what he was supposed to do. I'm willing to give him the benefit of the doubt."

I'm not. Brooke remembered when Rakesh mistakenly slid his scalpel through the wrong transverse spinalis muscle. She couldn't stop herself from shouting, startling him so much that he dropped the scalpel into the thoracic cavity, but at least she had saved their cadaver from a misguided dissection.

Xander was nodding in agreement with Rachael.

"Okay." Brooke patted the air with her palms, sensing she had no choice. "I'll text him to send us his part. But we should write it, just in case he doesn't get it to us."

"We can't write it." Rachael enunciated each word as if the suggestion was preposterous. "It's his work, he needs to do it, and I'm sure he already has. Don't worry about it." Rachael rose from her chair.

"I agree. We don't have time to do it anyway. It's due in the morning. It will work out." Xander yawned. "I need to study for the histology quiz. I sort of failed the online self-test this morning."

"I can get it done. And I think I should," Brooke insisted.

"No," Rachael said firmly. "You can't do it. It's not right. It will work out." Then she turned and followed Xander out of the lounge, leaving Brooke alone, fuming.

How dare she tell me what I can and can't do!

She took deep breaths, dangerously close to losing her cool and chasing Rachael down the hall to strangle her. She hated to be in situations that were beyond her control.

She texted Rakesh and left him a message.

Hi Rakesh. Sundeep told us about your father. So very sorry. If there's anything we can do, just let us know. And any chance you could email me your anatomy project section? We have to hand it in tomorrow. Thanks.

Brooke knew not to text or call Rakesh again, that would be overkill.

I have to be patient. How long does it take to get to India? Will he have cell phone reception there? Will he forget about the anatomy project if his dad is dying?

The waiting and not knowing made her feel helpless.

She needed to do something active, as she was becoming increasingly anxious, but she had already been for a long run and taught a sculpt class.

She was certain she had no hope of going to sleep when she was this worried about the project and her grade. Just as with any good medical care, it made more sense to take care of the problem itself, when possible, instead of focusing only on alleviating the symptoms. She could easily write Rakesh's piece of the project. She knew exactly what his piece entailed; she had all the necessary notes. And, she expected to do a better job than he would have done.

Three hours later she had finished the work, and she was glad, because she still had not heard from Rakesh.

Chapter Twenty-Five

"Drop your completed lab report sections on my desk," said Dr. Sarcough.

Relaxed and confident again now that she had secured their project grade, Brooke handed in her work and, separately, the piece she had done for Rakesh. With the first quarter test and report behind them, each group could begin dissection of a new area, the abdominal region. Their cadaver was covered in plastic from the chest up and the pelvic region down. With only the most superficial muscles exposed, Xander seemed to be fine, although he did appear tense throughout, as if bracing himself for a possible flashback. He made it through the class without incident.

"I'm okay today," he murmured to Brooke, as the group finished the steps required to preserve their cadaver. "I just wish I could trust my mind not to freak out on me ever again."

Dr. Sarcough approached their table. "Brooke and Rachael." He sounded pleased. "Just wanted to let you know that the two of you did the best on the test of the first quarter material. You had an identical score, and it was the highest."

Rachael smiled. "Wonderful."

"Excellent. Thank you for letting us know." Brooke clenched her jaw. *Only one person can be the best.* "Can you tell me, was it the highest grade of all the first-years or just this lab section?"

"Just this lab section. It was the second highest overall. Connor Reed had a perfect test. Very impressive. But you two came very close."

"Oh." Brooke forced a half-smile on her face and turned to leave.

"Brooke." Rachael waved. "I need to tell you something. I was going to tell Xander too, but it looks like he already left. And it's you that seems to really care."

Brooke narrowed her eyes. "You had the whole class to tell us."

"I'm telling you now."

Peter was waiting in the doorway. "I need just a minute," said Rachael, with a tight smile. "I'll see you in cell bio, okay?"

"Sure, I'll get coffees."

Peter walked away, leaving Rachael and Brooke alone. Rachael's smile disappeared.

"What is it?" Brooke would have happily traded in Rachael, the bossy do-gooder, for any other lab partner. And finding out that Connor Reed had scored higher than her on the first quarter test had put her in a foul mood.

"Look, Brooke, about the anatomy report. I don't know if we're going to get full credit for it after all. I know that's clearly a huge issue for you, but the entire project is less than ten percent of your grade. I'm not happy about it either, but it's life."

"Don't worry about it, Rachael. Rakesh sent me his work last night and I handed it in this morning. He did an excellent job. It's all good."

Rachael stared at her for a few seconds. "No, he didn't."

"Yes, he did. He sent it to me. It's taken care of. I handed it in for him at the beginning of class."

Rachael frowned and put her hands on her hips. "No, he didn't. That's why I wanted to speak with you. Rakesh emailed me minutes ago, as class was ending. He said he hadn't finished his section before he had to leave. He was sorry that he didn't get it done. His dad just came out of his second surgery and his mother and sisters need him. I told him the anatomy project was the last thing he needed to be worried about."

Brooke glared at Rachael as heat rose to her face. Brooke had called and texted Rakesh, done her very best to sound sweet and concerned, and he hadn't responded to her. Yet he had communicated with Rachael! "Why did he email *you*?"

"Probably because he knew you would freak out and he can't deal with it right now." Rachael stepped closer to Brooke, holding her gaze with her own angry scowl. "So how is it you got his work then? Since he didn't do it."

"He must be confused." Brooke felt a vein twitch at her temple. She dug her fingernails into her palms. "Which is understandable because of what he's dealing with. He sent me his work, the part he finished."

"He said he didn't have it. He didn't send it to you." Rachael squared her shoulders and looked Brooke right in the eyes, unwavering. "You wrote it, didn't you? You did the work and pretended it was his."

"No, I didn't." Brooke crossed her arms. "Not all of it. Rakesh sent me a file. And what's the big deal if I just finished it?"

"The big deal is that it's lying and cheating. He didn't send you anything. It's supposed to be his work. Maybe he doesn't want to receive a grade for your work. Did you ever think of that?"

"I think he could do worse than getting a grade for my work. What's your problem? I thought we were supposed to be a team working together. Isn't that the point of teamwork? Don't you realize that each of our grades is at stake if we don't hand in the whole thing? I'm not taking a chance that Rakesh is going to get an extension, if he even finishes it. How is he ever going to get caught up? He's going to miss at least a week just getting to India and back. It's not exactly a hop, skip, and a jump on the subway." Brooke did her best to hold her anger back and keep from shouting.

"This is not acceptable, Brooke. That's plain as day to me. You need to tell Dr. Sarcough what you did." Rachael held Brooke's gaze with a determined intensity and Brooke glared back at her with pure hatred.

"It's also your grade I'm helping save—"

"You need to tell him."

Brooke glanced back at Dr. Sarcough's desk. The box with the reports was gone. She clenched her jaw. "I'll just ask Dr. Sarcough to give me back the section I finished for Rakesh and we'll all take our chances with the grade."

"No. You did more than finish it. And after we specifically told you not to do it. You need to tell the professor what you did. You have the weekend to tell him or I'll do it for you on Monday morning."

"You can't be serious." Brooke threw up her arms and forgot to keep her voice in check. "It's just not a big deal, Rachael!"

"Standing your ground is important when it comes to principles and integrity. And I think you might be lacking in those areas. Your moral compass might be in need of repair." Rachael stood with her legs apart, only inches away from Brooke. "I told you explicitly not to do that section last night and you did it anyway. I think your type-A personality is almost overboard, teetering on the edge, about to fall over in the waves of insanity. I've given you an opportunity to own up and make it right."

"How generous of you!" Brooke wanted to kill Rachael right then and there. The obnoxious scent of her flowery perfume was reason enough. She never wanted to see or hear her again. *Don't do it. Don't do it. Not here. Not now.* She forced herself to spin around and stomp away.

"Fine, be that way." Rachael shouted after her. "But you've been warned . . . "

You have no idea what you've done, Rachael Kline.

Brooke stormed left out of the anatomy room and slammed straight into Xander.

"Whoa, slow down. What was all the yelling? Are you okay?"

"I'm fine." Brooke marched around him without making eye contact, like a roaring cauldron of anger that was unlikely to simmer down. A switch had been flipped and bitterness churned from deep inside her stomach. At times like this, and there had been plenty, she could sometimes exhaust her body and calm her mind with a long hard run, but there was no time for that now. Cell biology started in less than five minutes. And she needed to stay on edge to survive this situation. She had no intention of bowing down to Rachael.

No one gets away with threatening me and no one, especially not Rachael Kline, is going to destroy my future.

***

During class, Brooke appreciated the intensity of her emotions. She imagined a whole section of her cerebellum set up solely to accommodate the amazing depth of her rage. It was obsessive, all encompassing, and so powerful, it lifted all her senses to a new level of heightened awareness. Instead of clouding her mind, she was able to think more clearly than ever. She truly didn't believe for a second that doing the work for Rakesh amounted to a big deal. Wasn't that the point of being on a team? Helping each other out? Or was there nothing more to teamwork than wasting time? Why was Rachael insisting Brooke had done something awful? Brooke pictured herself telling Dr. Sarcough exactly what had happened, hoping he would understand. But what if he had the same opinion as Rachael? What if he also decided she had a broken "moral compass"? There was no way Brooke could take that chance and jeopardize her reputation. That would be the end of the surgical scholarship that was going to pay back all her debt. And Dr. Sarcough might tell the other professors and then no one would recommend her for the cardiothoracic fellowship. Brooke gulped. What if she was expelled? She could not take any chances, and she did not take orders from Rachael.

Rachael is not going to ruin my life.

A dozen variations of that sentiment looped through her brain, until she realized with sharp clarity what needed to be done. Piece by piece her fury channeled into a plan to accomplish her goal.

***

By the time medical ethics started later in the day, Brooke was keenly alert, her senses fine-tuned to the important mission ahead of her. She sat down in the auditorium next to Julie and behind Rachael, Connor, Peter, and Xander.

Rachael turned her head to the side. "Connor, I heard you got the highest grade on the first quarter anatomy test. Good for you. Did you know there's an award for the top first-year student? It's announced in May. I think you've just positioned yourself in the lead."

Xander gave Connor a congratulatory slap. Brooke listened, her face stony.

Strands of Connor's short dark hair were trapped in the fibers of his wool sweater. While Julie was reading from a book in her lap, Brooke plucked several hairs off Connor's shoulder and discreetly stuffed them in her pocket.

She forced a smile when he glanced over his shoulder.

Connor raised his brows. "What are you doing back there? First time I haven't seen you in the front row."

Brooke shrugged and smiled. "What type of *p*hysician do you want to be, Connor?"

"Sports med." He returned her smile, although he was almost always smiling.

Lucky for him that he didn't say surgeon, or he might have to watch his back later. I don't want competition. "Oh. Nice. I'm curious, what does everyone have planned for tonight?"

"Dunno, but we should all go out." Connor twisted around in his seat to face her. "Last weekend we found a bar on Third Street that plays student bands. It was good."

"So, you're the self-appointed social director for the first-years?" Brooke batted her eyes.

"If you'll all have me."

Xander leaned forward. "I'm in."

"I hate to be a party pooper, I know how important it is for us to bond outside of class, but I'm not going out tonight." Rachael looked at Connor and leaned forward so she could also make eye contact with Xander and Peter, but acted as if Brooke wasn't there. "I think I'm coming down with something. I'm going to bed early."

"Oh, okay." Peter kept staring at Rachael and they seemed to be silently communicating. "I guess I'm up for going to the bar." It sounded like a question.

"I'm not sure yet." Julie closed a book in her lap. "My boyfriend is visiting for the weekend. I'll see what he wants to do."

Brooke kept her smug grin in check. Julie and her boyfriend were as good as a fire alarm for forcing everyone out of the dorm, at least in her hallway. That would only help with her plan. She twirled her ponytail around her finger and did her best to look disappointed.

"Unfortunately, I can't go out tonight. There's something important I have to take care of."

Chapter Twenty-Six

Brooke waited until two AM. She didn't drink anything caffeinated, but it wasn't hard to stay alert. She was pumped with adrenaline and used the extra time wisely; studying for the next anatomy lesson and getting a head start on a paper for medical ethics. Unfortunately for her, she was forced to listen to Julie having noisy sex with her boyfriend, and not just once, but twice. Just when she believed it was finally over, they started up again.

On their first go around, Brooke blasted music through her speakers hoping to alert Julie and her guest to the fact that if they could hear her music, then she could hear them. To her amazement, it didn't work. She considered banging on the wall and decided that while it might help with the immediate situation, it would create more embarrassment down the line. The second time, she put on her headphones so she couldn't hear much aside from her own workout songs.

Will Jeff ask me to escape with him like the last time? No, I forgot, he went to New York City for the weekend to visit friends.

At least a quarter of the dorm's residents left campus every weekend. The rest were probably out blowing off steam. As the hours passed, doors slammed in the hall and voices rang out as people returned to their rooms for the night. With the exception of Julie's bedroom, it had been a quiet night in the dorm.

When her chosen time arrived, she changed into a pair of red skinny jeans that she almost never wore. They were a gift from her sister and slid down her backside when she walked, requiring her to constantly yank them up. She didn't mind parting with them at the end of the night if it came to that. She pulled her sheets and blankets off her bed and folded them loosely over her desk chair. She used her scalpel to slice through the thick, heavy plastic protecting her mattress, opening it at the top end, enough to slide it off.

So glad I never got rid of this.

She piled things into her large duffel bag: the plastic, towels from Performance Fit, an entire box of heavy duty black garbage bags from the cafeteria kitchen, five pairs of gloves from the lab, a hat, a borrowed lab coat, her taser, a scalpel and her own bone cutting saw. She carefully remade her bed and waited a few more minutes to be sure no other signs of life existed outside in the hall.

Yesterday morning it seemed an impossible task to take care of Rachael without having access to a car. But Brooke had devised a simple but detailed plan. She was in awe of her own competence. Life periodically dropped obstacles in your way; removing them was up to you. Brooke wasn't going to just walk around a roadblock, leaving to chance that it might get dropped back in her path farther on down the road. She aimed to destroy it.

She crept out of her room with her large duffel making as little noise as possible because anyone might still be awake studying. That was a risk she had to take. It was also conceivable that someone had a few too many drinks—it was Friday night after all—and would be needing to use the bathroom. A few of her classmates were super serious during the week and then let loose with alcohol every weekend like the world was ending. She went into the stairwell and climbed down one flight of stairs. Rachael's room was located two doors down from Brooke's, on the second floor at the end of the hall, between the stairwell and a custodial closet. With no neighbors on either side, Rachael didn't have to be subjected to anyone's noisy sex-capades on a regular basis. Not that you needed to be adjacent to Julie's room to be aware of what was going on in there. The whole end of her hallway was acquainted with her boyfriend's skills.

Brooke knocked lightly. The hallways were always fully lit even in the middle of the night. While she waited, she ran her eyes over the ceilings. Every exit to the dorm had a security camera, but there were none in the halls or in the stairwells.

"Who is it?" Rachael opened the door part way, squinting, her movements sluggish from sleep. She saw Brooke and straightened, her eyes opening wide.

"Hi. I want to talk to you about what happened between us this morning." Brooke sounded calm and reasonable even though her heart pounded and every nerve fiber was hyper-alert. She felt the same way before delivering a big speech, like the valedictorian's address at Everett's graduation ceremony—full of nervous energy and anticipation, but confident and prepared.

Rachael wore a pink cotton nightgown with scalloped lace edges. Mouth hanging open, she peered at Brooke and the empty hall beyond her. "Excuse me?"

"Our conversation this morning, about the anatomy project. I want to discuss it with you."

"Are you out of your mind? It's like three AM."

"It's two."

"Oh, my God," she muttered. "It can wait until the morning, don't you think? You're really unbelievable." She shook her head and started to close the door, but Brooke shoved her foot inside.

"No. It can't wait. It's really bothering me."

"Well you know what you need to do, and once you do it, it won't be bothering you anymore. I'm going back to bed."

Rachael tried to shut the door again. With one last glance behind her, Brooke moved swiftly inside, gently closing the door and reaching into her duffel bag.

No turning back now.

Rachael lifted her arms. "What the—"

Brooke lunged, pulling the trigger on her taser and Rachael stumbled back against her bed. With a stunned look on her face, she fell unconscious.

Thank you, uncle, once again. That's twice this thing has come in handy.

Brooke locked the door and pressed her back against it, closing her eyes and controlling her breath.

Time to go to work.

Crouching down, she unloaded items from her bag. She tucked her braided hair under her wool hat to avoid leaving dozens of long blonde strands behind. A few would be no problem, since it was feasible that she had been in and out of Rachael's room a few times, as had most everyone in the dorm, but she wanted to be careful. She donned a pair of gloves and the borrowed lab coat. Almost everything she needed had been readily available to her.

"I didn't want to do this, Rachael. I even made a vow. . ." She spread the opening of the thick plastic mattress cover. "If you had simply thanked me for saving our project, both of us would be sleeping soundly right now."

Rachael let out a soft moan as Brooke lifted her and deposited her inside the bag. *Does she even weigh ninety-five pounds?* The effort was nothing compared to maneuvering Jessica Carroll's heavy body around.

Brooke yanked a thick wool blanket off the bed and spread it down to protect the floor. Carefully layered garbage bags followed on top of the blanket. *Not one drop of blood will touch this floor.*

Once the floor was adequately covered, she rolled the plastic-bound Rachael onto its center and tased her again, for far longer than recommended.

"I was willing to talk it out, to wait for you to understand that what I did was the best possible solution to our problem." She gripped her scalpel. "But *you* didn't even want to discuss the issue."

With Rachael slumped unconscious inside the mattress bag, the plastic pulled up high around her, Brooke made a deep, clean slice through the carotid artery. An instantaneous, powerful spurt burst forth, splattering the inside of the bag. Brooke pushed Rachael's head forward. Her blood rushed out, coating her collapsed form. A pool of the thick, dark liquid quickly accumulated at the bottom of the makeshift containment bag.

Brooke pulled the sides of the mattress bag upward as Rachael's pulse ebbed away until it ceased completely.

That was peaceful.

She grabbed her bone cutting saw, old and dull from use over many years.

I'll have to throw this out after tonight, and I probably can't ever keep another hidden in my room.

Those realizations made her angry at Rachael all over again.

Hot, sticky blood plastered Rachael's skin, making her difficult to grasp. To contain the mess, the cutting and sawing had to be done inside the mattress bag. Brooke settled onto her knees and bent over, her head inside the tube created by the stiff plastic, with Rachael anchoring the bottom. Her range of motion was limited, but she took excruciatingly care not to rip the mattress bag with her tools. The plastic was thick, but no match for the slightest nick from her bone saw.

She made progress with tiny, incremental movements. Sticky steam built up inside the bag. Her scalp itched and perspired under the wool cap, but she ignored it. When drops of sweat ran down the ridge of her spine, her legs cramped, and her back and shoulder muscles screamed in protest, she recharged her determination by ruminating over Rachael's unnecessary, indignant behavior.

I can't believe the trouble Rachael caused me.

Brooke remained focused, imagining herself a seasoned surgeon working with controlled patience under difficult conditions. A smile flickered across her determined expression, she was pleased at being able to name most of the joints, ligaments, and tendons she detached. Sawing in silence, she viewed the situation as a project with a deadline. With exceptional skill and impressive strength, she single-handedly took care of her problem.

Noises in the hallway interrupted her concentration. She froze with the bone saw firmly entrenched in Rachel's right femur. Someone had exited the stairwell and was clunking around nearby in the hall.

Who could it be? What if Peter is coming for a middle of the night booty call?

She listened, gripping the sides of the plastic and the saw, holding her breath. Staring at the door, she willed whoever was out there to go away. The discomfort in her back had evolved from an ache to a throb. Her frozen stance intensified the tension in her muscles. Rolling her neck from side to side made little difference. Sweat pooled and ran down her face. She resisted the intense urge to wipe her forehead with the back of her hand, so as not to touch anything with her blood-soaked gloves and sleeves. A door creaked open and clicked shut. Brooke exhaled and resumed her work, ignoring her aching, burning muscles.

The dismemberment continued until only one big piece remained. Brooke grabbed Rachael's hair and lifted her dripping head out of the bag. She licked her lips. It was time to satisfy the craving that had haunted her since her first day in the dorm. With one swift slice, she cut off Rachael's mole and deposited it into a sample container.

Inhaling deeply, she looked around. *I've got thirty minutes to clean up.*

She transitioned slick, blood-soaked parts from the mattress bag into the black garbage bags. When finished, the room resembled its original state, with the exception of the five heavy-duty, triple-lined garbage bags, each about one quarter full. They contained Rachael, a ruined lab coat, Brooke's tools, and other debris.

Almost forgot . . .

She removed a small zip-lock bag from her duffel.

Just in case . . .

She deposited Connor's hairs into each of the garbage bags.

The mattress bag holding gallons of fluid was tightly secured and triple bagged, the soiled towels, and Rachael's blanket thrown inside to absorb some of the blood.

Brooke circled her arms to release her cramped shoulders, clasped her arms overhead and arched back.

Stretches never felt so good before.

Bent halfway over, she arched and rounded her back while she surveyed Rachael's room. For the past two hours she had been so intent on what she came to do, it was as if she was seeing the room for the first time. A poster of a crew team with the caption "Together we achieve more" represented Rachael's days as a coxswain.

The perfect job for Rachael, someone who lived to call the shots and bark out orders.

Rachael's shoes were inside her closet, scattered about the floor. Lying haphazardly on top of other footwear were black flats that Rachael wore often.

I'll take these.

Brooke dropped them into one of the trash bags.

And these.

She slid Rachael's purse and phone off her desk and into her duffel. Rachael's keys went into her front pocket.

Atop the dresser sat Rachael's signature earrings. What had Xander said about them during one of their labs? Either, he liked them, or his sister would like them. With a sweep of her hand, the earrings slid off the dresser and into the back pocket of her skinny jeans, which were so tight she could feel the earrings pressing against her backside.

Brooke yawned and stretched her arms again. The night had proved exhausting. She was ready to wrap everything up and go to bed. *But it's not over yet.*

She tied the top of each trash bag so that nothing inside could come spilling out. Fortunately, Rachael wasn't Connor's size. Peering out the peep hole to make sure the hallway was empty before beginning, she crept out, making the first of three trips back and forth from Rachael's room carrying garbage bags inside her large duffel. On her last trip, she glanced at Rachael's clock. One more hour of darkness remained before sunrise. She had to hurry. Using Rachael's room key, she left for the final time, locking the door behind her.

The trash bags now sat in the center of Brooke's room. A gust of cold air entered when she opened her window. She grabbed one of the heavy bags, extended her arm out the window and allowed the bag to drop into the dumpster below.

She'd done her research during her first week in the dorm, when the newness of the city noises had prevented her from falling asleep. Connecticut was the first state in the country to stop dumping garbage into landfills. The majority went into incinerators; they processed thousands of tons of trash into fuel and ash every day. Trash to ash, it was that simple.

When she had dumped all five bags, she carefully and quietly shut her window. After removing Rachael's phone from the duffel, she turned it off, and placed it in her own backpack. The container with the mole went into her refrigerator.

I can't wait to section it and check for cancer cells.

Finally, she pulled off her clothes and her sweaty wool hat and stuffed them in her dirty laundry bag.

Should I wash them right now, or would that be suspicious so early in the morning? It wouldn't be the first time I've done a very late load of laundry. I could come up with an excuse, but . . . no, it can wait until tomorrow, I'll take a quick shower instead.

After a thorough look around to make sure nothing had been forgotten, she tiptoed out of her room to shower, scrubbing every inch of her skin. Her last thoughts before she fell asleep were about her bone saw. She'd had it for years. It wasn't possible to clean it well enough to remove every last microscopic drop of Rachael's blood. She couldn't very well march over to the hospital and ask to run her personal bone saw through their sterilization machines. So, it had to go. She was probably the only person who had brought her own bone saw to campus anyway. It would have been considered odd if anyone knew, even if nothing had happened to Rachael.

I don't want people to think I'm odd. Correction. I don't want people to know I'm odd.

She was still miffed at Rachael for forcing her hand and costing her that bone saw. But there wasn't anything to be done about it now. And honestly, it was worth trading her future for an old bone saw.

Chapter Twenty-Seven

Across the hall and two doors down from Brooke, Xander lay in bed, uncomfortably alert, bracing his body and mind for the visions that remained after waking from another nightmare. This one contained more of the same new images. And this time he was carrying something. He couldn't see what it was, but he could tell that is was heavy. And he was running full-force, hot and sweaty, powerfully strong, but he knew it wasn't a memory from a football practice because he was savagely angry, charging towards something, and there was so much blood.

He wished he had a television to occupy his thoughts. With no other available distractions—Julie and her boyfriend had finally called it quits—he listened to the strange noises coursing through the walls. The rattle and knocking of the water pipes, the hiss of heat pressing through the ducts. He concentrated on anything that might keep him grounded in the present; that could convince him he was at school in Connecticut. A nearby door opened and closed. From the proximity of the sound, it had to be Julie or Brooke. Just a few minutes later he heard it again, and yet again a few minutes after that. By now he was certain it was coming from Brooke's room. Why was someone else awake? It was too late to be finishing the night, too early to be starting the day. He hoped her reason for being awake was more pleasant than his own.

He paced his room, anxious for the sun to come up so he could begin the day's routine. A good workout might help him feel normal. Hours later, decked out in his running gear, at what he considered a reasonable hour, he headed over to Brooke's room. They hadn't agreed to any set times for running but since they had identical class schedules and meal times, he generally knew when she was available, provided she wasn't teaching a class at the nearby gym. It was Saturday, but he wasn't sure if she would even be awake since, while struggling to get a grip on reality, he thought he heard her coming and going. Perhaps she wasn't feeling well. He couldn't think of any other reason that would require so many trips in and out of her room.

He knocked gently, in case she was ill. "It's Xander. You up for a run?"

"Yes!" She surprised him by responding immediately, more enthusiastically than usual, from behind the door. "Give me five minutes. I have to use the bathroom. I'll meet you outside."

The bathroom again. But she didn't sound sick. She sounded full of energy. He waited outside, stretching his hamstrings, when Brooke came through the front doors. She pulled her hoodie up over her head, bent down to tie her shoes in a double knot, started the stopwatch function on her phone, and put her gloves back on.

"Let's go." Her smile was contagious.

Their newly established default route, unless one of them suggested otherwise, consisted of an eight-mile loop that took them out to the football fields, past the stables, back through some residential neighborhoods and around the entire undergraduate campus. Although they conversed a bit, comfortable silence prevailed over talking. Xander used the time to completely clear his head. It usually happened about a mile into the run, he could focus solely on the exertion, the healthy rhythm of his breath, the pulse of his pumping muscles. He pictured his cardiovascular system working at peak efficiency; it was easy to imagine exactly what was occurring now that he had studied it in class.

They reached the football stadium, a massive structure that resembled a Roman coliseum more than a modern day football arena. They usually stopped there for a drink of water. Brooke bent over and placed her lips on the fountain's stream of cool water.

I'm glad she's not asking about my Afghanistan memories. But I've got a question for her. "What was going on with you and Rachael yesterday?"

Before answering, Brooke watched students coming off an activity bus. "What do you mean?"

"I heard you arguing after anatomy. I know the two of you don't always see eye-to-eye, but you need to get along if we're all going to work together for the rest of the year, especially since it's just the three of us until Rakesh returns."

"Oh. That." She waved her hand to the side. "Don't worry about it. We'll be fine going forward. I've taken care of my issues with Rachael."

"What was the issue yesterday?"

"Nothing. It was nothing."

They started running again. Brooke picked up the pace and Xander dug a little deeper to match her strides.

"You know . . . it didn't look like nothing. Is there a problem?"

"I said, don't worry about it."

"Was it about the project?" He could tell she wanted him to drop it, but he also remembered how persistent Brooke was when there was something she wanted to know, whether it was medical knowledge or personal information, it was exhausting to deny her when she kept pressing. With that in mind, he tried a little harder. "Was it about Rakesh and his piece of the project? I know you had a difference of opinion on that." He was just guessing.

"No." Brooke frowned. "It wasn't about the project. Look...I shouldn't tell you, it's not really for me to tell, but your insistence is making me feel like I have no choice." She exhaled loudly. "It's about you."

Me? The heat of shame spread over his face. He supposed he expected to hear something like that eventually. Since the first day of school, he had not been himself. He was more withdrawn, less friendly. But, no one at Rothaker knew him previously, and that had worked in his favor. Still, it was inevitable that someone would eventually notice or complain if he didn't get a grip on his symptoms. Maybe he should have told everyone what he was going through, since they were all going to be physicians. If they couldn't understand, then who would?

"I'm sorry, but if it's about me and my symptoms affecting the group then I should know. She should have said something directly to me first." Then another disappointing thought occurred to him. Perhaps all his classmates had been commenting about his strange behavior for weeks, behind his back, without his knowledge. "I don't need you to protect me from what anyone is saying. I can handle it. Even though I'm like a low-grade, anxiety-riddled version of myself right now," he finished with a bitterness in his voice.

Brooke turned to face him, slowing a bit. "Xander, it's not what you think. Rachael doesn't have any problems with your . . . your standard of work, your symptoms . . . or anything like that. She doesn't know there's anything going on with you right now. She probably just thinks you're out partying with Connor and feeling the after-effects once in a while."

"Connor doesn't party. He may give that impression, but he's like the god of pure living."

"Hah. I know. I know."

"Then what is it then?"

"Oh, what the heck. She confronted me, so I don't know why I'm feeling like I need to keep a secret."

"What? Please tell me."

"It was about you and me. She was asking about you and me."

"Why?"

"She likes you, Xander. She totally likes you. She wanted to know if you and I were more than friends. And I said no. She didn't believe me. You know how she is." Brooke scoffed. "She thinks she knows everything. I told her we were good friends and she could think whatever she wanted to think."

"Oh." Xander was not expecting that. "Hmm. We are good friends. You and I."

"Yes, of course we are."

Suddenly, he had much to consider. He watched his running shoes hitting the pavement, one of his shoelaces flopped with each stride. "I have to say I'm surprised to hear that Rachael liked me, more than a friend that is. I didn't pick up on that, not in the slightest."

"You have a lot going on, you know, with your post-traumatic stress symptoms. I guess you just didn't notice. Guys don't always pick up clues like that, even when they've got all their wits about them, or so I'm told."

What else might I have missed or misinterpreted? Are Brooke and I just good friends or have I missed something there too?

They shared work, stress, recreation—that's what Brooke considered their runs, and their most personal problems—well, he had shared with her. Attraction wasn't an issue. Anyone would find Brooke attractive, and the slightly unorthodox aspects of her behavior, too difficult to precisely define, were almost endearing. They certainly made her unique. He was also significantly blessed in the looks department.

I'll be direct with Brooke. What do I have to lose?

She was unusually direct all the time; it was one of the most salient quirks of her personality.

Xander took a deep breath. "Have you ever considered being more than good friends?"

Brooke shrugged, keeping her gaze forward. "I like this. It works."

"Um, okay." He laughed.

Near the end of their typical route, Brooke nudged his arm. "Are you up for one more mile?"

"Sure. Why not?" Physical exhaustion increased his chances of sleeping through the night and helped keep the nightmares at bay. He enjoyed seeing how much he could push himself. "Let's run to the pond."

"No, I'd like to go this way." She turned in the opposite direction, past the hospital parking lots and the busy side streets toward the outpatient clinics and the Greenwood Circle area. "It's not exactly a scenic route."

"Not by a long shot."

"But still, it's interesting to see how the hospital and its satellite facilities have taken over the area, spilling into these impoverished neighborhoods."

Xander pointed at a shabby one-story building. "I think that's where Rachael volunteers."

"Oh. Does she?"

"I think she goes there twice a week. The area is . . . sketchy."

Brooke wiped the back of her hand over her forehead. "I hope she doesn't go alone after dark. It can't be safe here at night."

"Wouldn't be wise." Xander kicked a crushed can off to the side of their path. "Are you looking for something particular? It looks to me like you're scanning the sides of the buildings."

"Hah! No. I'm just checking it all out. Pretty depressing."

Located a half mile from the clinic, a dilapidated park, the size of a football field, had seen better days. It functioned primarily as a night-time gathering space for derelicts. On each corner of the mostly concrete space existed a dense outcropping of overgrown trees and bushes providing just enough cover for someone to do things they wouldn't want to be caught doing.

Brooke murmured, "Perfect."

Chapter Twenty-Eight

Brooke felt unusually good the morning after killing Rachael, in spite of her lack of sleep. She experienced a grand feeling of accomplishment as well as a weight off her shoulders, as if she had turned in a massive project worth half a course grade. Similar to completing the final draft of her senior thesis after pulling an all-nighter to perfect the finishing touches. Happy. Satisfied. On track. Until she peered out her window . . .

Two vultures circled the dumpster. Lumpy white trash bags, some random boxes, and a mangled lamp already covered the surface, but the bulging black bags containing Rachael weren't too far below.

A past biology course taught her that vultures had an excellent sense of smell, particularly for methanethiol, a byproduct of metabolism produced after death. Was it sensitive enough to detect Rachael's dismembered body decaying through triple bagged plastic? If they sensed what those bags contained, if they pierced them with their beaks and claws . . . well, that could prove disastrous. Hurriedly she opened her window and waved her arms around as if it was her last chance to flee a sinking ship.

God, I hope no one sees me!

Her movements were enough to send their shriveled bald heads and sinister bodies flapping away into the sky. Somehow, she needed to keep them at bay until the dumpster was either emptied or full enough that they couldn't reach the bags that were surely calling to them.

After showering, she traveled down to the basement to wash a week's worth of workout clothes and the giant duffel bag. Sunday was usually the busiest laundry day in the dorm, but there was no one else in the basement when she arrived. She brought her laptop, intending to stay and study while she waited, although she was worried about the dumpster-diving vultures.

Brooke had no regrets as far as Rachael was concerned. She was disappointed only because last night's incident was exactly the type of situation she had sworn to avoid at Rothaker. Why did Rachael have to force her hand? Rachael turned into an obstacle that wouldn't get out of her way, leaving Brooke no choice but to take care of her. And once again, everything had worked out in her favor, although there were still several important loose ends to tie before she could completely wash her hands of Rachael Kline.

Messing with Xander's head by telling him Rachael liked him had not been planned, but he was backing her into a corner with his questions, and truly it didn't matter now.

Brooke thought about her end goal. Since she started high school everything had been about becoming a surgeon. She was compulsively interested in the human body and the science behind life. She was fascinated with the way physiological systems could come close to shutting down and then be revived or repaired, or just let go. It had been challenging to wait for the opportunity to acquire the knowledge and skills required to have that power over the human body. But she had made do with her own private experiments in the woods behind her house and occasionally in the labs when no one was around, until an incident at Cedarhurst when she had been caught off guard. Working with the cadaver at Rothaker had been so good for her. It had been enough. Finally, she was as close as she had ever been to becoming her true self, performing her true purpose. And Rachael had tried to ruin everything.

The cardiothoracic fellowship Brooke hoped to match with out of medical school was extremely competitive. One bad anatomy grade might have cost Brooke one of those coveted spots. Did Rachael not understand that? Either she hadn't understood or hadn't cared. Maybe she wanted to see Brooke squashed like a bug with no scholarship, no fellowship, not even a medical degree. The more Brooke thought about it, the more relieved she was that she had dealt with Rachael in a timely manner.

The hum of the washing machine lulled her senses. She struggled to keep her eyes open, but succumbed to an overwhelming sense of relaxation, falling asleep on the floor, her computer on her lap and her head against the wall. She slept until the buzz of the completion cycle woke her.

When she returned to her room, she rushed straight to the window. The vultures were gone and the dumpster was almost full now. Sundays must be when everyone threw out their trash.

She flopped onto her bed, smiling, filled with relief.

Chapter Twenty-Nine

Brooke sat at her desk with Rachael's phone, scanning through her texts and emails. Lack of cell phone activity would get noticed and send up a red flag before Rachael's physical absence did. Brooke wasn't going to let that happen.

Most of Rachael's text history had been recently cleared, with the exception of messages to her parents. There were more than enough texts between Rachael and "Mom" and "Dad" from which Brooke was able to get the gist of their exchanges. Rachael tended to text them early in the morning, so Brooke sent a message that fit in seamlessly with the rest.

"Hi Mom. I have a cold bug or virus. Plan to stay in bed most of day and get better. Anything new? XOXOXO"

Rachael's phone had registered several missed calls from Peter over the weekend, but no voicemails. Peter had also sent several texts asking where she was, the tone of which progressed from nice and neutral, as in "are you okay?" to sounding pissed off, as in "did I do something to upset you, because if I did you need to tell me." There was a group message from Connor about getting together on Saturday night, and Julie had sent two messages asking if Rachael wanted to meet up with her on Sunday, apparently after the boyfriend had left. There were other messages from contacts Brooke didn't recognize. Brooke responded to all of them with variations of a simple message—*Sorry, I've been sick. Hope you had a good weekend.*

As far as she knew, no one had commented on Rachael's absence from the hallways, bathrooms, and the cafeteria yet. The weekends were unpredictable. Students left campus, slept in, missed meals, and went out to eat. There was no way to tell if something unusual had happened to someone. That would change with Monday morning's arrival. The weekday routine was about to restart.

***

And then there were two.

Brooke and Xander stood on either side of their anatomy class table. Brooke had done her best to keep their cadaver mostly covered for Xander's sake, which is what they were supposed to do anyway so it wouldn't dry out.

"Where is Rachael?" Dr. Sarcough scrunched his brows together.

Students missed class occasionally, but not often. It wouldn't be noticeable in any other room, but because of the way the gross anatomy course was organized, the professor expected to see four students around each table. Rachael's absence was more obvious because Rakesh was also gone.

"I don't know where she is." Brooke clutched a scalpel, ready to make the first incision of the day. Now that there were fewer people in their group, the opportunities to personally dissect and explore had doubled. It was much easier to examine their cadaver with only two heads leaning in and blocking light.

Xander tugged one side of his lab coat. "Rachael's sick, sir." Word had traveled.

Brooke faced the professor. "I sure hope it's not a virus that's going to hit us one by one."

"Just wash your hands frequently." Dr. Sarcough hung around their table for a few minutes and Brooke took the opportunity to ask several questions from her list of items that required further clarification.

Later, during cell biology, Brooke excused herself briefly from class. She hated to miss even a minute of the lecture, she would have a gaping hole in her otherwise perfectly recorded notes, but it was part of her plan and she needed to carry it out meticulously.

She hustled to the ladies' room, peeked under the stalls to make sure she was alone, and turned on Rachael's phone. She sent a message to Xander, Connor, and Julie, all of whom seemed to be friends, based on their communication over the weekend:

Hi All. I'm sick and contagious so I'm staying away from classes for your benefit. You can thank me later. Please take legible notes so I can borrow them.

She hurried back to class and did her best to catch up.

Jeff raised his eyebrows when she stood up again and left during medical ethics. From behind a stall door in a different restroom, she made a few calls to students from Rachael's contacts whose names she recognized. Since she had just left them in class, she knew none of them would answer and their phones were turned off. She let the phone ring just enough to reach their voice mail and then she hung up.

Jeff teased her when she returned. "I falsely believed you would rather pee in your pants than miss a minute of class."

"Well, maybe I had to do more than pee." She didn't care if they thought she was suffering from a bout of diarrhea or anything similar. And if she had to miss part of any class, her choice was medical ethics. The course revolved around figuring out the correct things to think and say to avoid getting in trouble. She had been doing that her whole life and was already an expert.

***

During lunch Brooke returned a message from Rachael's Mom.

Not feeling any better, but getting lots of sleep.

On Monday afternoon Brooke chose to study in her room instead of going to her usual spot at the medical library. She settled into Chinese splits while she read from notes on her laptop. Beside her, Rachael's phone chirped several times with incoming messages. Almost everyone Brooke contacted earlier was now responding to say "feel better" and "let me know if you need anything."

Peter wrote—*I'm sorry you're sick. I've been knocking on your door all weekend. Where are you? Are you mad?*

Brooke didn't answer that one. Intentionally she had left Peter off her earlier text. It worked in her favor if Peter continued to think Rachael was mad and ignoring him. She stood up to take a quick break and was spreading peanut butter on a graham cracker when she heard the screech and clank of the hydraulic arm. Its tell-tale sounds, insignificantly muffled through the concrete walls and windowpanes, indicated the black bags containing Rachael were on their way out of Rothaker, headed to become a tidy collection of ash and steam. Brooke scrambled to her feet to watch. She didn't know how much time would elapse from when the trash arrived at the processing facility to when it was loaded into the furnace, and she couldn't research it now. It was possible that Rachael's impending investigation might involve checking everyone's computers. She didn't need "how long does it take for trash to be incinerated in Connecticut" to be part of her recent browsing history. She just hoped it was a quick cycle, a few days at most. That might be all the time she had. Very soon, things would get heated around the dorm. She learned that from college.

Chapter Thirty

The last texts from Rachael's phone were delivered on Tuesday morning, shortly before the cell battery died. Brooke sent one to Rachael's parents, one to some of the first-years to say she was still sick, and one to herself, which said—*Please let me borrow your notes when I get back, I know yours are the best.* She couldn't resist.

On Tuesday night in the cafeteria, Rachael's absence was one of the topics of conversation. No one could remember seeing her since Friday.

"I tried her room a few times and I called the health affairs office right before dinner," Peter sighed. "She's not there."

"She must have gone home." Connor set his glass of milk down. "If she was sick she probably wanted to be at home. That makes sense. Where does she live?"

"Outside Philadelphia," Peter answered. "And she doesn't have a car."

Brooke set down her knife, finished chopping her salad into tiny pieces. "Her parents came and got her then."

"It's strange that she didn't mention it to any of us." Peter looked around the table. "And if she was that sick, she could have gone to the hospital here."

"She did call us." Julie nodded. "Yesterday, while we were in class. Maybe that was to tell us she was going. If only she had left a message."

"She might be out getting food and fresh air right now." Jeff examined the chunk of meat on his fork. "Whenever I get over the flu I crave fresh melon. It's like a thing. I need chunks of fresh cantaloupe and watermelon. And it has to be cold."

"I always get Super C Protein Shakes from the Juice Factory when I feel sick, in fact, as soon as I start to feel something coming," said Connor. "They definitely help."

"It's just odd that no one has seen or spoken to her in days, don't you think?" Peter frowned. "It doesn't make sense."

"We need to open her room, in case something happened to her." Julie raised her hands to her mouth. "I hate to say this out loud, but what if she was sicker than we realized."

Peter clasped his hands and shook them. "It's ironic that someone could become invisible with so many people around."

"It's because we're all too busy and self-absorbed." Jeff smirked. "It's true."

"Maybe there are things about her we don't know," said Xander. "After all, none of us have known each other for more than a few months. Could she be with a guy?"

"No. She's not." Julie shifted her gaze to Peter.

Xander looked over at Brooke. "What are you smiling about?"

"Me? Nothing." *This is exactly how I thought it would play out. I knew her absence wouldn't be noticed right away. Jessica Carroll was missing from Everett for days before any alarms were raised.* "She's probably fine." Brooke waved a hand. "She just needs the rest. We heard from her this morning."

"Did you get a text from her too?" Peter scrunched up his face.

"Yes."

"I didn't think you two were texting buddies." Peter had a strange look on his face.

"She asked for my notes. What can I say? I take good notes."

"She wouldn't be the first student to unexpectedly pack up and go home to be fed and pampered while someone washes and folds her panties," said Jeff.

Julie rolled her eyes. "No. I can't see Rachael doing that. She's not the type to freak out from stress and take off. And she knows how to wash her own panties."

"Like Xander said, how well do we really know each other?"

Brooke closed her lips tightly around her spoon to keep from smiling again.

***

The following morning, Wednesday, a subset of first-years was sufficiently concerned enough about Rachael's whereabouts to take action. By that time most of her friends had already asked "any sign of Rachael?" and shook their heads in wonder at least once, while continuing to do nothing. They knew she had been sick, but no one had seen her come in or out of her room in days, even to use the bathroom. They hadn't seen her in the cafeteria, so where and how was she eating? Why wasn't she answering her door or her phone? She must have left, but when? And why didn't she tell anyone? They had asked all of those questions, but done nothing to find the answers. They speculated scenarios, some of them grim. But no one person was clearly responsible for taking action. So, no one did. At least not immediately. It was Connor who finally got the ball rolling.

"You know what?" he said, waving his hand around and sounding angry. "This situation would have played out way different if Rachael was here and it was one of us who had dropped off the radar. Rachael would leave no stone unturned in an effort to make sure we were okay. We need to step up. Even if we aren't sure anything is wrong. Especially because we aren't sure anything is wrong."

"Connor's right. This is pathetic. It's past time to figure this out." Peter's voice cracked. He took a deep breath and closed his eyes. "I'll call security."

***

On Wednesday night, Peter and Julie accompanied two members of the campus security staff to open Rachael's door.

"Her room should have been checked before now." The security officer huffed and searched through his ring of keys. "Someone should have called us."

The door opened to an empty room and they all expressed relief. Initially it was a good sign. She hadn't died of a sudden hemorrhagic fever, one of the more outlandish speculations, since they had several viruses—Ebola and bubonic plague, to name a few— in the third-floor epidemiology lab. Neither had she choked on a granola bar while studying.

The security officer nodded to Julie and Peter. "Can you check if anything's missing?"

"I'm calling her phone," said Peter.

They heard nothing in response.

Scanning the room, Julie sighed. "Her backpack and laptop are both there, but there's no trace of her purse or her keys. She always plops them on her dresser." She crouched down and sorted through the shoes on the closet floor. "Her black flats aren't here. Rachael wore those all the time; they were her most comfortable shoes. She would have put them on to go out."

"That means she went out, somewhere," said Peter.

Security officially decided that the unaccounted for items indicated Rachael had left the dorm. What happened to her outside the building was anyone's guess and not as much their responsibility as she was an adult and could go wherever she pleased. But it was school policy to call a primary contact in the event that a resident is reported missing.

"She must have gone home," Peter said.

"All the way to Pennsylvania and leave her laptop and books behind? I don't think so." Julie sounded stressed.

The security officer called Rachael's mother, introduced himself, and then turned the phone over to Julie.

Julie pressed the speaker button and explained who she was, in her sweet, shy voice. "We haven't seen Rachael in a few days. And she's not answering her phone. We were just wondering if she had gone home."

"Here? To our house?" A muffled sound came from Mrs. Kline's end. She was calling to someone.

"Yes. Any chance she's home?"

"Rachael isn't here. Excuse me a moment please, I'm going to ask my husband if he's heard from her, if it's possible she's on her way home."

She returned to the line a few seconds later. "He hasn't heard anything about Rachael coming home. She doesn't have a car, so I don't think she would come home without letting us know. She could take a train, but we'd still need to pick her up from the train station. She told us she was sick earlier in the week, too sick to get out of bed and go to classes. You haven't seen her? Have you checked her room? Hold on please, one moment, I'll be right back."

Julie put the phone on mute. "Oh no. They don't know where she is. Mrs. Kline asked me to hold again. I can hear the panic in her voice. I can't imagine what a call like that would do to my own mother. She would be devastated. She's from a different era. She'd have a heart attack if she even knew we had coed showers. She has no idea how much independence we have here."

"Too much apparently, if one of us can disappear and none of us even know when it might have happened." Peter dropped his head, his shoulders slumped.

"I'm going to start calling my mother every night. I at least want someone to know *when* I go missing, if it happens to me." Julie sounded frantic.

"Hello. Julie? I'm back. I have my cellular telephone now. I can see when we last heard from Rachael. We haven't talked to her in two or three days. That's not unusual. We message each other frequently. I'm putting you on speaker phone so I can search my phone and pinpoint my last communications with my daughter. Here it is . . . last Tuesday. Just two days ago. She said she was still sick, first flu and then laryngitis, and she was upset about having to miss class time, but she was starting to feel better. Did you say you checked her room?"

"We're standing in her room right now. We know she's been sick. But because we haven't seen her in a few days, we asked the school's security officers to open her room. She isn't here."

There was silence on the other end of the phone. Julie pressed the mute button.

"Oh my God! What do I tell her? This is so terrible!" Her hands shook. "We don't even know where Rachael is or if she's okay!"

Suddenly Brooke was in the doorway, then striding past the security guards and reaching for the phone.

"Mrs. Kline. Hi. This is Brooke Walton. I'm one of Rachael's friends, one of her anatomy partners. We didn't mean for you to worry. We think Rachael left the dorm to do an errand; maybe she needed tissues or cough drops, maybe some fresh air. She took her purse and phone with her. If anything was wrong she would have called one of us. We just wanted to check to make sure she hadn't gone home, since she wasn't feeling well. We try to look out for one another."

"Sometimes days pass without us hearing from Rachael. We usually text. She's always busy; she's involved with so many wonderful things. We've learned to be patient and wait, imagining all that she's learning and accomplishing, but now . . .," her voice cracked, "now I'm worried."

"I'm sorry. We'll call you as soon as we hear from her, unless she calls you first. She's probably going to be upset with us for causing such a fuss. She's entitled to some peace and quiet when she's sick."

Brooke hung up the call and handed the phone back to Julie.

"Thank you for handling that," said the security guard. "There's no reason to jump to conclusions yet. It's only been a day since you heard from her." He was looking directly at Julie, who was near tears. "Students go off for much longer than that without telling anyone. We've seen it happen. More than once."

"But you don't know Rachael! She hasn't been to the cafeteria all week, and if she's not at home, where would she be?" Julie wrapped her arms around her body and Peter placed a hand on her shoulder.

Brooke scanned the room, just in case. It appeared she was being helpful, searching for potential clues to Rachael's whereabouts.

"What should we do?! My gut is telling me something is very wrong." Julie looked from person to person.

"Me too." Peter turned to Brooke. "You said she took her purse. How do you know that?"

“Brooke lifted a hand. “What do you mean, how do I know? I . . . I heard you say it, I was standing outside the door.”

“When we first came in? I didn’t see you.”

“I was there. I want to know what’s going on as much as any of you.”

Peter kept his eyes on Brooke and he didn’t look happy.

Julie caught his attention. “Can you study in your room tonight, keep the door open, sit by the doorway so you’ll be sure to hear her if she comes in, even if she comes up the stairwell?”

“That’s a good idea. I’ll do that.” Peter placed his palm against his heart and rocked forward on his shoes.

“If she hasn’t returned in twenty-four hours, the police should be notified,” the security guy quoted from the policy handbook.

“We’re calling the police if she doesn’t come back tonight,” said Julie.

Brooke walked past them and out of the room, calling over her shoulder, “Sounds like a good plan.”

***

Brooke taught the last late-night yoga class at Performance Fit. She didn’t like teaching so late, but at least Mike wouldn’t be around. She was tired of him questioning her about the stupid certifications, although, several weeks had passed since he last asked. That was good.

If he’d kept up, I would have had to put a stop to it, somehow.

Winter was upon them, and the wind chilled her bones while she rode her bike. Her discomfort was relative, thanks to two winters at Everett, where it was truly freezing, but her nose still ran and her cheeks grew numb.

She took a detour on her way back from the gym. The area was almost deserted. The streets were dark, businesses had closed for the evening. She stopped her bike alongside the large pond, or small lake, depending on who you asked, that marked the outer edge of the undergraduate campus. A biking and running trail snaked around the pond’s perimeter. With her bike still between her legs, she swung her backpack around to the front of her body and unzipped the outer front pocket. There was a lone jogger about twenty yards ahead, sticking to the path directly under the lamp lights. Brooke shook her legs to keep herself warm while she waited for the distance between them to increase. Once the person was no longer visible, she heaved Rachael's phone toward the center of the pond. It was too dark to see ripples spreading toward the shore. She briefly wondered what else might be under the water deep in the middle, then rode away, shifting her thoughts to what she needed to accomplish when she got back to her room.

Chapter Thirty-One

Peter and Julie attended classes the next day and temporarily forgot about Rachael because they had not one, but two quizzes. When they reconvened at lunch, they called security, who alerted the police. It was Thursday afternoon. Six days had passed since Brooke killed Rachael.

***

Brooke had one more task, and then her plan would be complete. This last step—getting rid of Rachael's purse—was risky. It needed to be placed somewhere it would be quickly found. Ideally, she would drop it at the clinic where Rachael volunteered. She needed whoever found it to immediately use Rachael's credit cards. Then, when they got caught, as they presumably would be, he or she would explain where they had found the purse and swear it had just been sitting there all by itself. That would cement the theory that Rachael's volunteer work near Greenwood Circle had somehow contributed to her disappearance. Of all the theories, it was the one that made the most sense, the explanation her friends would bet on if forced to choose. A little evidence would help it solidify.

During her last run with Xander, Brooke had scanned the area around the clinics for surveillance cameras. There had to be some. But she couldn't find them. If she left the purse there, and there were cameras, then eventually it would come down to the simple matter of looking through video footage to see who had put it there. Should she wear a disguise and drop off the purse? Wear a disguise and pay someone else to put the purse there? She didn't want to see her image on the news below the words, "Do you know this person?" She had given the matter some serious thought and if she couldn't tell where the security cameras were positioned, it just wasn't going to work. Fortunately, she had discovered the neglected park a few blocks away from the clinic. It was the perfect alternate spot.

The biting wind was unusually strong and cold; the way it blew against her chest led Brooke to imagine it was personally out to accost her. She was used to running at night, on isolated dark roads, but not in this type of neighborhood. A neon-rimmed older model SUV drove by at a menacingly slow speed; the passenger rolled down his window, whistled, and hollered "Hey, baby. Hey, baby. Whatcha doing?" Brooke was uncomfortable, and that was an unusual feeling for her. But she wasn't afraid. Her pace quickened. Turning into an alley allowed her to avoid further interaction with the car, even though it sent her heading in the opposite direction of where she needed to go, and further into darkened and questionable territory. Two homeless men covered in blankets huddled against the side of a run-down building beside two grocery carts and a row of trash cans. One of them garbled "that's one way to stay warm," between his missing teeth when she passed. Their stench, filth and old urine, followed her down the alley. Needing to loop around the next set of buildings to get back on track, she ran even faster, her backpack and its contents sliding around and annoying her.

In the derelict park, all the lamplights were purposefully shattered to allow occupants the cover of darkness. *Am I crazy to be here alone at night?* Anyone there at night was up to no good. Herself included. She kept up her pace, aware of movement on the other side of the park. The sound of scraping feet. A hacking cough. A grunt.

Squinting in the dim light, she jogged over to some mangy bushes. She swung her backpack around and unzipped it, dumping the purse unceremoniously in plain sight beside the shriveled branches. She hoped it would be found before sunrise. As she turned, her foot kicked something light and plastic. A discarded syringe. With her gloved hands she scooped it up, holding it almost at arms-length all the way back to the hospital. Outside the ER, she dropped it in a trashcan, in memory of Rachael.

Chapter Thirty-Two

The disappearance of Rachael Kline presented a milestone opportunity for Lieutenant Arty Sanchez. The lieutenant's boss, Captain O'Brien, was near sixty. Why didn't he retire already? Heading up a case like this would provide Sanchez mounds of exposure. The number of different people and organizations that he would be working with would be, for him, unprecedented. The FBI would be making an appearance any time now. Not to mention the coverage the case was going to get.

Sanchez parked his Toyota, put on his navy sports coat, and walked to the medical school dormitory. "Not the madhouse scene I was expecting," he told O'Brien when he called.

"Colleges don't like the publicity that goes along with losing a student. It's not supposed to happen. Their applications for next year are going to take a hit. Rothaker higher-ups are doing all they can to keep the news internal for as long as possible. You might have another day or two before the media is involved, but be prepared. The precinct has already assigned you a full-time media liaison."

"I'll keep you posted throughout the day."

"Did you shave?"

Sanchez ran his hand over his thick stubble and mumbled something indiscernible.

All the trouble could be worth it if the case turned out to be a kidnapping or a homicide, and if he solved it, he would prove himself. He would be well positioned to replace O'Brien. But along the way he would have to handle the soon-to-be circus show surrounding the case.

There was no evidence of foul play, but Sanchez was betting on finding some. Campus officials made it very clear that this was still a "missing persons" case, not a suspected kidnapping or homicide investigation, but Sanchez knew the statistics. A student was considered a missing person if their absence was contrary to their usual pattern of behavior. Rachael Kline was responsible, reliable, in good mental health, so it was out of character for her to go away without letting anyone know. Most disappearances involved students who were younger and made unwise decisions regarding alcohol consumption. They turned up eventually, rarely with a beating heart if they were gone more than two days; bad timing, terrible luck, the stupidity of youth and untested freedom contributing equally to their misfortune. But Rachael Kline was a graduate student, with no history of irresponsible drug or alcohol use, and no behavioral problems. And it wasn't exam time, which was when a stress-induced suicide would be most probable. Sanchez had directed one of his Sergeants and his squad to check out the Connecticut River Bridge and the large pond on the outskirts of the Rothaker campus. If they found Rachael in either location, he might be willing to bet that she didn't jump in on her own. Learning more would help him decide.

Sanchez had sent a quarter of the shift's staff over to the medical school dormitory to interview its residents because Rachael's dorm was the last place she was seen. His detectives had made it to the end of the third floor already, interviewing thirty-something students along the way, but not everyone had been in their rooms. They would have to revisit until they had made contact with every resident. Hopefully the labor-intensive interview process would uncover a useable lead. Sanchez was doing some of the interviews himself to get a feel for every angle of the investigation. He used the following questions:

"When did you last see Rachael?"

"Did she mention any plans to leave school?"

"Did she say or do anything suspicious?"

"Where were you last weekend?"

The last question was guaranteed to generate a mountain of useless information to comb through. There were ninety-eight full-time dorm residents, each with immediate proximity to Rachael. There was no such thing as a strong alibi with everyone coming in and out all weekend, mostly staying out, which was to be expected of people living in tiny spaces with no toilets. The residents also spent a significant amount of time alone in their single rooms, hours that no one else could vouch for. And no one had a clear idea of when Rachael had disappeared.

The lieutenant's phone rang. It was his wife calling again, probably about his son, her step-son, most likely in trouble again, or about to be in trouble if Sanchez didn't intervene with some serious repercussions to prevent him from ever stepping near Greenwood Circle again. But he wasn't going to deal with it right now. It would have to wait.

***

Brooke lay on her bed trying to focus on her studies, aware that the police were making rounds. Below her window, two detectives rattled around the dumpster. They removed every bag of trash and loaded it into the back of a cart. A man inside the dumpster scraped residue samples from the metal sides. Brooke let out a deep sigh.

So glad I triple bagged everything and got rid of that purse.

She was confident the vultures had not gotten into the bags because the dumpster had filled quickly. And her taser was now locked away in a locker at Performance Fit. It had been useful to her too many times to dispose of it.

When an official sounding knock arrived, she was ready. Squaring her shoulders, she opened the door.

"Hi. I'm Lieutenant Sanchez." He straightened his posture and sucked in his gut. "The East Dalton police department is asking everyone in the dorm to cooperate and provide us with any information that would help us determine the whereabouts of Rachael Kline. Please state your name."

"Brooke Walton."

He added a check mark on his clipboard. She could smell coffee and cigarettes on his stale breath. She hated that smell.

"Do you know Rachael Kline?"

"Yes, I do. I'm a first-year also. Rachael is in my anatomy group.

It's particularly unfortunate that she's missing because one of our other group members had to go back to India unexpectedly, so now we're down to two. But that's not relevant for you. Sorry."

"No. That's okay." Sanchez nodded with encouragement. "I'm interested in anything you can think of. There's no way for you to know what information might prove to be useful in finding Rachael."

That's pretty amusing, since I know exactly everything you need to know. You're the one who is clueless.

Not for the first time, she felt like a master puppeteer making everyone around her dance. She maintained her pleasant almost subservient expression, thinking it would look best to come across as somewhat intimidated by the lieutenant.

"Can you tell me when you last saw her?"

"I think I saw her at dinner on Friday, but I didn't sit with her, so I'm not positive."

"Did she mention anything to you about going anywhere this past weekend?"

"No. Nowhere in particular. In our last class on Friday I remember she told some of us that she was feeling sick and staying in to rest. But she was disciplined about visiting the outpatient clinics around the hospital. She did that a few times a week to stock up the pamphlets for a program she worked with. So, knowing Rachael, I expect she took care of that anyway, so the clinics would be set over the weekend."

"That would be her volunteer work for Mercy Street," the detective nodded.

"She also rode around with a mobile needle exchange program in the city. And she worked at an HIV clinic. She might have followed through on her volunteer commitments this weekend regardless of how she was feeling. I don't know."

"Do you remember what you did last weekend?" He intended to record the whereabouts of every student in the dorm, just in case.

"Last weekend? Hold on, let me think," Brooke responded in her soft voice, completely unfazed by the situation.

The lieutenant made small talk from the open doorway while Brooke bent over her desk to open her calendar on her computer. "I don't know why I'm looking at this." She laughed and tossed her thick, blonde ponytail to the side as she closed out of her calendar function. "I didn't go anywhere. I was here. I stayed in the dorm on Friday night. I went for a long run with a friend on Saturday morning. Then I was here in my room most of the time or in the library, except for meals in the cafeteria. I taught two classes at Performance Fit on Sunday. I almost never leave the dorm, except for classes, the library and when I work at Performance Fit. Oh, I did my laundry on Saturday. I hate how this sounds…what a homebody right?" She rolled her eyes and laughed at herself and Sanchez chuckled right along with her.

When the detective peered into her room, Brooke pictured the mole in her refrigerator. She still hadn't created a section from it. Was there any chance the lieutenant would open her refrigerator? Would he have any idea what he was seeing if he did? Of course not. If she wasn't a medical student, it might be weird to have random tissue in her fridge. But she was, and so it was most likely fine. Plenty of explanations and no reason to worry.

"Down to my final questions. Do you own a vehicle?"

"No, just a bike."

"A motorbike?"

"A Schwinn."

"Do you have access to a vehicle?"

"Unfortunately, no. I haven't driven a car since I arrived here in September. And now that you mention it, I miss it." She offered a small laugh, because anything more would have been inappropriate considering the serious nature of the investigation.

"That's all of my questions. If you think of anything, anything at all, give me a call." He handed her a business card with his name and number. "I don't mean to scare you, but watch yourself. We don't know that Miss Kline's situation involved foul play, but a young woman your age, you always want to be careful of anyone suspicious."

"Thank you, lieutenant."

She waited at the door with a smile until he walked away. Her corded muscles were well hidden under her loose jeans and winter sweater. Nothing about Brooke would lead a detective to envision her sawing through bone after bone with a look of steel determination until Rachael became an ensemble of dripping parts pooled inside a mattress bag.

***

Detective Sanchez knocked on three more doors, but their occupants were elsewhere. He would let his detectives finish the rest. His shoulders slouched. He craved another cup of coffee.

One of his detectives was charged with reviewing the footage from the dorm security cameras. He was on his second pass through, a long and tedious process. Sanchez called him to find out how it was progressing.

"Hey, boss," Detective Sandberg answered.

"Have you finished the security tape review?"

"We have, we went all the way back to Monday, but there is no sign of that girl coming out of the dorm. Not unless she was wearing a disguise. She's just not there."

"Okay, get another officer, a fresh pairs of eyes, watch it again, and go all the way back to Friday night. That was the last time anyone saw her. This time look for anyone carrying a large suitcase or anything large enough to hold a body. If you don't see her coming out, we'll get the search warrant." He sighed and rubbed his neck. *Can't believe we've got nothing.* "What about the cell phone records? Who went through those?"

"Officer Myerson did. All the girl's calls went directly to voicemail starting last Saturday morning. She sent messages and responded to messages from friends and her parents, mostly about being sick, last one was Tuesday morning. No activity since then. The cell records show the signals were received from the closest tower to the college, so all of those texts could have been sent while she was still in the dormitory building."

"It's a university, Sandberg. Get that right when you're talking or they'll have a reason to thumb their noses up at us. Trust me. Tell Myerson to print out a record of all her texts. Have a timeline on my desk when I get back to the office. Concentrate on screening the video footage from Tuesday morning through Wednesday late afternoon, but like I said, start with Friday night."

"Got it."

"Any activity on her credit card?"

"Nope. Nothing on the credit cards. And no ATM activity."

"Damn. Okay. I'm on my way back now. I've sent a few guys over to Greenwood Circle to ask questions."

"Finding someone suspicious in Greenwood Circle is like finding a piece of hay in a haystack."

"I know." Sanchez rubbed his tired eyes. "They have her picture to show around. I want someone to track down the elderly man who recently threatened her, the one whose family was murdered."

A few yards away from a sign that read "No Smoking Anywhere on the Medical Campus," Sanchez leaned against the outside of the dormitory building to light a cigarette and review the information he had so far. Fifty dorm room interviews had revealed nothing of significance, nothing he didn't know before they started. No one had seen the victim since Friday night and no one had heard from her since Tuesday. If she made it to a nearby store, she didn't purchase anything, unless she used cash. He needed to find out when Rachael Kline left the dorm, who she was with, and where she was going.

Sanchez took a long inhale of his cigarette and wrinkled his brow.

Where are you, Rachael Kline?

Chapter Thirty-Three

Rothaker University retained the right to search student's dorm rooms without a warrant, at any time, if they had probable cause. But the student needed to be present. With a warrant in hand, the East Dalton police could investigate every room without rounding up the residents. With no evidence that Rachael had left the dorm, Sanchez made the call to O'Brien to obtain a warrant, and fast. He didn't know how many days had passed since their victim went missing.

The warrant came through first thing Friday morning, as Sanchez was driving in to the office. He made a U-turn to pick it up. On the way, he called George Lay, the head of security at Rothaker.

"Is there a time when all the students are out of there?" asked Sanchez.

Lay put him on hold for a moment before returning. "They'll be in class starting at 8 AM. Their first break is at noon."

Sanchez hung up and called Detective Sandberg. "I want us in and out of every room before noon. Get every available officer over there now."

By the time Sanchez arrived at the dormitory with the warrant, two detectives and half their squads were waiting along with Lay and Dr. Ernest Sinclair, Dean of Rothaker Medical School. Sanchez needed a cigarette bad, but he started giving directions immediately.

"Every room, every closet, under every bed. Scour every corner, every stairwell, unlock every door in this building. Tunnels, roof-shafts, elevators, under the ceiling tiles, everything in the kitchen. Inside out and upside down. Every inch. I don't want any students or staff walking around while we're searching. They can wait. Let's be quick. Find me something."

Dr. Sinclair gave him a critical look. "This is unexplored territory, Lieutenant. We don't know anything happened to Rachael Kline here, or anywhere, and we don't know that another student was involved if something did happen." It sounded as if Sinclair was giving a warning.

"According to your security footage, the girl never left this building, so chances are she's still inside. It would have helped if you had security cameras in the hallways."

Lay stepped forward, addressing the officers. "If it doesn't pertain to Rachael Kline, don't find it. You don't need to mess with the reputation of the medical school and its students as a byproduct of your search."

"Agreed," Sanchez said. To do otherwise would only mean more paperwork, more distractions, and potentially—attorneys. "Don't be bringing me joints, or anything that amounts to less than a grand felony crime. This isn't the time. I don't want to hear about it if it doesn't pertain to Rachael Kline."

"If the staff are going to have to clear out, start with the kitchen." Lay puffed out his cheeks, gripping one of his wrists. "The culinary team starts preparing lunch right after they finish cleaning up the breakfast. They'll need to get back in there."

"Sandberg, start your guys in the kitchen," Sanchez repeated, pointing in that general direction and showing the university honchos just how cooperative he could be.

***

Three hours later, at the end of the thorough but fruitless search, Sanchez got a call from Myerson. "How's your search going boss?"

"We're finished. We didn't find anything. Zip. Not even drug paraphernalia. Medical students don't seem very interesting. Maybe that's why they're more likely to crack later on, higher suicide rate, all that."

Lay and Sinclair were as relieved as Sanchez was disappointed.

"Well, sir, I'm calling because we have a hit on Miss Kline's credit card. Purchase made fifteen minutes ago at Radio City. Car stereos."

"Why didn't you tell me that first?" Sanchez slapped his clipboard against the back of a chair. This could be their break. "Get someone to the store, get the security footage. Find that person and get him in to the station now."

They had a lead. A car stereo purchase with a stolen credit card—it sounded like their suspect wasn't the sharpest. If he had anything to do with the girl's disappearance, it would be an easy conviction. Sanchez couldn't wait to interview the guy. Hopefully his officers would have an identification by the time he finished his twelve-inch meatball sub and a few cigarettes.

***

Just as Detective Sanchez drove away from the Rothaker campus, Jeff stopped at Brooke's door, practically bouncing with excitement, bursting with news he couldn't wait to share.

"Are you in there?" he called to Brooke, tapping lightly with the back of his knuckles.

Brooke opened the door and Jeff started talking as if he couldn't contain himself.

"Oh my God! I feel like I'm living in a real-life episode of CSI Connecticut. The police watched surveillance videos of everyone who left the dorm all weekend. A detective just grilled me because I left the dorm on Friday night with a suitcase! I had to open it up and show it to him and he wiped it down with some tape that's going to be analyzed. Can you believe it?"

Brooke was impressed.

"As if I put Rachael in my suitcase and kidnapped her, stuffed her in my suitcase! I mean . . . this is a suitcase I can fit in an overhead bin! This is nuts!"

"It is," Brooke said, feeling omniscient. But the police were being logical and thorough. More so than she had imagined.

"They sprayed chemicals all over Rachael's room. Isn't that what they do when they're looking for blood?"

Brooke's face drained of color, although she was certain they would find nothing. She was too good, too careful.

"Security organized a campus-wide search for Rachael tomorrow. With scent tracking dogs. They're asking for volunteers so we're all going. So terrible, but just crazy too."

"Oh. Great. What time?"

"Seven. Seven in the morning. And Connor made flyers that we're going to hang up everywhere."

"I got his message about that. It's great. Hey, I need a few more minutes. I'll see you downstairs, okay?"

It was getting crazy. Brooke hated drama, but it was difficult not to feel a small sense of pride that she was the one responsible for all the hoopla. But had she been careful enough in Rachael's room?

Chapter Thirty-Four

On Friday, after the police finished scrutinizing every inch of the dormitory, news reporters from all the media outlets descended upon Rothaker Medical School. Any medical students interested in two minutes of fame could answer questions for reporters. Jeff snuck back to his room during a break to choose a better outfit. Julie exchanged her weekday sweats for one of her chic weekend outfits with just the right accessories. Everyone dressed a little better than their usual. Eventually, the reporters' constant requests of "excuse me, do you have a minute?" would get annoying, and in the absence of new information, everything anyone could say had already been said, but in those first few days, their presence was an interesting and exciting turn of events.

Julie made hundreds of "Find Rachael" ribbons—a tiny button with the letter R, secured to a loop of purple ribbon by a safety pin. She distributed the ribbons, asking people to wear them until Rachael was found. Everyone at the medial school appeared to be wearing one.

Brooke couldn't believe how many people claimed to be missing Rachael. The media was keeping her disappearance fresh in their minds. Meal times had temporarily become "the Rachael hour."

"Rachael was the most caring person."

"Rachael was a fearless leader."

"Rachael tried to help all of us to be close friends."

Brooke forced her most practiced empathetic look into place as she nodded her head to the many testimonies about how Rachael helped someone with this and someone else with that.

One man's trash is another man's treasure. But what she said out loud, feeling the need to carefully contribute to the conversation, was "stop saying that Rachael *was* all of those things. Why is everyone acting as if she's gone forever? I think Rachael just got stressed or tired and needed a break. I'm going to believe she's coming back."

"Stressed from what?" Jeff frowned.

"Where could she have gone?" asked Julie.

"Stressed from school. I think she went to India to visit Rakesh and help him get through his troubles. That's the kind of person she was." Brooke smiled in a way that indicated she knew what she was saying was ridiculous, but it was what her concerned heart wanted to believe.

"That's nice," Jeff said. "I appreciate your optimism. If only it could be true."

Julie shook her head, wringing her hands again. "Rachael wouldn't leave without telling anyone and put her family and friends through this nightmare. It's inconceivable. Something terrible has happened to her."

Jeff had told everyone about the detective's interest in his suitcase. It only proved that the police suspected the worst.

"She's probably doing something with that project of hers," Brooke said, wondering why there was still no news about the purse or any of its contents being found. Once it was found it would change the entire course of the investigation. What was taking so long?

"It's her projects, her volunteer work around the Greenwood Circle area after dark, that worries me," Xander said.

"What about that old man she told us about, the one whose family was murdered. He threatened her, pointed his finger right at her and said she was damned to hell, or something like that, for enabling drug addicts," Peter reminded them.

***

Xander finished the cafeteria's dried out chicken breast, his third, while he listened to the conversation going on around him. Like almost everyone else who knew Rachael, he was both worried and curious. He had been consumed with his PTSD and his studies since the semester started. He hadn't even picked up on the fact that Rachael had a thing for him. Not one clue. Each scenario he imagined to explain Rachael's absence seemed far worse than what he was experiencing because of his stress symptoms. He felt guilty. How many times had his mother said that if you want to help yourself you need to help others first? That was the key to happiness and contentment. Maybe he should be volunteering in the city, getting over his issues by reaching out instead of turning inward for self-analysis. He was friendly with everyone on campus, but he hadn't made many close friends. He enjoyed spending time with Connor, and Brooke, and truthfully, with everyone in their class. He had certainly spent enough time with his anatomy group to know them well. But first Rakesh had left and now Rachael. That left only him and Brooke from the original group. He felt protective and unusually sentimental about their situation.

Across from him, Brooke was getting up from the table. She gracefully swung her legs around and stood up, wearing those form fitting workout pants that revealed every curve and taut line of her lower body. A body that was strong and healthy, he had seen it do some amazing things before and after their runs. He noticed her long, dark eyelashes, a nice contrast to the blonde ponytail that fell over her right shoulder. As she walked away, he realized he would be especially upset if he lost Brooke. In fact, it pained him to imagine being at the school without her. He only had a second to dwell on his unexpected realization before Jeff whispered to him.

"I feel bad for Peter."

Peter and Sundeep sat together at the end of the table, having a private conversation. Peter shook his head. Sundeep leaned toward him to say something. Peter looked down, one hand absentmindedly pushing a fork through the rice on his plate.

"What's wrong with him?" Xander asked.

"He's either having a tough time dealing with Rachael's disappearance or the police are being particularly hard on him."

"What are you talking about?"

"He and Rachael were an item, sort of."

"You're kidding me. Since when?"

"I don't think it was anything official, but they've been discreetly hooking up for a while. Not so discreetly that a bunch of us didn't know about it."

"I had no idea."

"He knocked on her door all weekend and when she didn't answer he thought she was mad at him because he went out on Friday, which he did because she said she wasn't feeling well. When she didn't return any of his calls, he thought maybe he was supposed to stay in with her and he was like 'how was I supposed to know that.' He thought she was blowing him off, so he stopped trying to contact her. He feels guilty now. Heck, maybe if he hadn't been so insecure about it we would have known she went missing earlier. Who knows how long she's been gone."

"She was in her room until Tuesday, right?"

"Or was she? Couldn't anyone take her phone and send a few texts saying she was sick? Anyone could do that once they knew she wasn't feeling well."

"I suppose, but that seems far-fetched." Xander felt terrible for Rachael. He knew what people were capable of, even if they didn't know it themselves until it happened. He wasn't beyond imagining the worst.

Jeff leaned back and looked around. "Peter's a nice guy. I don't think he did anything to her. This whole situation is just horrible."

"Of course he didn't," Xander said sternly, "none of us could ever hurt Rachael."

Xander rubbed the back of his neck and thought. Jeff's story didn't fit with what Brooke told him. How could Rachael have been into him if she was hooking up with Peter? Not that he ever thought she was; he had never seen any hint of it. So why would Rachael say that to Brooke? Then, finally, it occurred to him—*why would Brooke say that to me?*

Chapter Thirty-Five

Straddling her bike, Brooke watched from a hilltop. The sky was overcast and ash gray. Over two hundred students and faculty gathered, many carrying umbrellas or wearing raincoats. Four search dogs had been made available to the university to help find Rachael. Her pillowcases were provided as scent articles. A handler announced that the scent dogs performed best on cool cloudy mornings.

Poor little doggies, you can sniff and sniff, but you aren't going to find Rachael anywhere.

Everyone was instructed to wear something purple so that they could be identified as part of the search party. When the searchers were assembled together, it looked like an outdoor concert was about to start. The head of security stood on a makeshift platform to outline the search plan. He provided guidelines on what to look for and how to search so that if they did find information relevant to Rachael, they wouldn't destroy pertinent evidence. He handed out maps split into grid areas so the search party could divide and conquer to cover five miles of territory. There wasn't much in the way of woods in East Dalton, but there were still plenty of half-hidden spots that needed to be searched.

Brooke planned to return after she taught two classes at Performance Fit. She wasn't particularly motivated to help look for someone who would never be found.

***

She left the gym and sent a message to Xander to find out where she could catch up with him and his group. He and Connor happened to be at the lake, which was not far from the gym. Brooke found it ironic that they ended up at the one area where they might find something of

Rachael's, but only if they searched the depths in the middle.

***

Xander and Connor were waiting for her when she arrived. Connor wore a cap from Northwestern, whose school color happened to be purple, along with his permanent grin. Xander had a purple t-shirt, worn over two long-sleeved shirts so he wouldn't freeze. Both had "Find Rachael" ribbons pinned to their chest.

"She. Is. So. Beautiful," Connor said to Xander as they watched Brooke's shapely form jogging to meet them.

"Yeah. She is. And you say that every time you see her. Did you know that?"

Connor laughed. "She's a little strange too. Don't you think? But that's fine with me."

"Yeah? If you want to talk about strange, let's remember that you told her about your hemorrhoid. Maybe not the most romantic way to start something."

"Dude, I told everyone about my hemorrhoid. We're all going to be doctors. You, my friend, might have to look at people's butts every day. And they won't all have butts of steel like me. You're going to see some ugly butts. Fat ones, old wrinkled ones, butts that make you wish you were an accountant."

They were both laughing when Brooke reached them. They stopped abruptly when they saw the serious and determined look on her face, a reminder that they were searching for Rachael and more solemn expressions were appropriate.

"How is the search going?"

"We're already done searching our assigned area," said Connor. "With so many volunteers, it didn't take long."

"Are they going to drag the bottom of the lake?"

"The police dragged it days ago. It was one of the first things they did, before they checked our dorm rooms," Connor answered.

"Oh. Wow. I guess they didn't find anything then. She's certainly not underwater at this point anyway, since she's been missing for days.

She would have reached a stage of decomposition that would cause her body to surface." Brooke gazed out at the pond and stretched her quads while she spoke. "So? Anything new?"

"We were assigned to a ground area. We were supposed to look for spots that might have been recently dug up. Unbelievable right?" Connor said.

"Oh, that's gruesome. What else? Tell me what I missed."

"We haven't heard any useful news yet, but there are people searching miles away. The entire campus was searched, but most of the police and volunteers were sent over to the hospital clinic and the Greenwood Circle area."

"Why is that?" Brooke asked.

"Oh. You didn't hear? Someone used her credit card. The police tracked him down and he has witnesses that swear they found the purse by itself at an old playground."

"That's the playground we ran by, remember?" said Xander.

"Yes, I do. I hope they took empty trash bags along so they could help clean up the area while they're over there. That would be a good use of time." She studied everyone in their purple shirts and Rachael buttons. "Too bad they didn't find anything, but plenty of the people around here needed a good walk and some fresh air anyway."

Chapter Thirty-Six

Xander adjusted his cap and gazed at the sky. "Might pour any minute."

Clasping her hands behind her back, Brooke folded forward into a straddle stretch, speaking to him from upside down. "Yeah. But it's been like that all day. Besides, I like running in the rain."

"Let's do a different route today." Xander bent his leg behind him, holding on to his foot, also stretching. "I want to check out where they found Rachael's purse. I know we ran by it before, but I didn't get a good look then. I just want to get a feel for where she might have been when she disappeared."

"Sure. Do you have tracking skills from the military you want to put to use?"

"I wish, but no, nothing that would work in this environment anyway."

They began their run by turning left instead of the usual right that took them through Rothaker University. They ran past the hospital buildings and some of its satellite facilities and outpatient clinics. The flyers Connor made were tacked to every vertical surface with the words "Have you seen me?" below Rachael's picture.

Just beyond the health care buildings was Greenwood Circle, and beyond it, a few other residential neighborhoods that had also seen better days. Each worn-out home in the impoverished neighborhood was fronted by a small dry, dirt covered area. Some of them had even been paved over, the concrete cracking, but otherwise requiring little maintenance. They couldn't be called yards, although that's what they were supposed to be. Twenty small homes crammed into the same space reserved for one house in his neighborhood. The roads were marred by ruts and rain filled potholes. Garbage and discarded items filled in the areas where there should have been grass and shrubs. There were no other runners around.

"This is depressing." Xander scowled. "Especially on such a dismal day. I shouldn't have suggested it."

"I would never come here alone at night, that's for sure."

"How do you think you did on the cell bio test?" Xander flinched as a nearby muffler backfired.

"I aced it."

"Gotta love your confidence. I thought it was a ball breaker."

"How was your last therapy session? Can you tell if it's helping?"

"Not yet. The sessions force me to face what happened, not just the facts but how it affected me. Emotionally."

"Cognitive therapy?"

"Yeah. My last session was good, according to my psychiatrist. I've probably never talked so much before without stopping. Telling him all sorts of things."

"Like?"

"Like my expectations for the enemy's behavior." He laughed. "I know it sounds nuts." Then his voice turned serious. "My flashbacks and nightmares aren't letting up."

They were silent for many strides.

"What about rapid eye motion therapy? That's supposed to work for PTSD."

"I think that's next."

"It's a neat concept based on a well-proven premise. Certain eye movements reduce the stress associated with traumatic thoughts. Directing your eyes a specific way while focusing on a disturbing image can eventually decrease the stress associated with that image. The initial trauma causes a change in neural elements, and the therapy is supposed to reverse it.

"Hmm. Interesting."

"Do you want to talk about it? I know you have the psychiatrist but sharing the events with family and friends is supposed to help."

"That's what Dr. Chavez keeps telling me."

"I just read about it. With you in mind, of course."

"I can tell. Either that or you really do know everything. But it's nice you were thinking about me."

Their eyes caught for a beat more than usual.

Xander looked ahead and picked up the pace. "I just want to focus on the run, let it clear my head. You're a great running partner, you're challenging me endurance wise."

"You're leaner and more chiseled than you were before."

"Yeah? You noticed that?"

"Yep."

A rusting sedan cruised by, its frame barely two inches off the ground, vibrating to the blaring base of rap music emanating from inside.

"Sorry if it seems like I'm pressing you, but just tell me what you saw. I'd like to understand what you're going through."

"It's not pleasant, Brooke. It's ugly. I don't want to fill your head with this stuff."

It started raining as they crossed the street. Rivulets of mud formed and traveled towards the piles of unpackaged trash waiting curbside. Two people standing at a bus stop opened umbrellas. One woman held her pocketbook horizontally over her head to protect her hair. The child next to her opened his mouth and tipped it up toward the sky. The woman smacked his head back down. "Close your mouth. That rain is dirty!"

Xander thought about how it had rained that morning, just before they left for Kandahar. The rain combined with the ubiquitous layers of dust, creating dirt trails that flowed over everything, including his body, before being washed clean, temporarily.

"Some of the things I experienced in Afghanistan made me question basic humanity and what a human being is capable of doing," he said suddenly.

"Can you stop being so cryptic and just tell me. I'm working hard to find the right questions. Since you were there to kill people, if need be, how is whatever happened so terrible? What did someone do that was so evil or sick that it made you question humanity?"

"We were there to keep the peace. To keep people from being killed. That's the point of war, to promote peace and understanding."

"Is it? I thought wars started when people tire of being pushed around by those determined to take what doesn't belong to them. I'd say wars are equally about destroying people who would otherwise destroy you."

"Uhh, no." He pressed his lips together as they ran across an intersection.

"So, what happened that was so terrible?"

"What I experienced involved someone who was sick. Out of control. Who the hell knows how someone gets like that? Screwed up childhood? Some of the Taliban are living like animals in the mountains and being brainwashed since the day they are born. I still don't understand why basic human decency doesn't prevail though. I'm interested, I'll tell you that. I'm thinking about going into psychiatry now. The more time I've had to spend thinking about what I saw, the more I want to know how someone can possibly kill another person when it's not necessary."

"When someone is out to get you, you have to take immediate action. And in those cases, there is no reason for guilt or shame. Feelings of guilt and shame can lead to PTSD. And generally, those feelings aren't warranted," Brooke said, sounding defensive.

Xander watched Brooke as she spoke, splitting his attention between her determined expression and the ground so he wouldn't trip over anything. "Some of the things I saw should not have happened, they served no purpose, and they were avoidable."

"It's hard for me to philosophize with you about this when I don't know what we're talking about here." Brooke's tone had a hint of indignity.

Xander didn't respond.

"The best soldiers are the people who have no remorse about taking a life." Brooke nodded as she ran. "I read that, too."

They ran for another five minutes in relative silence, aside from Brooke's frustrated sighs.

"Can you just tell me this—what did you see when we unveiled our cadaver that reminded you of Afghanistan?"

Xander began exhaling more forcefully; his forehead tightened. He understood from his sessions with Dr. Chavez that it wasn't what he had experienced in Kandahar that upset him as much as the capability for evil that it represented. He didn't want to talk about it or think about it, but his symptoms weren't getting any better. And, he was becoming increasingly uncertain about what had happened. Raindrops slid off his eyelashes. He squinted, then closed his eyes for a second even as he kept running. He needed to take the plunge, tell everything he knew, get it out of his system, and do it fast before he changed his mind.

Sighing, and feeling sorry for dumping the information on Brooke, he began. "Okay. Since you're being so persistent, I'm going to tell you."

He shared the background story he had described to Dr. Chavez, how his mission team had left the city with his two wounded comrades and returned a few hours later with an additional unit. Brooke listened intently, not once interrupting.

"The village, the stores and marketplace, they were empty when we returned. We had to make sure it was all clear before we went back inside. The building was a crazy design of hallways and shoddy rooms that had been added on one after another, most of them were destroyed. We found the rest of our guys, together, and they were all dead, as expected. I was the first one to find John. His eyes were open, looking straight at me as if he was alive. He was hanging sort of sideways, suspended from a beam that was jutting out from the wall. He was covered with blood. At first, I thought he had a bloody rope around his neck. Then I got closer, and I saw it wasn't a rope. His intestines were ripped out. Pulled straight up his torso, split across each shoulder and over his head. That's what was suspending him. He was hanging by his own intestines."

Xander felt tears in his eyes and the acrid taste of vomit in his throat. "I'm sorry. You shouldn't have to hear this."

"No. It's okay." Brooke hadn't flinched in the slightest. "You can tell me. You should tell me. It will be good for you."

Xander puffed up his cheeks with an exhale and waited until they crossed a busy road before he spoke again. "After his autopsy I learned that what happened to him was pre-mortem. He was alive for all of it. And he was an unarmed civilian helping them. I still can't get over it."

"I'm picturing the scene from anatomy," Brooke said calmly, "the Y-shaped incision marks on our cadaver could look the same as the small intestine arrangement you described. I understand how seeing it jump-started your PTSD. I took neuroanatomy. The brain is a complicated network of electrical impulses and connections. Almost anything is possible with the right spark of ignition."

"What bothered me was how a person has the capacity to hurt another human being like that."

"I see." Brooke spoke so softy that Xander didn't hear her.

Xander had shared one of his most disturbing visions with Brooke. But he had a nagging feeling that there was still something more, a deeper memory that wanted to come out. It was eating away at his mind in panicky waves. It was somehow linked to the terrifying, Hulk-like image of himself, soaked with blood. But it couldn't be real because he didn't remember it happening and he had never been wounded. He stopped running and leaned over, hands on his thighs. He was going to be sick and he truly didn't understand why his mind and body kept responding so violently.

Brooke didn't ask any more questions. She waited silently while the rain fell, dousing them. Xander was frustrated and confused. He had been sick to his stomach many times during two a day football practices, but at least then he understood why and it had nothing to do with his mind. Once he recovered, he stood up, wiped his mouth on his sleeve, and started running again.

Brooke's blonde hair was so drenched it appeared to have turned brown. "What about the other guys?" she asked, as if they were talking about a good movie, as if he hadn't just emptied the contents of his stomach on the side of the road. "You said they were all dead. How were they killed?"

At that moment Xander decided Brooke should be a psychiatrist. Instead of looking horrified or turned off, she seemed to care about getting to the bottom of his issues. She was almost pushing to hear the details, as if she wanted him to dig down deep and get it all out. But he was finished.

"I appreciate your help, I really do, but I need to talk about something else." He had hoped to have a catharsis of some sort after telling that story, but as far as he could tell, he had not. He only felt guilty about planting those ugly pictures in Brooke's mind. He couldn't imagine what she was thinking now.

Chapter Thirty-Seven

Xander had an appointment with Dr. Chavez the next afternoon. He recounted the same story he told Brooke about returning to Kandahar and finding John. After he finished sharing the experience that he remembered, he still didn't feel any different, even though it was now his second re-telling. There was no magical lifting away of his symptoms. At Xander's request they spent an entire session delving into the incident and discussing man's capacity to hurt another man. Where did it come from? Was it innate in every man? Even in those who never imagined they could do something so atrocious and barbaric? Did that make them evil? He needed to understand.

After that discussion, which was as philosophical as it was scientific, Dr. Chavez thought it was important to talk about the issue of trust.

"You said the ambush in Kandahar was started by people you knew, people you trusted and with whom you thought you had built relationships."

"Yes."

"I'd like you to talk about that so we can get deeper into this conflict surrounding trust."

"Okay. Well, the problem was corruption within the Afghanistan security force. We found out who was responsible later. They were all guys we knew. Guys we had met. They were Afghan security, supposed to be totally on board with this project John was working on. It would have helped them and their families immensely, made their lives better. They were corrupt, and we didn't know. Hell, the Afghani people didn't know either. These people we thought we had built a relationship with, they were in the room with John and the rest of the guys from our unit the whole time, every time. They weren't who we thought they were. It's still hard to swallow."

"They had earned your trust."

"One of them had a conscience, or maybe he was clued in enough to realize what they were planning would only sabotage their own welfare. He tried to warn us right before it went down. He approached the guys in the MRAP. That's how we got a heads up to go to the meeting place before there was any gunfire. He was too late. Why he waited until it was almost about to happen . . ."

"Have you thought about them much since then?"

"I've thought about them a lot. Azhar Kassir, he was the leader of the ambush. And here we were thinking we were working together, sharing our f-ing food with the guy. He's the one responsible. Corruption is like a disease, it's like a cancer, it spreads silently and unless you know where it's originating from you can't stop its spread. And if you find out too late, it doesn't matter."

Xander thought about his anatomy class cadaver and the cancerous cells that had spread silently throughout the man's lymphatic system. His group had been correct weeks ago with their initial diagnosis. It was definitely non-Hodgkin's lymphoma that ended his life too soon. Where had his cancer started? If any part of that man's body had given off a warning sign a little earlier, would the cancer have still been able to kill him? Instead of laying on a cold table in the refrigeration unit at Rothaker, would he be going home to eat pizza in front of a football game if just one part of his body had sent out a clear signal earlier, before it was too late?

"I'm wondering if you're comfortable working in groups now. Do you feel you can trust the people on your current teams?" Dr. Chavez's question brought Xander back into the moment.

Xander thought about it. He had always been on official teams that trained together and lived together and shared a common goal, first for football and then for the military. He didn't have anything like that now.

He participated in activity-based groups for some of his classes, but the group members switched around frequently. Only his anatomy group was set for the year, and now it consisted of only him and Brooke. Did he have issues with trusting her or the former group? No, he didn't. In Afghanistan he had been completely fooled and his misplaced trust had culminated in murder. And it wasn't just him who had been tricked. His entire unit and everyone in his regiment had been completely unaware. The medical curriculum at Rothaker was serious and important, but things were just completely different here. There was no Azhar Kassir equivalent. How could there be? School didn't cultivate that sort of extremism. He trusted his classmates.

Chapter Thirty-Eight

Robert started his work days with an egg and cheese croissant and a coffee; his leather loafers up on his desk while he perused several online news subscriptions. He always began with a quick glance through the NFL and college football headlines to find out the scores and to see if there were any major injuries or arrests. He wasn't much interested but that provided the extent of what he needed to know, in case someone assumed that because he was a man he wanted to engage in a conversation about sports. After that he did a similar scan through the social section and the financial news, again, in case there was anything big or breaking he should know about. With those subjects out of the way, he was free to read leisurely about national and global events as well as political news and opinions, processing and critiquing every word.

Europe had been a great experience, and now that he had recently returned, he was enjoying the gift of appreciating what he already had, particularly the simple things in life. The news in America was more comprehensive, less filtered, and far more interesting. As he read, one of the first national headlines grabbed his attention. He put his feet on the ground and sat up straight.

<u>Medical Student Missing from Rothaker.</u>

Police are searching for a missing student at Rothaker University. Rachael Kline, 22 years old, is a first-year medical student. Rachael is from the Philadelphia area. She received her undergraduate degree in biology from Rothaker in May. She was last seen on the evening of

Friday, November 1st, inside the medical school dormitory. She used her cell phone to call and text friends and family over the next few days. Her phone was turned off on November 5th. Police were called in to investigate on November 8th. Authorities searched the medical school campus and even sifted through a dumpster behind her dormitory. Classmates said she vanished, taking some of her essential belongings with her, but investigators reviewing security camera footage from outside her building cannot find her leaving the dormitory. Classmates say Rachael is a wonderful friend and student.

"The most reliable person you will meet," says fellow medical student Julie Chow.

Rachael volunteered regularly at a local HIV clinic near the Rothaker University Hospital, and with the East Dalton Needle Exchange Program. Rachael is the co-founder of Mercy Street, an outreach program for victims of domestic violence. She was recognized by Rothaker University at her graduation with an award for citizenship and service.

"Rachael was petite, but she was feisty and she always took a stand when she believed in something. She wouldn't back down," said the director of her college, Lisa Welsh.

Authorities believe Rachael was abducted from the Greenwood Circle vicinity because her purse was reportedly found in a park in that area.

Rachael weighs ninety-seven pounds and is 5'2". She is Caucasian and has shoulder length brown hair. Rothaker officials said the investigation is ongoing. The Kline family is offering a reward and asking anyone with information as to her whereabouts to call the state police department at 860-222-5000.

His first thought when he saw the headline—*Brooke is missing!*

It was impossible to see or hear the words "Rothaker" or "medical student" without a vision of Brooke popping in to his consciousness, if he wasn't already thinking about her. He was relieved to discover the article was not about Brooke, and surprised that it was about the one and only other medical student he had met. To have a classmate mysteriously disappear not once, but twice, would be harrowing for anyone. He worried about Brooke dealing with the fear and uncertainty of the situation. Surely she was scared and feeling vulnerable, at the least. He knew what she was going through, having been through it himself. He remembered enduring a long period of sadness for Jessica filled with the difficulty of not knowing what had happened and imagining the worst. He hated for Brooke to be going through that again, alone. Actually, he did want her to be alone until he got there. She needed someone who could empathize with her and help her through this. *She needs me.*

He was thrilled to have an immediate excuse to see her. Now he wouldn't have to wait until after he proposed the dormitory remodel project.

Within minutes Robert left his office to go home and pack a bag. He was going to drive straight to Rothaker so he could say "I came as soon as I heard the news." There were a few things he could do while he was on campus, if he had time, to help him propose the dorm remodel project at the Mending Foundation's next board meeting. As he left his office without having to ask or tell anyone, he appreciated the perks of having a family business.

***

On his way to Connecticut, Robert attempted to reach Brooke twice on her cell phone. He figured she was in classes, but tried anyway. He mulled through a constant stream of thoughts about what he would do when he arrived. He felt both hopeful and racked with doubt. One of his closest friends in college had been caught making out with another girl just when his actual girlfriend had arrived from another school to surprise him with a visit. Robert had felt terrible for the girl. She couldn't return on the bus, so she stayed with Robert until the next morning. Robert was painfully aware of her crying well in to the night. Robert wasn't even Brooke's boyfriend yet, so if he caught her with another guy it wouldn't even be like she was cheating on him, but it would certainly feel like it.

What if she *was* with someone else? If that was the case, he would say he was there to do work for the Foundation and he just wanted to say hello. Or he could tell her the truth no matter what, that he rushed there to be with her because he was concerned. If the situation proved too troubling for her to discuss, they wouldn't talk about it at all. They could find other things to do, maybe. . . hopefully . . . the kind of things he had been thinking about doing with her for two years now.

He didn't want things to be weird. He had waited this long. He didn't need to rush anything, particularly not at a time when she must be freaking out, wondering and worrying about who else around her might suddenly vanish. He would arrive on the auspices of being a true friend, which is absolutely what he wanted. It just wasn't *all* that he wanted. He pictured a scene with her falling into his arms, crying softly while he held her and told her everything would be all right. Then he reminded himself that Brooke was not demonstrative. Her relationship with Ethan was longstanding yet physically limited, as far as he knew. He needed to be patient. She probably wouldn't cry in his arms. But it would be great if she did. He wished it hadn't been seven weeks since seeing her last, but he was enormously glad that he had returned just in time to take advantage of this very unfortunate situation.

It was noon when Robert arrived at the medical school dorm. Brooke's phone was still turned off, but he hoped to catch her in her room during her lunch break. He parked his car and walked right in through the front door of the dorm. The lack of security was appalling; within a few minutes he had taken the elevator to the third floor and was standing outside Brooke's room. That would have been relatively impossible to accomplish at Everett, where the front doors were always locked and manned by someone working the front desk.

During the drive from Boston, Robert had instructed his voice command tablet to read him every article it could find about the recent disappearance of Rachael Kline. One of the pieces detailing the investigation had mentioned that Rachael was seen going in to the dorm on Friday, but never coming out, unless she was significantly disguised, which was highly unlikely. There were no security cameras inside the dormitory. That would change. He would specify it in the terms of the Foundation's gift for the remodel. Now that he had seen how easy it was for anyone to walk right up to the rooms he was disgusted that there was little regard for the safety of the building's occupants, especially since one of them was Brooke. When he compared it to what he had to go through to enter his office building each day, it seemed shameful. He had to show an ID badge to security guards at multiple check-points before a retina scanner allowed passage through a glass and steel door contraption. His plan to revamp the dorm could not have come at a better time. The plan should still improve the building aesthetically and bring it up to date, but now, the emphasis would be on improving security. He would try to meet with the head of security as soon as possible. That would give him a jump-start on the project.

Robert was about to knock on Brooke's door.

"Are you looking for someone?" asked a muscular man wearing a flannel shirt with jeans and boots. Every student on campus was probably on alert about strangers now. But this guy didn't really look like a medical student.

"I'm Robert Mending. I'm a friend of Brooke's. Do you live here?"

"Robert." The man's eyes moved as he thought. "Oh! Robert the flower guy?" He shook his head. "I've been cramming my brain with medical terminology. I'm amazed I came up with that."

"Excuse me? How do you know me?"

"You sent Brooke flowers earlier in the year. A few of us saw them outside her door." Xander now appeared to examine Robert critically, looking him up and down, while Robert did the same.

"Oh. Yes. I did send flowers. After our date. It didn't occur to me that anyone else would see them. Do you know if Brooke is around?"

"Your date, huh?" The man stared, then extended his arm as if remembering his manners. "Hi. I'm Xander." They shook hands. "Brooke is one of my lab partners. And I live right across the hall." He pointed to a room and it's proximity made Robert cringe inside.

"She's probably at lunch."

Robert's eyes lit up. "Oh, here she is now."

Brooke stood in the hallway. "Robert? What are you doing here?"

Arms open, he walked toward her. "I was reading the news this morning, about the medical student that disappeared. I came as soon as I heard."

"Why?" Xander tapped his foot. "Did you know Rachael?"

"We've met. But I was worried." His gaze shifted from Xander, who was making him increasingly wary, to Brooke. He put his hand on her arm. "I was worried about you."

Brooke hurried to her room and quickly unlocked her door.

Robert saw the confused, critical look on Xander's face. He also couldn't help noticing the guy's solid build, with a rugged cowboy effect that might take hours to perfect for a photo shoot. Except Robert feared that Xander's look was effortless and unintentional. He hated that this guy lived across the hall from Brooke. He wanted to get the dorm remodeled immediately and put the men and women on separate floors. He didn't like thinking about this guy showering anywhere in Brooke's vicinity.

Brooke motioned for Robert to follow her into her room. Although he wanted nothing more than to join her, he felt compelled to explain himself to Xander.

"I rushed here because I knew Brooke might be having a particularly difficult time because of what happened at Everett."

"What happened at Everett?"

Robert's jaw dropped. Xander didn't know? Wouldn't it have been one of the first things Brooke mentioned to her new friends when Rachael Kline disappeared? Wouldn't she have told them that something similar occurred to someone she knew at college? Maybe this guy wasn't a very good friend of Brooke's after all. But he still seemed to fill the hallway, commanding attention, hands on his hips in a territorial way.

"A friend of ours disappeared from college two years ago." Robert wouldn't say more. It didn't seem appropriate to remind anyone of Jessica's fate while this Rachael Kline was still missing. Rachael's family and friends were surely holding out hope that she would turn up safe and sound. He didn't want to upset Brooke especially.

Before Xander could ask a question, Brooke pulled Robert into her room and closed the door.

"I've never had an unexpected visitor in the middle of the school week." She looked a little angry. "Why are you really here?"

"I was worried about you. I imagined what you must be going through here, after something similar happening with Jessica. It would make anyone nervous. I thought you might need to see someone who could understand."

Brooke narrowed her eyes at Robert. "You came all the way from Boston?"

"I had some things to take care of on campus for the Foundation," Robert added, disappointed that he was already making up an alternate excuse for his visit. "I need to meet with security on campus. But first I wanted to see you and make sure you were okay."

"Yes. I'm okay." She sighed and looked out her window. "Do you want to go to lunch or something?" she said, as if it wasn't a good idea. "I only have an hour. It has to be quick."

"Yes. That would be great. I would love to take you to lunch."

"I'll have to go to class right after we eat. It has to be quick. And if you're busy, I understand. You don't have to say yes."

"Of course I want to go. We'll get a quick lunch and I'll drop you off in time for your class. You won't be late." He planned to make the most of every minute.

"I would have suggested dinner if you have stuff to do on campus first. Or did you already do it?"

"No. I came here first." He would love to stay for dinner.

"But I have to teach an exercise class right after my last lab. Then I have to study."

"I understand. I didn't give you much of a heads up."

She turned on her phone. "No, you—" The screen showed two missed calls and a voicemail from Robert. "Oh. You called. Sorry, my phone was turned off. How is Ethan?"

"He's fine. I haven't talked to him much since I've been away." He didn't want to use the little time they had discussing Ethan.

"Oh, I forgot . . . how was your trip?"

Robert tried not to let his posture deflate. *I guess she wasn't exactly pining for me in my absence.*

Robert shared the highlights of his trip on the way to the Café. He wanted to hold her hand but he was too apprehensive.

After getting their food, they settled into seats.

"Why didn't that guy know about Jessica?" He had dropped everything and driven all the way to Rothaker on the pretense of talking things through with Brooke to help her out, but now that he was here he discovered that the last thing he wanted to talk about with Brooke was Rachael's disappearance, or anyone else's disappearance for that matter. Yet he was curious. "Doesn't everyone know about her?"

"They do," Brooke answered, taking a bite of her turkey sandwich. "Most of my classmates know about her and read the big article in People magazine, the one with her picture on the cover. A lot of people asked me if I knew her at the beginning of school."

"What did you say?"

"I said I knew who she was. I didn't know her like you did, obviously. Other than that one trip to Boston with you and Ethan, I think I only talked to her a few times. I didn't know much about her. I knew she drove a blue Volvo."

"Really?" It surprised him how little Brooke knew about his former girlfriend. Jessica always had something nasty to say about Brooke, so he assumed they had spent more time together. According to Jessica, Brooke didn't dress well enough, ("always and only in workout clothes"), she studied too much ("a huge nerd lacking in social etiquette"), she didn't go to the right high school ("public") or the right college (some no name place before Everett, Cedarhill?), her dad was a teacher (as opposed to a corporate executive, as if that was a crime, and Robert had corrected her on more than one occasion and informed her that Mr. Walton was a professor). He could go on and on remembering the number of times Jessica had criticized Brooke. If not for his massive crush on Brooke, her criticisms might not have grated on him as much. How strange to learn, after all this time, that Brooke had barely known Jessica

Robert tried his best to remember Jessica in a positive light, but hearing Brooke say she barely knew her made him appreciate the difference between the two women. Brooke kept remarkably busy achieving academic success. She helped pay her way through college with money she earned from teaching exercise classes. In summary, Brooke was wonderful. Meanwhile, Jessica had worked endlessly to find superficial reasons for putting other people down.

He wasn't going to think about Jessica anymore. He didn't want to remember her like that; it didn't seem right. He would much rather focus on Brooke.

"Xander doesn't know, I guess because he's from Nebraska." Brooke pressed the home button on her phone and glanced at the screen.

"They have news there." Apparently, Xander was a dumbass who didn't pay attention to what was going on in the world. He was one of those people interviewed on the street during The Wright Way program who couldn't identify pictures of the Vice President or the Secretary of State but effortlessly recognized trashy celebrities who were famous for nothing except their own bad behavior.

"You're right. I don't know why he doesn't know. He's a few years older than us. He was in the military after college, in Afghanistan. He was involved in some terrible situations there. It took him awhile to even be able to tell me about it. He might have had a lot going on when the stories broke."

"Oh . . . he's a veteran?" And were all of Xander's fellow medical students privy to his stories or only Brooke? How was Robert supposed to hate the guy now that he knew he was a veteran? It also meant that the rugged protector look Xander had going for him was the real deal.

"If Jessica had been found alive, I would tell everyone about her to keep their hopes up. But considering how things turned out with her, it's probably best not to talk about what happened at Everett."

"Of course, of course, that makes sense. I hope that Rachael will be okay. But from what I've read, it sounds like she was an exceptionally responsible woman. If she had her act together, well, that makes it more likely that someone else is responsible for her disappearance. And that can't be good."

"What do you mean by that? The part about having her act together? As opposed to Jessica? Do you think Jessica killed herself?"

"I hate to say this, but I think she may have, but definitely not on purpose. It wasn't a suicide. Suicide would never cross her mind, she's too . . . never mind. But I do think she was responsible for her own death. She took several different pills, I could barely keep track of them, and she was always drinking something, a Red Bull, an espresso, alcohol. I've learned more about it since then. Different drugs don't always mix well, even if they're not illegal. And I'm sure you've learned that we had a big argument before I left. The fight heard round the world."

"Yes, I did read about it in People magazine. There was a lot of speculation."

"And for the record, I never raised my voice. I wouldn't have considered it an argument, not on my end. She was freaking out because I didn't invite her to Aruba with my family for the holidays. I was just trying to calm her down."

"Interesting," Brooke said sincerely. "But why do you think she was found so far from campus? No one seems to have a good answer for that."

"I've asked myself that question hundreds of times and I've thought up all sorts of reasons, but I haven't thought of any that make sense. Jessica hated to be cold. But she wasn't in her right mind." Talking about it was not particularly painful for Robert because the situation had been discussed on so many levels on so many occasions that the associated emotions had faded away.

"Before they found her body, I jogged out there a few times, to the place where they found her, near that bridge. She must have been there the whole time, under the snow," Brooke said solemnly.

"How frightening for you, to think that you had been there." Robert placed his hand on Brooke's arm. "I didn't know that bridge existed before Jessica's body was discovered. No one did. Did you know that afterwards it became one of the most visited destinations in the area? Everyone wanted to see it for themselves."

Brooke shook her head. "That's morbid, if you ask me."

Chapter Thirty-Nine

Xander dropped his bag on top of his bed and opened his laptop. He heard Brooke talking to her friend Robert in the hallway. He wondered what they had done on their date. He was grateful they were only in her room for a few minutes, and he was somewhat surprised to feel that way.

Once his internet browser was open, he typed "Everett College, student disappearance." He didn't know if the student in question was male or female. Countless references appeared.

Body of Missing Everett College Student Found After Five Months
College Student's Mysterious Disappearance Remains Unsolved
Jessica Carrol's Body Finally Discovered…What Really Happened?
Missing Everett Student's Cause of Death Unknown
Police Confirm Body to be Missing Everett Student Jessica Carroll

He read a few of the articles. Why hadn't Brooke mentioned Jessica Carroll, in light of Rachael's disappearance? Brooke wasn't one to gossip or go for dramatic effect like plenty of other people he knew, which is something he appreciated about her, as opposed to Jeff who couldn't tell enough people about his suitcase search. But bringing up what happened at Everett was hardly gossiping. The articles implied that Jessica's death may have been her own doing, but there were many open questions. The mystery surrounding the situation kept it in the tabloids. The two disappearances were too much of a coincidence for Brooke not to mention. What if there was some kind of link? With two top-notch schools only a few hours apart, there could be one sick guy with a connection to both places. Were the police aware and had they searched for connections between the cases? He certainly thought they should.

"Have you seen Brooke?" It was Jeff, the only person he ever saw

Brooke talking to outside of class and meals. Besides himself.

"She just left with her *friend*, Robert Mending."

"Who?"

"The flower guy," Xander added.

"Oh! The flower guy in the flesh? What did he look like?"

"Like a guy."

Jeff rolled his eyes. "Very helpful. Wait . . . there's a science building here named after a Robert Mending. I just read an article about it in the Rothaker magazine."

"This guy is too young to have a building named after him."

"You never know. I'm going downstairs to see if I can catch them. I want to see Robert Mending for myself. Jeff popped his head back in a second later, grinning. "You aren't jealous are you?"

"No. Why would I be? What are you talking about?" Xander scowled.

"Just checking." Jeff laughed. "Not everyone is in tune with their inner feelings."

Xander turned back to his laptop and typed "Robert Mending" into his search bar. It returned dozens of results and images. Robert the flower guy was the grandson of Robert Mending, an enormously wealthy graduate of Rothaker University. Robert the grandfather had created the Mending Foundation as a means to distribute his wealth, which was apparently of such magnitude that it could not be spent by one family alone. The science building was *one* of his grandfather's generous gifts to the university.

Brooke apparently had quite a catch after her. But she didn't seem to be too enamored with him. She had treated him more like a strange cousin who made an unannounced visit. Xander did not like the way he felt when he saw Robert touch Brooke. He experienced an unwelcome pang of jealousy. Even worse when they went into her room and shut the door.

Suddenly, something Xander didn't even realize he wanted became of utmost importance. It had taken thoughts of losing her to wake him up to his true feelings. He hadn't asked for it, or anticipated it, but now he was determined. He knew how to go after what he wanted. Slow and steady had always gotten the job done. And now, he wanted Brooke. Whether or not she knew it yet, they were going to be more than friends.

He did one more search before he shut down his laptop for lunch. He typed Everett College again . . . searching for similarities to whatever had happened to Rachael. He quickly scanned through the links but didn't open any. On a whim he typed "missing college student" to see what else came up. After that he tried "college, student, dead." It was sad to see how many links appeared. Most related to accidents but some attributed to foul play. He scrolled through the pages, scanning headlines until he came across,

<u>Beloved Cedarhurst College Professor Found Dead by Student.</u>

Cedarhurst sounded familiar. It took just a few seconds to remember why. It was the school Brooke had transferred from. He clinked the link. The professor, Director of the Science Department, had died unexpectedly in his office on school property and had been found by a student. It happened three years ago. If Brooke attended the school at that time, she would have known about the incident, particularly since it was a science professor and she had been a science major. He made a point to ask her about it later. And then, for the next few hours, as he decided how to act on his feelings, he completely forgot about his PTSD.

Chapter Forty

Brooke literally ran from Robert's Audi when he dropped her in front of the academic building, yelling goodbye without turning around. She was going to be a few minutes late for her one o'clock class because of that lunch. It was a blatant reminder of how socializing leads to trouble. She had known for years that when you let other people into your life you relinquish some control. Here was proof.

She rushed in, full of mounting despair, only to find that the professor wasn't even in the room yet. Xander was seated near the end of a row, second seat in, and the seat next to him was unoccupied, as if he was saving it for someone. She sat down next to him, noting with a hint of anger that someone had taken her usual front row center seat. The nerve.

Xander's eyes lit up when he saw her. "I thought you weren't going to make it. It's not like you to get here after me. What happened to your friend?"

"We ate lunch. He left." Brooke removed her notebook and pen.

"He's not sticking around for dinner then?"

"I have to teach a Pilates class after our lab."

"What time? Because I think I'll go with you."

"Really?" Brooke turned and wrinkled her nose up. She nudged him in the shoulder, unsure if he was joking.

"Yes. I've done a lot of Pilates in my time. For football. Keeps the core strong, protects the back. You'll see."

"Okay then. It's at 5:30. We have to leave right from the lab so you'll need to go back to the dorm and get a change of clothes before then. I'll get you in for free. I have a pass."

"It pays to know the right people."

Then their professor came in and apologized for getting a late start.

Brooke muttered, "If you're going to be late, you better be sincerely apologizing or half dead."

Xander laughed.

Not really joking.

Chapter Forty-One

"Good job," Xander said after Pilates. He walked behind Brooke as she maneuvered through the crowded studio and down the stairs. The class had been full, everyone treating Brooke like some sort of exercise guru.

"Is that all you have to say about it?"

"What do you want to hear?" he teased. "That my abs are going to be sore?"

"I hope so. Listen, I still have to do cardio today. I'm going to get on a bike. Do you want to join me?"

"No, but I will so you don't think I can't keep up."

"It's fine with me if you don't. I already know you can keep up. I was going to study while I rode. You can find your way back to school on your own." Brooke was already adjusting the seat and handlebars of a racing bike.

By now Xander knew what was important to Brooke. First came studying, then exercise, then everything else. He could work with that. There was room to fit in.

"I can bike and study at the same time too, you know. As long as we're not facing those televisions. Too much of a distraction. There's two reasons I don't have a TV in my dorm room. Football and basketball." He raised the seat and handlebars of the bike next to Brooke and then watched her pull a water bottle and notebook out of her backpack.

"What are you going to study?" Xander hadn't brought his books along.

"Immunology and then cell biology."

"How about if you quiz me? And then we'll switch," he suggested.

"Okay. Ready or not, why do you need immunosuppression meds to prevent graft rejection for a 2-haplotype matched kidney?"

"Because not all the minor antigens will match," Xander answered immediately.

"What could activate cytotoxic T cells and result in rejection?"

"That would be . . . let me think for a second . . . class II MHC proteins killing donor cells."

"What do helper cells and macrophages indicate?"

"A delayed hypersensitivity reaction."

Brooke smiled at him and Xander continued to answer with confidence. He had already done some review for this quiz. He was feeling clear-headed. His sudden awareness of his feelings for Brooke seemed to have lifted him out of a fog, and the exercise helped too. After fifteen minutes, Brooke handed her notebook over and he quizzed her.

"These are good notes." They were a perfect rendering of the lecture with the addition of all the relevant information from their book.

"Thanks. Hold on, I'm just going to get you a towel so you don't drip sweat on my notebook." She hopped off her bike.

"I need some of your water. Do you mind?" he called after her.

"No. Go ahead." She stopped to yell back. "I'm okay with acquiring your germs; they'll only boost my immune system. What doesn't kill you makes you stronger, everyone knows that."

They spent an hour on the bikes, heart rates in an aerobic zone, amiably sharing mnemonic devices while plowing through three quarters of the material they needed for the next day's quiz.

"You know," she said, "bringing another person into the mix usually reduces my efficiency—"

Xander snorted. "Your efficiency?"

"Yes, but, tonight, it worked. So far Xander you've been an asset without—"

"Did you say ass or asset?"

"I said asset. You haven't messed anything up, or wreaked havoc on my agenda . . . yet."

He shook his head and laughed. "I'm honored."

***

After taking quick showers, they walked back to the dorm. Brooke's Rothaker hoodie wasn't enough to keep her from shivering in the chilly moon-lit night. She glanced at Xander, who wore several layers of shirts with the Levis that Jeff admired. He looked comfortable. And capable. And strong. Like the type of man who could protect someone, who could do *whatever* needed to get done. Even if it meant taking a life.

"You're cold." He removed his flannel shirt and draped it around her shoulders. "We missed dinner, and I'm hungry thanks to you cracking the whip." He stopped in front of Café Connect. "Let's get something to eat."

"Yes!"

Xander smiled. He was a very handsome man. "It's like he walked straight off the cover of a steamy romance." Jeff had announced a few days ago, pretending to fan himself after seeing Xander leave the showers shirtless.

The Café was buzzing with Rothaker students and their laptops. Xander ordered a huge sandwich, soup, and chips. Brooke ordered soup and a salad. She found a table available near a gas fireplace and opened her notebook to study while they waited. Instead of sitting down across the table from Brooke, Xander sat next to her. They began quizzing each other from where they left off and continued until their food was ready.

"How long have you been teaching?" Xander made quick work of his sandwich.

"Six years. Since I was sixteen. Five to ten classes a week ever since."

"Wow. It shows. That was a good hard class, very professional. So you're twenty-two?"

"Almost twenty-two. How old are you?" Brooke raised a spoonful of soup to her lips.

"Twenty-seven. Almost twenty-seven."

"Oh." *Four years behind schedule. But being a veteran was part of his plan, so I guess it's okay. Sort of intriguing that he's so old.*

"Why was Robert visiting?" Xander picked up the second half of his sandwich.

"Robert is a friend from college. He's coordinating a huge donation for our dorm, actually. To remodel it, improve security, things like that."

"I'd say that's a coincidence." Xander cocked his head. "Don't you think?"

Brooke shrugged as she slid the spoon from between her lips.

"He seemed to be worried about you."

"He doesn't need to be."

"I did an internet search on the girl from Everett. The one Robert mentioned. Did you know her well?"

Brooke tensed slightly. "No. I knew her, but I wouldn't say that I knew her well. She was Robert's girlfriend. I only know Robert because he was best friends with my closest friend, Ethan. Robert had been planning to break up with Jessica the day she disappeared. He didn't because she was acting crazy. And then she was gone."

"Your closest friend was a guy?" Out of all the information Brooke had just shared with him, that was the piece he questioned.

"Yes. Do you think that's unusual? Aren't you my closest friend? You and Jeff?"

"I think it's a little unusual, nothing wrong with it though."

"Well, maybe Ethan was my boyfriend, I suppose."

"Ahh. I see." Xander's gaze seemed more intense. "Lucky guy then."

Brooke stared at him, and he stared back with a hint of a smile. No words were exchanged and their eye contact didn't waver, but something stirred inside both of them. His leg moved to press against hers under the table. A warm sensation tingled through her body. He reached for her hand and she clasped his fingers. They stayed that way, nearby gas flames adding to the charged atmosphere, until both leaned in confidently to share their first kiss. PTSD symptoms and immunology test terms were temporarily forgotten. And from that moment on they stopped being just friends.

***

Jeff opened his door as Xander simultaneously exited Brooke's room. It was midnight. Xander didn't have his laptop or any notebooks with him. Jeff was confused for an instant and then he knew.

"Yes!" he said, pumping his fist in the air, grinning from ear to ear, looking sincerely happy. "It took you long enough."

Xander grinned back at him, he couldn't help himself.

"Tell Brooke I didn't hear a thing. Truthfully." Jeff laughed.

Chapter Forty-Two

Brooke studied Xander through breakfast while he ate two bowls of cereal, toast, eggs, and a generous helping of bacon. She had jumped into the physical aspect of their new relationship head first. It was adventurous, new, and wonderful. She had been amazed by what he could do for her, and the power she had over him. After breakfast they walked toward the medical school tower together. With one arm through his, Brooke checked her emails on the way.

"Listen to this," she said, "Rakesh isn't coming back. He sent a message to our anatomy group. I'll read it. 'After more than two weeks in a coma, my father died. I'm staying in India to help my family make arrangements. I've missed too much of the first-year curriculum to catch up, so I've decided to return next fall and start after the first quarter. Rothaker applied my tuition to next year, and there's a spot waiting for me."

Brooke was relieved by the news. Rakesh would never know or care that "his piece" of the gross anatomy project had been turned in without his knowledge. And he would never know that his irresponsible behavior, leaving his work until the last minute, started the chain of events leading to Rachael's demise.

Now that he was gone, that was one less person from her class vying for the surgical scholarship, the prize that would erase all her debt. Thank God he was repeating the year, or he might have received the scholarship over her just because they felt sorry for him.

While they waited for Dr. Sarcough to arrive and start his lesson, Jeff caught Brooke's eye from across the room. He was smiling at her like a hyena. She made a face at him and he gestured toward Xander with a discreet toss of his head and another sly smile.

How does Jeff already know? Just to see his reaction, she clasped Xander's finely muscled arm with both hands and placed a gentle kiss on his cheek. She laid her head against his broad chest for a few seconds where she could hear and feel his steady heartbeat. It felt exciting and reckless to touch and kiss him in the classroom where they had acted so formally and professionally until now. Xander wrapped his arm around her shoulders and gave her a firm but gentle squeeze in response. Across the room, Jeff crossed his arms over his chest and swooned like he was watching the final scene of a love story.

Dr. Sarcough approached Xander and Brooke after his lecture, just as they were getting ready to identify the vessels he wanted them to locate.

"How are the both of you doing?"

"Fine," Brooke answered.

"We're fine," Xander responded sincerely.

There were many reasons why they should not feel fine: his PTSD symptoms, which weren't improving despite multiple therapy sessions, their classmate's suspicious and most likely tragic disappearance, the overwhelming amount of material they were expected to memorize and understand, and their other lab partner's withdrawal for the remainder of the year. But there was one unexpected change that made everything else seem less important – their new relationship.

"Unfortunately, it's down to the two of you for your lab group." The professor rubbed one side of his bowtie between his fingers, making it crooked in the process. "I don't remember this ever happening before. Would you like me to assign someone from another table? That's probably what I should do."

No! Brooke shouted inside her mind, while she groped for the appropriate way to politely decline before Xander might say otherwise. The fewer people involved the better. They spent less time taking turns, deciding who would do what. And considering her new relationship with Xander, it felt like their partnership in the lab had been destiny all along.

“I don’t think that will be necessary,” she calmly answered. “We’re all hoping Rachael will be back. What do you think, Xander?”

“It’s fine with me, sticking with the two of us. I think we function well together.”

“Okay then,” Dr. Sarcough nodded. “Let me know if you need any assistance, now that you only have two minds instead of four working together. But, you should be fine.”

When their professor left, Xander said, “For their own sakes, I wish Rachael and Rakesh were still around, but I’m not complaining about having you to myself. And, you’re somewhat intelligent.”

“Really? Do you think?” She laughed, only because she knew he was being facetious.

***

Xander leaned down and whispered to Brooke. “How are you managing to look so unbearably beautiful when you’re wearing the same exact lab coat as everyone else in the room?”

“You don’t look so bad yourself, Xander.”

They worked together comfortably. Brooke was sensitive to Xander’s issue with the cadaver, and Xander was okay with Brooke being in charge. And with all that had happened in the last twenty-four hours, he forgot to ask Brooke if she knew the professor who died at Cedarhurst.

Chapter Forty-Three

Brooke did an internet search to find the latest reports on the "Mystery of the Missing Medical Student," as it was being called. It was okay for her to be searching, it was not suspicious behavior because everyone at the medical school was checking the internet on a daily basis, even if it was only in hope of finding a picture of themselves in the news. She found nothing new. No traces of anything unusual were discovered in Rachael's room, or anywhere in the dorm, news that Brooke received with pride. It was well reported that a young man named Antonio Delmar had bought three high-tech car stereos with Rachael's credit card. He had been with four members of his posse when he found the purse ("without an owner") in the park near Greenwood Circle. Despite their combined lack of credibility, with four other witnesses, it wasn't possible to connect him to Rachael's disappearance. The only helpful evidence to come out of his arrest was that Rachael had been in the vicinity of the clinics and Greenwood Circle before she went missing. The police turned their efforts to casing those areas, forgetting about the medical school campus.

Any evidence was a tiny pile of ash, and with nothing left behind, there was nothing to find.

***

Rick Copeland, however, wasn't willing to let the Rachael Kline hype fizzle away. It was too newsworthy, in a morbidly curious "we should all be outraged" sort of way. Yet it was dying out like a giant candle with a broken wick before his very eyes because the police had no leads and there was no new information. What was a rising reporting star from WXRC TV to do?

The one piece of information that continued to intrigue Rick was that the front and back entrance security camera footage did not contain any images of Rachael leaving the building. The interior of the dorm had been searched top to bottom and there were no signs of Rachael. If there was any other way out, he wanted to be the one to find it.

It was a mystery, with all the elements that made people want to follow it. An upper-middle class Ivy League graduate, attractive, loved by all until the very moment she disappeared into thin air after a few days of a self-imposed quarantine. Rick was poised to capitalize. If no new information was forthcoming, he would find some himself. He and his camera man, Nicky Demaine, had just finished filming a brief segment on Rothaker's hockey team. Since they were already on location, they did some snooping behind the medical school dorm. They poked through the dumpster, which they knew had been processed and dumped since Rachael disappeared, and found nothing aside from garbage and disgusting debris. They gazed up at the windows, but the sun's glare shot straight into their eyes.

"Let's check the doors to see if any are unlocked." With Nicky trudging a few steps behind him, Rick walked to the building and reached for the handle. The door flew open and he stumbled backward, spinning his arms to maintain his balance.

A gorgeous, blonde woman wearing tight black exercise pants and a fitted running jacket strode through the door. She was looking down, zipping her back-pack, so her face was not the first thing he saw. When she glanced up, clearly startled, his jaw dropped open. She had to be someone famous. All she needed was that Grande Starbucks cups all the celebrities carried with them when they wore their workout gear outside hoping to get photographed. Her make-up had been applied with so much skill that it appeared she didn't wear any, yet no one could have skin that glowing and flawless without it.

Rick thought fast. That's why he was good at what he did; he could improvise and make the most of an opportunity like no other.

***

Brooke stared, temporarily taken aback and about to apologize for almost running into someone. She was confused about seeing a well-groomed man in her path where she was not expecting anyone.

"Hi." His smile revealed super white teeth. "Do you live in this building?"

"Yes." With a glance around him, she spotted the camera man. "Ah." She should have known who they were from the face paint the first man wore. What they were doing behind the dorm was not clear. Most of the media people had given up on getting any new Rachael content days ago.

"We're looking for someone to give us a comment on what you think happened to Rachael Kline. Would you be willing to answer a few questions for us?"

The cameraman hoisted his equipment from his hip to his shoulder.

It wasn't the first time a reporter had tried to ask her a few questions about Rachael, but it was the first time anyone with a camera had stopped her. She was usually surrounded by other students who were hoping to be filmed, they had spent the extra time getting ready just in case, whilst she purposefully walked by, making it clear she had places to be.

If not for her connection to Rachael's disappearance, she would have had no problem telling him "No, I'm on my way to teach an exercise class. I can't be late. I don't have time. Sorry." But her involvement invoked a sense of duty to provide appropriate commentary so she wouldn't look culpable.

"Sure. Okay. It has to be quick though." She continued down the stairs. "I'm on my way to teach a class."

"Are you a teaching assistant?" The reporter walked by her side.

"It's an exercise class at a gym nearby. What exactly are you doing behind the dorm?"

"Looking for clues, the old-fashioned way. I'm Rick Copeland from WXRC TV channel ten news. The man with the camera is Nicky Demaine. Thanks for helping us. We won't take more than a few minutes of your time. Ready Nicky?" Rick maneuvered his hair across his forehead to achieve that feathered, soft look the female market favored.

"The two of you are going to look excellent standing together," Nicky said. "If only the backdrop was better." He swept the camera around the dirty concrete and rusted metal.

"I'll work that into an angle somehow, there's no other way around it," Rick said before turning his attention back to Brooke. "Are you a student?"

"Yes. I'm a first-year medical student. I knew Rachael. We had classes together."

"What's your name?"

"Brooke Walton."

"Okay, Brooke. Thanks again for helping us out here. I'm going to ask you a few questions, look at the camera on Nicky's shoulder when you talk so your gaze isn't wandering around."

"Got it." She adjusted her posture, standing straight and tall but still appearing relaxed. Brooke sensed it was important for Rick to put on a good show. She asked herself exactly what her face and body language should do to convey what she wanted people to see. Her tactics resulted in the perfect head tilt and a thoughtful expression as she stared into the camera with concern, aiming for intimate eye contact with the viewing audience.

"This is Rick Copeland from WXRC TV Channel 10 reporting from the Rothaker Medical School dorm where Rachael Kline, a first-year medical student, disappeared at least six days ago. I'm speaking with Brooke Walton, a classmate who knew and worked with Rachael. How well did you know Rachael?"

"All the first-year students know each other pretty well. We live, eat, and work together every day. Rachael and I were especially close because we were assigned to the same group for anatomy lab."

"How did you first learn that Rachael was missing?"

"Let's see. She had been sick for a few days, Monday and Tuesday, and couldn't go to class, so we were already missing her, but then no one heard from her on Wednesday. Initially we imagined she went home. We called security to see if she was in her room, and when she wasn't, we called her parents. That's when we knew something wasn't right."

"What is the mood on campus, amongst the medical school students?"

"We're all so worried for her. Hoping she'll be found soon and that she'll be okay.

"Do you think the university and state police have done all they could to find Rachael?"

"Absolutely, yes. So many people have been involved. I was interviewed by Lieutenant Sanchez from the East Dalton City Police. I think he interviewed everyone in the dorm, right away. Detectives also searched every bit of the dorm and each of our rooms. I heard they poured through days of video camera footage from around the dorms. Some students handed out and posted flyers all around the medical school campus, in the neighborhoods where she did outreach volunteer work. I think hundreds of people have searched the campus for her, with dogs. I even saw detectives searching the dumpster behind the dorm when they realized she disappeared. I can't imagine why, or maybe I don't want to imagine why, but yes, I think they've done a commendable job. I've been impressed. And I'm only aware of what they've done on campus. That was before her purse was found near Greenwood Circle. If they've been just as thorough investigating other parts of the city, then they're doing a great job."

Rick wasn't getting anything from Brooke that everyone didn't already know, but people would still enjoy watching this beautiful young woman provide a comprehensive summary of the case from her perspective. The police department, particularly the Sanchez guy she mentioned, would also appreciate her plug.

"That's good to hear, Brooke. Now, if you had to provide an answer, what would *you* say happened to Rachael Kline?"

Brooke put on her pensive face, it was expected and appropriate to pause and think until she came up with something.

"Rachael was an active volunteer, involved with several admirable efforts, East Dalton's needle exchange program for example. She spent a lot of time in areas like Greenwood Circle. That has to be where she ran into some sort of trouble, while she was helping someone. I think she may have been in the wrong place at the wrong time. But I hope and believe that she'll be back here soon." She stared into the camera, blinking. "We miss you, Rachael."

Rick nodded. "It sounds like Rachael was an exceptional woman and you cared deeply about her."

"Yes, that's true."

It irked her to present Rachael as some hero, when in reality Rachael had been out to destroy Brooke's entire future, but it was the right thing to do. Rick's questioning reminded her of a job interview, and she excelled at those. And medical ethics class had helped refine her ability to deliver what people most wanted to hear.

An ambulance roared by, turning its siren on as it passed behind the dorm. Nicky swung the camera away from Rick and Brooke to catch it on film.

"I'd like to remind our viewers that we're standing directly behind the medical school dormitory right now. It's not what people expect when they picture the medical school for one of the top universities in the world, is it? The dormitory is located across the street from the world renowned Rothaker teaching hospital. Its emergency room treats more victims of violent crimes than any other hospital on the East Coast. This vicinity is where Rachael Kline was last seen."

Nicky turned in a slow circle with his camera to capture the unattractive dumpster overflowing with trash and boxes, the parking garage, the highway ramp, all of it looking seedy and suspicious.

"I'm Rick Copeland from WXRC channel 10 news." They cut the scene. Rick grinned. "That was excellent. Can I get your number in case we need you for further clarification?"

"Sure. It's 203-554-3845. I have to go now."

"WXRC news at 11. Be sure to watch."

"Okay." She was already jogging away from them.

***

When she returned from the gym, she mentioned the interview to Xander, who insisted they watch and made a big deal about setting his alarm so they wouldn't miss it. Since neither of them had a television, just before eleven, they went down to the first-floor lounge with their books to sit in front the dorm's large flat screen TV.

The station ran the entire four-minute interview. Even in her workout clothes, Brooke appeared just as polished and professional as the reporter by her side.

"Wow. You look incredible." Xander squeezed her into a hug. "And I'm glad that Rachael isn't being forgotten. She's an impressive woman."

It still bothered Brooke to hear people discussing Rachael as smart and wonderful, but up until now, she had managed to deal with it. Once in a while, she even had to swallow her pride and sing Rachael's praises. But listening to Xander call Rachael "impressive" was too much. And she was tired of having to pin the little purple "Find Rachael" ribbon to her shirt every single day. They were supposed to wear them until Rachael was found. Since Rachael was never, ever going to be found, were they stuck wearing them until the end of the year or could they finally stop over Christmas break?

"Rachael wasn't so perfect you know. But I suppose no one ever says bad things about a person once their gone."

"Yeah, they do. But who has anything bad to say about Rachael? She was nice to everyone."

"Yes, she was nice, but she was also a little bossy, don't you think? She seemed to really enjoy being an obstacle in my path."

"You and she had a bit of a rivalry going. Maybe you can't see it, but I'm telling you now, it's because you're too much alike."

"I wouldn't say that," Brooke snapped, upset that he found any truth in that statement. "I don't think we're alike at all and I don't care enough to have anything 'going on' with her."

"You don't have to believe it, but it's true. You're both very similar. Granted she couldn't drop out of med school to be a super-model like you could, but she was brilliant and hard-working, passionate about medicine. She accomplished more in a week than many people do in a month. You had a lot in common. That's probably why there was tension. If opposites attract, then sames must repel."

"Sames isn't a word." Brooke moved closer to Xander and knelt before him on the floor. She gazed mischievously into his eyes while her hands worked at undoing his belt buckle. She would show him how un-Rachael like she could be. "Would Rachael do this? In public where anyone could walk by and see us at any moment?"

Xander was unable to answer.

Chapter Forty-Four

Brooke and Xander were inseparable, except when she worked at Performance Fit and he went for his psychiatry appointments. And Brooke didn't mind at all. In fact, to her surprise, just the opposite. Xander's easy-going personality complemented her well. He said he felt constantly on edge because of his PTSD symptoms, but she considered his personality laid-back. The physical aspects of their relationship were new and exciting. Each time they got together it felt like taking a leap out of an airplane, with a parachute, of course. She appreciated his hard and toned, zero-fat physique. His body would make the most fantastic cadaver ever. She benefitted from their physical connections, which left her feeling the same as after a long, exhausting run. Since he had almost all the same commitments and assignments she did, it worked perfectly. Their relationship was effortless, convenient, and exhilarating in every way. It was also nice that he lived across the hall. Even when they weren't together, he was literally a few steps away.

The change in her behavior toward Xander was remarkable and people noticed. Notoriously aloof, Brooke was now openly demonstrative with her lab partner. Jeff had returned to calling them "Ken and Barbie" and the nicknames had spread throughout the first-year class. Xander knew the evolution of their relationship had become common knowledge when Dr. Sarcough good naturedly asked "Ken and Barbie" to come up to the front of the room to demonstrate a lumbar puncture.

Brooke was irritated by the reference. "I don't look anything like a Barbie doll. Barbies have huge breasts and their feet are permanently messed up from wearing only high heels."

"I bet you spent a lot of time playing dress up with your Barbies when you were a little girl," Xander said, straight-faced.

"No, I didn't! I didn't have a single Barbie." Brooke's hands flew to her hips and she frowned. "I had books and science kits."

Xander laughed. "I know. I'm just messing with you." And then Brooke was laughing, punching him playfully until they were making-out in the hallway outside the lab as if it were their last day on the planet.

So, it was not unusual that they were together, studying in her room, when her phone rang.

Xander stretched to edge her phone closer. "It's Robert Mending."

"I'm not going to answer it," she said, eyes never wavering from her laptop. "He'll leave a message."

"I think you should return his call sometime soon and mention something about us."

"Why?"

"Because it would be very awkward if he made another surprise visit and found us together. I wouldn't wish that on anyone. You need to give him a heads up."

"Okay. I'll let him know that you and I are more than friends and he might not want to barge into my room without knocking." She was laughing, but Xander's suggestion made sense. There was no need to embarrass Robert or make him uncomfortable. And she didn't want their relationship to move beyond friendship.

In fact, once Robert knows about Xander, he'll stop visiting. We can still be friends, but we'll be friends who don't have to see each other and don't waste each other's time.

"Go easy," Xander said.

"He won't mind. He's rich. He can probably have any girlfriend he wants. Did I tell you his company is going to remodel our dorm, put in a whole new security system?"

"You told me."

Brooke was very glad the dorm hadn't been previously upgraded with security improvements. She would have come up with an alternate plan to get Rachael out of her way, poison definitely worked, but in this case, she had the outdated dorm to thank.

Her phone rang again.

"It's not anyone in your contact list."

"Probably a marketing call."

"Hello," Xander answered and hit the speaker button.

"Hi. This is Rick Copeland from WXRC TV news. May I speak with Brooke?"

"This is Xander Cross, her personal assistant. Hold one moment for Ms. Walton, please." He smiled and handed her the phone.

Brooke poked his arm before she took the phone. "Hello?"

"Hi, Brooke. This is Rick Copeland. From WXRC TV news. Did you see your interview on television last night?"

"Yes. I did.

"What did you think of it?"

"It was fine." Unexpected phone calls did not sit well with Brooke. Xander was listening and grinning at her. It was difficult to concentrate.

"You were a hit, Brooke Walton. We have emails, texts, and calls coming in about you. That's what happens when people like what they see. We would love to have more time with you on camera."

"Time on camera doing what?"

"I'll need to figure that out. Perhaps further discussion on the Rachael Kline disappearance. We'd like to do that for sure if there are any new developments. If not, I'll think of something else. Are you on board? If you are, we'll work out the details and the pay schedule with the finance department, probably on an interview by interview basis."

"Uh, okay. That's exciting. But, can I wait and give you an answer when you have something more specific? I don't have a lot of time with school."

"Sure. I just wanted to congratulate you. You and I looked great on camera together."

"Thanks. Thanks for calling." She hung up.

"You're famous now, Brooke Walton." Xander wrapped his arms

around her from behind, kissed her temple and then nibbled suggestively on her ear. Ear nibbling led to "taking a break." In the past, Brooke's study breaks had always consisted of stretching sessions. With Xander around, stretching had been replaced with other activities, unless they happened to be in the library together, although they had already found creative ways to feel reckless there as well.

After, Xander stood up from her bed, and said, "I'm thirsty."

"You sound like a caveman," she laughed.

"Do you have bottled water?" His hand grasped the fridge handle.

"I have water that came from that sink over there and was poured into a previously used container. I hope you're not a bottled water snob."

"I'm not. Water is water." He opened the fridge and peered inside. "You wouldn't believe some of the food we had to eat overseas. High tech but low, low taste. I think I can handle water from a tap in Connecticut . . . Huh?" Xander straightened, holding the plastic container with Rachael's dissected mole. "What the heck is this thing that was in the back of your refrigerator?"

From where Brooke sat, it resembled a tiny clotted brown piece of beef sirloin.

"Did you take this from the lab?" He rotated the container, studying the sample from every angle. "Do you want to get yourself dismissed, young lady? Nothing leaves the lab or else." He imitated Dr. Sarcough's voice, laughing, but suddenly his smile disappeared, and he pursed his lips. "Wait—"

"It's not from the lab. It's . . . it's just a sample of . . ."

"Of what?"

Brooke shrugged. "It's nothing."

Xander's face relaxed. "This is odd, you know. Even for a med student. You are definitely interesting." Xander placed the container back in the fridge.

Brooke didn't want Xander to think she was odd. Perhaps it was a mistake to let someone get so close. She wished she had discarded the mole. If she hadn't made the time to look at it by now, it probably wasn't going to happen. As soon as Xander left, she would take it out of the container and flick it straight out her window into the dumpster. A tiny treat for the vultures.

Chapter Forty-Five

"How was your week, Xander?" Dr. Chavez's face reflected no expression.

"Great week. A really great week. But, unfortunately, it had nothing to do with my symptoms improving. The depression and anxiety have lessened. I think that's the medication. But the flashbacks, disturbing memories, and the nightmares . . . they're still occurring."

"Have you found other people you can talk to about what you're going through?"

"There is one person I've been talking to. She's my anatomy partner. We run together. And now she's my girlfriend. That's why I had a great week. I've told her everything. She's very encouraging about having me share what I've been through."

"Hmm. Let me ask you a question, it might seem off topic. Do you know the medical student who is missing? She's a first-year also."

"Yeah. She was another one of my anatomy partners. I knew her well. She's a great person. She's nice, responsible . . . It's crazy. I don't know what to think. I feel guilty."

"Why?"

"Because she disappeared. There one minute, gone the next. No explanation. I feel like it happened right under my nose and I should have been there for her. We all feel like that." It occurred to him that Brooke was experiencing this strange sense of loss and confusion for the second time, although she said she didn't know the girl from college as well as she knew Rachael. Did that mean it was more troubling for her or less troubling because it had already happened once?

Dr. Chavez interrupted his thoughts. "It's disturbing."

"Yeah. She did a lot of volunteer work around Greenwood circle and something happened to her out there. I told her it was dangerous, but she felt comfortable, it was routine for her. Sort of like Kandahar for me, we were less aware once our mission became routine, we thought we had built solid working relationships. Maybe the more comfortable Rachael felt, the more she put herself at risk."

"As I said, it was off-topic, so let's get back to your issues. I am concerned that you haven't seen improvement with some of your symptoms, but not discouraged. We'll try another course of treatment. Different strategies work for different people. We'll start the rapid eye movement therapy today, if that's still okay with you."

Xander nodded.

"It's an eight-step protocol. We've already made it through the first step, the initial evaluation. You're going to recall scenes from Kandahar, the distressing images in your flashbacks."

"I'm familiar with the process. My girlfriend, Brooke, she explained it to me."

The psychiatrist folded his hands in his lap. "Let's begin. Focus on your memories of finding your unit when you returned to the Kandahar village. While you do this, you will move your eyes laterally."

Xander concentrated.

"What other memories are you associating with that disturbing event?"

"I don't know." He didn't want to believe that the blood soaked, brutally savage image of himself from his nightmares was a real memory.

They repeated the exercise five times.

"During the next phase you'll visualize an image that *represents* the disturbing event. For example, the cadaver from your anatomy class. Then you will replace it with a positive one."

Xander did his best to follow the directions.

"Where are you feeling tension?"

"Shoulders, forehead."

“Are you feeling any additional physical discomfort?”

“Nausea, a little.”

***

Dr. Chavez repeated the association exercises with Xander as he had been trained to do. He had attended a workshop on rapid eye movement therapy last spring. It was nice to have the opportunity to put it to use and he hoped it would prove effective. But, he was perplexed as to why their earlier therapy sessions hadn’t lessened Xander’s symptoms. Why hadn’t it worked as it should?

Chapter Forty-Six

Robert was frustrated after his last visit with Brooke. It was ridiculous that he couldn't make any headway with their relationship. He felt increasingly uncomfortable and insecure about the whole situation now that he had met Xander, who had immediate access to her any time of the day or night just by walking across the hall. Robert wished he had applied to medical school. Maybe it wasn't too late. His grandfather had so much influence he could probably get Robert in without taking the science courses and the MCATs and all the other required stuff. But even if that were remotely possible, Robert wasn't a fan of the type of studying that would be necessary to survive there. Still, he would have been willing to pretend for a few months, or however long it took.

He was planning to ask Brooke to accompany him to a fundraiser that he had to attend with his parents in two weeks. His mother wanted to meet her. It seemed like a good idea, although he would rather have more time getting to know her one on one until they were more than friends. How could she not fall in love with him, eventually, when he cared for her more than anyone else possibly could?

He waited patiently until four-thirty to call. He knew she should be available then; her school classes would have ended, and she had a break before dinner, unless she was teaching an exercise class. He could have texted her earlier but then he would have driven himself crazy waiting for a response. If she didn't answer his phone call, he wasn't going to leave a message. He would just try again later.

She answered on the third ring.

"Robert. Hi. I was going to call you."

He felt ridiculously happy to hear it, remembering that Ethan claimed he called Brooke an estimated fifty times for every time she called him. "What's going on?"

"I was just wondering how you were doing."

"I'm doing great. Just busy with work." He cringed as he said it. It wasn't exactly truthful. "How are you?" He had been following the Rachael Kline story and he knew that it wasn't any closer to being solved but perhaps Brooke was so busy that it wasn't on her mind.

"I'm fine. I've only been teaching a few exercise classes every week. That's been kind of strange, not what I'm used to, but there's more school work here than I've ever had before."

"Oh. I bet your body appreciates having some down time."

"Maybe. Although I think a body gets used to whatever it is you do. I never felt like I needed a break before."

"Well, I need a break often." *What am I saying? That makes no sense. It makes me sound lazy!* "I was calling to ask if you would accompany me to a fundraiser here in Boston. The weekend after next. I could come and pick you up. It's at the Museum of Fine Arts. I think you'll enjoy it. I know I'll enjoy it if you go with me."

"Oh. Thank you for thinking of me. I would like that, but I don't think I can."

"Oh. Do you have plans?" He was already feeling dejected.

"Just plans to study. But the thing is, I have a boyfriend now, and I don't think it would be appropriate for me to go with you, even if we were just going as good friends."

Robert felt like someone had driven a sword through his heart. The boyfriend had to be Xander from across the hall, he just knew it, but he couldn't bear to have his fears confirmed. *Shit. Shit. Shit.* If only he hadn't gone on a f-ing, six-week vacation!

"Okay. I understand," he said, but he couldn't believe this was happening to him after patiently waiting for so much time.

"So, I hope you have a good time there, at the fundraiser. It sounds special."

"Yes. Thank you. Good luck with school."

As Robert hung up, he experienced the urge to kill someone. Seriously.

***

Brooke tossed her phone on top of Xander's sweatshirt on the floor. "I'm glad I got that over with."

Xander untangled his legs from hers. "I totally feel for that guy. I can understand where he's coming from. I wouldn't want to be in his shoes."

"Well, you're not in his shoes. His shoes are much fancier than yours." There was a gleam in Brooke's eye as she edged closer and wrapped her arms around his shoulders. "And I like for his shoes to stay on," she said in a sultry voice, "but I want yours to come off."

"Why would you want to take my shoes off." His voice was low and deep.

"Along with your shirt, and your shorts, and your boxers . . ."

Knock. Knock. Knock. Brooke rolled her eyes. There were too many interruptions this afternoon, although she was solely responsible for some, and she needed to finish memorizing the immunology material before dinner.

Shirtless, Xander opened the door. "Rakesh!" He reached out to slap Rakesh on the arm and ended up in a manly version of an embrace.

Rakesh pushed up his glasses because they had fallen forward. "I stopped at your room first to say hello. Someone said you might be here."

Xander grinned. "Yeah, glad you found me. It's great to see you. Are you moving back in?"

"I'm packing up to move out. I left everything I owned here. I've been wearing two pairs of pants for months, so it's nice to get the rest of my clothes. And I picked up all of my school work." He lifted the large collection of folders under his arm. "I'll need it for next year. Now I'm just saying goodbye to everyone."

"Hi," Brooke said, attempting to echo the warmth that Xander conveyed.

"Hi, Brooke." Rakesh's voice didn't have the same level of comfort it had when addressing Xander.

"I'm so sorry about your father and what your family is going through," Xander said, his hand returning to Rakesh's shoulder for a few seconds.

"I appreciate all the kind words and prayers everyone sent."

I wish someone had told me that everyone was sending thoughts and prayers. I would have sent out a few heartfelt-sounding messages of my own, if I'd known that was going on.

"And I heard about Rachael. I can't believe it. No one knows what happened to her?"

Xander shook his head. Brooke did the same.

It was sort of your fault, for not getting your work done, but I'm sure Rachael would have found some other way to try and ruin my life. Brooke stood quietly beside Xander, wishing Rakesh would go away.

"It's terrible," Rakesh said.

"Yeah. None of us can believe it either. Hey—do you have some time?" Xander tugged at the waistband of his shorts. "Want to go sit in the lounge?"

"I can't. I'm about to meet with Dr. Sinclair to finish working out an arrangement for next year. It was great to see you though. Good luck with everything. I'll be looking to you for guidance since you'll be a year ahead when I come back."

"Anytime. If I don't forget everything by then!"

"Oh, I almost forgot." Rakesh pulled a thin report from the stack of papers he was carrying. He held up the radiology section of the gross anatomy report, the one Brooke completed. "It had my name on it, but this must belong to one of you. I know I didn't get it done. I dropped the ball on this because I had to leave unexpectedly. So, thanks for putting it together. It helped me a lot. I'll receive full credit through the first quarter because everything got done. It must have been a real effort to write this up last minute. It's very good by the way. I hope you weren't put out."

Brooke didn't respond, so, after a few seconds, Xander said, "It was nothing, glad it helped," with some uncertainty in his voice.

"That's what teamwork is about," Brooke said, smiling.

Rakesh said goodbye again.

Xander closed the door, still clutching the report. "Um . . . did you write this?"

"Yes. And we got an A on the project. Remember you said you just didn't have the time to do it? But I did."

"Yeah. I'm learning that there's nothing you can't get done."

Brooke moved against him, wrapping her arms around his back. As they stood together, her body relaxed against his.

"I totally forgot about his section," Xander said, without moving. "So much has happened since then. I knew we got an A on the report, but I was so busy with our curriculum, and my psych appointments, and keeping up with you, and admiring your butt, that I didn't give any thought to how or if it got done."

"Did you hear what he said? He gets full credit through the first semester because I wrote it for him."

"Right. That's good. Rachael didn't want you to write it, did she? That's what I thought you were arguing about the next day, remember? Rakesh is lucky you did what you thought needed to be done."

Xander held Brooke as she nuzzled her head against his chest. Her fingers stroked his neck and then pressed lightly against his carotid artery, as if she was taking his pulse.

He loosened his grip on her shoulders. "So, it's all good . . . right?"

Why doesn't he sound convinced?

Chapter Forty-Seven

Robert couldn't get Brooke out of his mind. He imagined he saw her blonde ponytail turning a corner when he was out buying a coffee. Only after he ran down Newberry St., spilling his dark roast across his sleeve, did he realize he was mistaken. Even though she clearly wasn't into him and she had that ridiculously good looking ex-military guy living across the hall, he still couldn't walk away. Did that make him a fool?

The medical school dorm remodeling project should probably be scrapped. It was important to him only for developing a relationship with Brooke, since he knew it would take time. But the last thing he wanted was to witness her and that Xander guy together. He considered buying her a Bentley convertible to see if that might make a difference. No, it would only make him look desperate.

He settled on doing an internet search for Rothaker Medical School and Rachael Kline to see if there were any updates, because whatever happened affected Brooke in some small way and would allow him an opportunity to feel a little connected to what was going on in her life. He was amazed when he clicked on a week-old video from WXRC TV. Under the video, there were far more comments about Brooke being hot than there were about Rachael Kline's disappearance or the content of the interview.

The first time he watched, he simply longed for Brooke with a pit forming in his stomach, but the second time through he actually listened to what she was saying. She sounded so concerned and so convincing when she said "We miss you Rachael" that Robert was surprised. Brooke didn't like Rachael. In fact, when she said she didn't like her, it was the only time he had ever heard Brooke say anything negative about anyone.

It wasn't so much that he expected her to tell the truth on camera. He just couldn't believe what a good liar she was. He decided to send her a message about it, something sort of humorous but not insensitive to the situation. That way he wasn't stalking her, by any standards, but he was at least keeping a foot in the door until she grew bored with the guy from across the hall.

Hi. Caught your news interview. Very convincing, I would have thought Rachael was your best friend. Hope you are well.

Chapter Forty-Eight

"Good morning, class. Today we're going to study the female pelvic region. If you don't have a female cadaver, join a group that does have one. I'll give you a few minutes. I'm just going to select the images of the structures and tissues I want identified."

Students shuffled around the room reorganizing until everyone was standing around a table that held a female cadaver. Xander was on edge as he and Brooke moved over to the nearest table. His heart rate spiked due to his apprehension. He never felt relaxed in this class.

"We're happy to share our pelvic region with you." Sundeep smiled. "Let me just reposition this over the areas we're not studying." He lifted the sheet into the air. Although the cadaver's incisions had been made with great care and respect, it appeared grossly mutilated, coils of dull gray intestine visible between the torn flesh. Xander felt an unwelcome surge in his adrenaline and for a split second of horror, realized what was about to happen to him.

Simultaneously the building's fire-alarm went off, startling everyone. The alarm shrieked through the lab, echoing in his ears, accompanied by a flashing light that spread a semi-circle of blazing glare around the room from one corner to the next before it snapped back and began again. His classmates rushed to retrieve their bags from the back of the class, yelling to be heard over the alarm.

For Xander, it was the perfect storm.

"Exit the class immediately," Dr. Sarcough shouted from the doorway. "I don't think this is a drill."

Xander's eyes locked on Sundeep, with his dark skin and his goatee, laughing about the unexpected fire alarm. What Xander saw was an insurgent, gloating about the dead body before him. Fury took over. Xander shot forward, his powerful arms grabbed Sundeep by the shoulders and spun him back around.

"What the hell did you do to him?" Xander shouted, his knuckles turning white as he tightened his hold.

Sundeep stared back with wide eyes, too frightened to respond.

Brooke hurried over to them. "Stop!" she commanded, pulling Xander's arm away and edging between them. Xander heard her, but he didn't take his eyes or hands off Sundeep.

"It's not what you think." Brooke had to shout to be heard over the alarm. "What you're seeing isn't real. That's Sundeep from Chicago. Let him go. He didn't do anything."

The veins in Xander's neck strained, his corded muscles rippled along his arms, and tension wracked his body. A few of their classmates shot him a curious glance, but they were in too much of a rush to see what was going on, and the resounding clamor of the alarm prevented everyone except Brooke and Sundeep from hearing his angry words. His eyes took on a crazed look, his nostrils flared like an angry bull.

Brooke placed her hands on each side of Xander's face, positioning herself in front of him so that he only saw her. His whole body trembled, and his breath came fast, eyes darting from Brooke to Sundeep. She held him with a firm grip. "You're having a flashback. You're in anatomy class at school. Everyone here is your friend. You need to come back to reality and calm down."

It all happened so fast. Xander let go. Sundeep hurried out, and Dr. Sarcough stormed over, chastising them because they hadn't left the room yet. "We don't know if this is a drill. Please exit the room right now!" They could barely hear him. The honking screech of the fire alarm was enough to drive anyone out of their mind eventually.

"We're going." Brooke took Xander's arm and pulled him along. With her other hand, she scooped up their backpacks and continued to lead him out the door, watching his face as they made their way out of the building. He squeezed his eyes shut, his muscles remained rigid.

Once they were outside she brought him to a quiet area away from the multitude of congregating people, away from the two fire-trucks that had just pulled up in front of the academic building, sirens roaring. She sat him down on a brick half-wall, dropping their backpacks and leaning in close, peering into his face, her knees touching his. He hadn't said a word since she had intervened. It was cold outside, and their coats had been left behind, but Xander's skin was hot and perspiration coated his forehead.

"Are you okay now?" She murmured, stroking his leg.

He took a deep breath. "I can't believe that just happened." He wrung his hands and his face flushed red. "I'm so embarrassed." He buried his face in his hands. "I'm afraid of myself, afraid of what might happen next time."

"No, don't be embarrassed. And maybe there won't be a next time."

Xander looked away. "I don't know what to say. Thank you. Thank God you were there, and you knew what was going on. I need to find Sundeep and apologize."

Brooke sighed, her body relaxed. "You recovered quickly. I don't think anyone saw. There was too much going on." She stood up and drew her shoulders back. Her eyes gleamed. "Wow. I am glad I was there, for Sundeep's sake. You could have killed him. Crushed him with your bare hands. Right in front of everyone."

"I know." Xander's shoulders shook. "Oh God. I can't believe that almost happened."

"You were so powerful, it was scary." A smile spread across her face. "And so incredibly sexy."

Chapter Forty-Nine

Startled from sleep, Brooke opened her eyes in bed. It took a second to process that it was Xander sitting next to her, sweating, and breathing like he had just sprinted a quarter mile. They hadn't meant to spend the night together; the beds were too small. But they had accidentally fallen asleep. It was obvious Xander had experienced a nightmare or one of his flashbacks. It seemed like he was getting worse, not better. She remembered the look in his eyes yesterday, during the fire alarm, and the raw power she witnessed.

"Sorry," he said, his chest rising and falling rapidly. Neither of them reaching to touch the other. "Again."

"It's okay. Were you having a nightmare? About finding John?"

"No." Xander exhaled forcefully as he struggled to steady his heartbeat. He'd had enough. He was exhausted and, as of yesterday's fire drill incident, he was turning into a monster. He had to move past this PTSD or it was going to ruin his life. And now . . . finally . . . with his recent nightmare, he understood what was going on. After the events in Kandahar he had subconsciously erected a mental blockade to protect him from the truth, allowing it to stand as a means to survive. But his experiences at medical school had destroyed key pieces of that barrier, and the truth had been slowly seeping through. He had to be brave and face it, to face what he had done, or he would never get better and he would continue to get worse until eventually the behavior that he most wanted to forget, the actions he was just now finally remembering clearly, would be acted out in public for the world to see. It had almost happened in the anatomy lab yesterday.

A shiver ran down his spine. "There's more to that story I told you."

"What are you talking about?" Brooke sat up under the covers.

"Everything I've told you. Everything I've told Dr. Chavez, there's more."

"What?" She put one arm around his glistening shoulder for support, pressed her body against his back.

"I've been remembering, just a little at a time. I didn't want to face it, but now I think I must. I know I do. I don't have a choice or I'm going to be dealing with this shit forever."

"It's okay. It's okay. But, I don't know what you mean. Please tell me." She gently stroked the back of his upper shoulder.

"I'm so sorry to put you through this."

There was a long pause before Brooke sighed and began speaking. "I've been in several situations where I had to take a big risk, I didn't feel I had a choice, so I had to risk everything, but it ended up being the right thing for me. In every instance I'm glad I did."

Xander scooted over so he sat on the bed, his back leaning against the wall, his legs on top of Brooke's legs. "I appreciate your compassion, but there's no way it could be anything remotely like what I've done."

"Why don't you tell me?" Brooke slid out from underneath him and curled her legs up in front of her. She wrapped her arms around Xander's arm. "You can tell me anything."

He needed to come clean. He wanted to get better and it wasn't going to happen unless he faced the truth and processed his emotions. That concept was the foundation of all psychiatric treatment, proven by droves of research. It was the whole point of going to therapy. Why did he think that he could receive the benefits of therapy without participating truthfully in the process? It had been unfair to Dr. Chavez and a waste of his time. He felt arrogant, foolish, and fearful. But he was more afraid of what he might do next if he had another flashback.

"Just tell me," Brooke said softly. "You need to get it out."

A voice in his mind warned him not to tell Brooke, and yet against all his better judgment, it was Brooke he needed to tell.

"Whatever it is, you can tell me. It will stay between the two of us and it won't change anything. I can keep secrets. I promise."

He sighed heavily, raised his head, and turned toward the window. An ambulance wailed past, he glimpsed its red flashing light visible around the edges of the shade. Taking another deep breath, he looked at Brooke. The sparkle in her beautiful blue eyes penetrated the darkness.

"Since that incident in Afghanistan that I told you about, I remembered things incorrectly, and I managed to forget the truth. Until that first day in the anatomy lab. That's when I started to remember. Just small, disturbing pieces at first, I didn't know what to make of them, but now I remember all of it. I remember it perfectly. I know exactly what happened during the ambush in Kandahar."

He dropped his head, questioning what he was about to do, but he wanted and needed to tell her.

"I didn't find John when I returned with the other unit. I found him before we left. I was alone. When the alarms went off and our unit leader called us back, Charlie followed them, but I didn't. I didn't follow orders. I was already so close to the building. I was close enough that I couldn't leave John."

Brooke placed her hand on Xander's chest, remaining silent and still.

"Smoke was everywhere, so it was hard to see. Three guys from my unit were down on the ground and I could tell they were gone. John wasn't there. The insurgents had run off, all but one. I saw him moving, he was wearing an Afghani uniform, he had a long straggly beard. I followed, into the next room, and the one after that, until I saw him. But first, I saw John. I recognized his civilian clothes. He was backed into the corner. I shouted to him, for a split second I was so relieved. The man I followed was there too, stepping backwards, away from John. He turned and stared at me, he held a knife in his hand, and he grinned."

Xander pressed his fingers against his head and groaned. "It must have happened in a split second. When I looked back to John, his hands flew up around his own neck, blood was pouring out, and his body slumped down against the wall. I was too late. Like an f-ing second too late. The insurgent had slit John's throat." Xander choked on his words. "He murdered my friend and he stood there grinning at me."

Brooke was gripping Xander's arm. "Is that it?"

Xander shook his head. "He turned and ran. And I lost it. I didn't think I would ever lose it under pressure, not that way, but I did."

Xander's voice was calm, but the emotion and distress he was experiencing were evident throughout his tense body and in his carefully chosen words, spoken for the first time ever.

"I must have forgotten about all the firepower I was carrying. I sprinted across the room, tackled him from behind, just like we were on the field at Memorial Stadium. He was bony, half the size of the smallest player I'd ever taken down, and I tackled him like he was a 250-pound fullback. He hit the ground like he'd fallen from a two-story building. I could have easily captured him, but I couldn't feel anything except rage. I wanted to destroy him. He killed my friend, a good man who had left behind the family he loved and traveled thousands of miles to help strangers have a better life."

Xander shuddered. "The knife flew out of his hand and skidded across the ground, and I grabbed it. He was yelling, nothing I could understand, angry, ugly, frightened words in Pashto. I flipped him over and pinned him down, I was like a crazed animal. I plunged his knife into his body and sliced through his abdomen. I was out of control, I didn't think about what I was doing or why. And I still wasn't finished. I lifted him up. I could have carried someone three times his size right then. I ran toward the wall with his body and smashed it face first against exposed beams. When I backed away, he was fastened there. His insides had spilled out of his abdominal cavity and he was caught, suspended sideways, hanging by his own intestines. It was horrific, and I turned away."

Xander took a deep breath.

"When I turned around, John's eyes were open, looking straight at me, and I realized what I had done. He was dead, and I was alone, covered in a stranger's blood and gore. I prayed John hadn't died while witnessing my barbaric actions. I was disgusted. Horrified. I vowed that no one would ever know what happened. I would never tell. And then, by some miracle, I managed to erase all of it from my memory. I carried John out of there, his blood pouring over me, concealing the blood of the man I murdered."

Brooke nodded. "Is there more?"

"All those rules I told you about, I'm the one that broke them. I'm the one who crossed the line. I'm the one who was sick and out of control. I killed someone I could have easily captured. I repressed the memory, and when it came back, I couldn't believe what I'd done. For months now, I tried to convince myself that the returning memories were only fragments of a disturbing nightmare."

Xander remained still in her arms, his shoulders slumped forward.

"It's okay. Everything is going to be okay now." She wrapped her arms around his body, squeezing him hard. His catharsis had left him exhausted. He fell back asleep in Brooke's arms. There were no more nightmares.

Chapter Fifty

Brooke woke before Xander. Her legs were cramped from sharing the small bed with his large body. She carefully extracted her legs from underneath his and got up to use the restroom. Xander was still sound asleep when she returned, so she quietly rolled out her yoga mat and began to practice.

Brooke pondered Xander's story. She was pleased that he had also taken a life. But the more she considered what he told her, the more obvious their differences became. When he finally revealed the truth, she perceived his deep-seated sadness and profound remorse. Killing had upset him so much that he developed partial amnesia and believed something altogether different had happened. And all because he didn't deem his actions necessary.

Brooke knew, with unwavering confidence, that every time she had killed someone—at Cedarhurst, Everett, at that Harvard party, and now, most recently at Rothaker—it had been necessary. In fact, it was for the greater good, because once she was a cardiothoracic surgeon, she would be responsible for saving hundreds or thousands of lives. She wanted Xander to understand. And that could only happen by sharing a piece of her true self. But would he get it? She was ready to try.

When Xander's eyes opened, she greeted him with a sweet smile, abandoning her yoga mat to jump onto the bed and hold him.

"Good morning." She snuggled into his arms. "I want you to know that nothing has changed and I'm not afraid of you." She began kissing his neck.

Xander ran his fingers gently through her long blonde hair, something he couldn't stop doing since they had begun touching each other. They stayed that way for a while until he got up to stretch and take a bottle of water from her fridge.

"I found someone dead once," Brooke began tentatively, watching his profile as he drank. He was so strong and cut that she could see the fascinating contraction of his muscles with every movement. "It was at Cedarhurst."

"Really?" His voice was thick from sleep. He put the bottle back and walked toward the bed.

"A professor, my mentor."

Xander raised his brows. "That science professor at Cedarhurst? The one who was found dead in his office by a student?"

Brooke sat up quickly, alert, her mood completely changed. "How do you know that?"

"It came up in a search for college and deaths when I was looking up information about that girl from Everett. I only read the article because I remembered you saying you went to Cedarhurst. It said he had died, I think of a heart attack, and that he was found by one of his students, but it didn't have your name. I meant to ask you about it back then, but I forgot. I never dreamed that could be you. Why didn't you tell me before?"

"It's not something I like to talk about."

"Wow. That's quite a coincidence." Xander narrowed his eyes and angled away from her. "You knew someone who either died or disappeared at every school you've attended."

Brooke gritted her teeth. In a split second her self-preservation instinct was on red alert and she was no longer willing or prepared to share a single secret.

Xander ran his hand through his hair and bit down on his lip. "I'm sorry. That was insensitive. You don't have to talk about it."

"No, it's fine. I was going to tell you that I also happened to find someone that I cared about, right after that person died. That was all. And . . . I don't know, I just thought that maybe I could relate to you just a little. I know it's different, but . . . never mind."

Brooke stood from the bed and paced around the room, picking at her fingernails.

"You're upset. Did I say something?" Xander moved toward her. "Let me help you, for a change." He wrapped her in his arms and held her, kissing the top of her head, then her nose, using one arm to lightly caress her shoulders. He didn't let go until long after he felt her body relaxing, and she finally tilted her head up to find his kiss.

Brooke leaned away to look into Xander's eyes. "I'm really happy about us." A smile curled the corners of her mouth. "We're good together."

"Hmmm," he murmured.

"Any obstacles, any roadblocks in our future, we'll destroy them together."

"Deal." He nodded, but she saw something pass behind his eyes, like something had registered and it wasn't quite right.

Chapter Fifty-One

"Let's reevaluate the work we covered in your last session," Dr. Chavez settled into his seat. "How have you been since then?"

"Well . . . I had a terrible flashback, and I almost hurt one of my classmates. I thought he was an insurgent. I thought he was the guy that killed John."

"You should have called me." Dr. Chavez frowned and moved forward in his chair. "If you're in danger of hurting yourself or anyone else, there are additional precautions we can take, additional meds."

"I also had a serious breakthrough." Xander smiled and watched the doctor's expression change. "It was huge. I think I should start getting better now."

A slight smile crossed the psychiatrist's lips. "Tell me about it."

"You're not going to like this, but once I started having flashbacks and nightmares I started remembering bits of things that happened in Kandahar. Except I didn't know they were real, so I tried to ignore them, you know, focus on what I thought had happened instead. It wasn't until recently that I figured it out. I had blocked out the truth, because it was terrible, more terrible than I told you." Xander relayed the story that he now knew to be the truth.

The doctor settled back into his seat. "It's all making sense, isn't it? All your questions about what humans are capable of doing—you were having issues trusting your *own* behavior. You were concerned about your own capacity for violence."

"I think I had some clues then, but I didn't have all the pieces."

"Your brain was designed to protect you. It set up a giant obstacle to protect you from the truth."

"Yes, it did." The word "obstacle" reminded him of Brooke. He had heard her say it a few times. Obstacles and roadblocks. She must have run into her share of obstacles in the past, although whatever problems they posed, she had clearly overcome them. If he was recalling correctly, she had even referred to Rachael as an obstacle, or had said that Rachael was putting roadblocks in her path. It was almost a familiar phrase for Brooke—'when obstacles fell in your path, they needed to be destroyed.'

"Any other thoughts?"

"Huh?"

"I said, any other thoughts?"

"Oh." He nodded. "I hope to never be in a situation like that again, but I have learned something important for going forward."

"And what's that?"

"I know what can happen to me when I try to block the truth. The next time I have to face an uncomfortable reality, no matter how difficult the situation, I'll deal with it head on."

Chapter Fifty-Two

Brooke and Xander returned from a long run and went straight to her bedroom where they released all remaining energy. When they were finished, they lay in bed for a short time, feeling luxuriously relaxed.

"We should have showered first," Brooke laughed. "We were so sweaty I have to wash my sheets now."

"Any other big weekend plans?" Xander joked.

While Brooke summarized their plans for the rest of the weekend, Xander appreciated that he hadn't had a single flashback in a week, not since he told Brooke and Dr. Chavez the truth about what happened. He didn't feel good about what he had done in Kandahar, but he had to move on and make up for it. He was reluctant to jinx his recovery, but all signs indicated his anxiety was greatly reduced and he was returning to his former self. Yet, there was a nagging feeling in the back of his conscience. It was like what he had experienced with his flashbacks, a basic awareness that something wasn't as it seemed, the puzzle wasn't fully together yet. The pieces were all available, but critical connecting parts were just out of reach.

Brooke left to take a shower and Xander planned to follow her, but her phone chimed and he grabbed it, without thinking. It was a message from Robert.

You never responded, so, I hope my last comment didn't upset you.

He should mind his own business, but with a message like that, he couldn't help himself, he needed to know what Robert was talking about. He wasn't going to let another man get away with upsetting his girlfriend. Brooke's phone had no password, so he went straight to her messages. There were very few that weren't from him. The last text from

Robert read: *Hi. Caught your news interview. Very convincing, anyone would have thought Rachael was your best friend.*

Xander didn't know exactly what to make of the message, but it sounded as if Brooke disliked Rachael more than Xander suspected, and she had told Robert as much. Unfortunately, he couldn't ask her about it without admitting to an invasion of her privacy. He would join her in the shower and forget about the texts.

His clothes were soaked with sweat from his run and he didn't want to put them back on. One of Brooke's many crisp white towels was all he needed to wrap around his waist. He didn't know where she kept them, but there were only so many places to look in a room of that size. Opening the door to one of her closets revealed a pair of cute red pants. He had never seen her wear them. She always wore jeans or her workout clothes. He lifted them towards him, imagining how the tight stretchy fabric would look great clinging to her curves. As he released them, he heard a faint "ping, ping" as something small hit the tile floor.

Whatever it was, it had fallen from the pocket of the red pants, and he needed to find it. He squatted down, picking up Brooke's perfectly arranged shoes one by one until he spotted a small silver earring. It was just like the ones his sister always wore. He found its mate, which had bounced off to the back corner of the closet. And then he remembered who else always wore those earrings. He froze. His heart beat faster, blood drained from his face and a terrible feeling rose from his stomach. The missing puzzle pieces fell into place and he could see the big picture. And once again, he hoped he was just having a bad dream.

Chapter Fifty-Three

Brooke returned from the shower to find Xander dressed and sitting on her bed. He was looking down but lifted his chin to face her as she entered. His serious expression sent a wave of trepidation coursing through her. "Hey. What happened to you? You need to shower."

"Where did you get these?" The commanding tone of his voice was new to Brooke. For an instant she frowned, even before she saw what he was holding, but she quickly recovered. He uncurled his fist to reveal the objects in his open palm.

"What do you mean, where did I get those? Where did *you* get those?"

"These are Rachael's earrings. They were in the pocket of your pants hanging in your closet. I just found them."

"Are you sure? Because I don't know how Rachael's earrings got in my pants. Seriously." She opened her eyes wide, returning his gaze with one that was equally as steady.

"You hated her, didn't you? I saw a message about it."

"No." She shook her head. "She wasn't my favorite person, but I didn't hate her. Why would you ask that? What message?"

Xander rose from the bed and strode toward the refrigerator. He yanked opened the door and scanned the interior, moving fruit and almond milk from side to side. "What happened to that tissue container?"

Brooke sighed and spoke slowly, as if Xander were a confused child. "I don't know what you're talking about."

"There was a specimen container in your refrigerator a few weeks ago." Xander scrubbed his hand over his face. "What was in it?"

"I'm sorry, Xander, but like I said, I don't know what you're talking [illegible]. Are you having another flashback?" She stepped back from him and wrapped her arms around her body, as if she was afraid. "Do you understand that you're in the medical school dorm, in your girlfriend's room right now?"

Xander dropped his gaze to the floor. She stepped forward and placed her hand gently on his shoulder. "There was never a specimen container in my refrigerator, Xander. I think you're confused." The look on her face conveyed understanding and compassion. "Here, let me get you a bottle of water. You should sit back down."

Xander accepted the water and allowed Brooke to lead him back to her bed and massage the back of his neck.

"Paranoia is one of the symptoms of post-traumatic stress disorder. It wasn't that long ago that you momentarily believed Sundeep was an insurgent. But don't worry, we'll get through this."

"No, that's not . . ." Xander squeezed his eyes shut and tried again. "You called Rachael an obstacle once, after we watched your news interview. And I remembered that you've told me several times that obstacles need to be destroyed." Xander's tone was questioning rather than convicting. "And you have her earrings."

"Rachael was my friend. And I'm your girlfriend. Did you stop taking your meds, sweetie?" She wrapped her arm around him.

Xander didn't say anything for several seconds. "I did. Recently." He clutched the edge of the bed. "I guess . . . I guess it may have been premature."

He leaned forward, dropping his head between his hands. A slight moan escaped his lips. "I don't know what to think right now. I really don't."

"Don't worry, Xander. I'll handle this." A smile slowly formed as she stared at the wall above him, eyes gleaming. "I'll take care of you."

The End

NOTE TO READERS

Dear readers,

First, thank you for reading! *Rothaker* is one of my very first books. I wrote it several years ago with this cliffhanger ending. I wanted the reader to use their imagination to conclude what Brooke really meant by "I'll take care of you." If you're really dark, you probably imagined the worst-case scenario for poor Xander. And if you wanted to believe Brooke is capable of truly caring for someone, then you might have chosen the option that she was going to make sure Xander was okay. That's how I wanted the book to end, with the reader choosing the outcome. There were no plans for a third book at the time.

A few years later, I guess I missed writing about my tenacious psychopath, who really needs a huge lesson in conflict resolution, so I started book three, *The Intern.* As a result, you'll know for sure what she meant. I hope it doesn't disappoint. The first two chapter are below.

Jenifer Ruff

EXCERPT - THE INTERN

Chapter One

Seven months had passed without another murder, and Brooke Walton intended to keep the streak going. She had too much to lose—her reputation as an accomplished medical student and her future as a surgeon— if she should ever get caught. And the drama that ultimately followed every death and disappearance exhausted her, carrying on for weeks and months after each incident. She wanted to focus on school and for everyone else to mind their own business.

Wedged against the door in the back seat of a small rental car with her two sisters, she stared at the disappointing scenery along Cancun's main road. Clumps of dry mangled shrubs and barren brown fields. Two rail-thin men on a decrepit front porch, tank tops exposing jutting collar bones. So far, Cancun bore no resemblance to the magical oasis touted on the resort's website. Still, it might be perfect. She shifted her gaze from the back of her father's head to her mother's. What they didn't know wouldn't hurt them.

Sydney lowered her paperback and squinted at Brooke. "What are you grinning at?"

Brooke avoided her sister's eyes. "Just . . . excited to be here." She lifted her long, blonde hair off her shoulders and rubbed her neck.

"She survived a grueling week of medical school final exams." Their mother gazed at a travel brochure about windsurfing, not bothering to look up. "She has every right to smile."

Brooke felt sorry for her father, who had single-handedly planned their four-night vacation, bought five plane tickets, and paid for the resort. She wondered how he had afforded it on his salary. Professors at Cedarhurst, a small private school, weren't exactly raking in a fortune. And now, in addition to helping with some of her medical school expenses, her parents were paying for Sydney to attend a special school for kids with learning disabilities. The tuition alone cost more than her mother's net salary as a social worker.

Brooke's legs twitched with pent-up energy. She'd been sitting still for too many hours, first on the plane, and now the car ride, attempting to ward off claustrophobia. She needed to go for a run.

After forty-five minutes of hoping the resort would be around the next corner, a large and colorful sign announced *Casa de Royale.* At the end of a long driveway lined with tropical flowers and swaying palm trees, a group of young men carrying colorful drinks sauntered by. The Waltons parked in the circular entry and a uniformed man approached. "Welcome Señor, and your beautiful family." He opened the passenger side door with a grand sweeping gesture. "If you will open your trunk, Ramon will unload your luggage."

"I'll get my own bag." Brooke leaped out and hurried to the back of the car. "I'll meet all of you up at the room. I'm going to take a quick look around. Check out the gym."

"Okay." Her mother glanced at the deepening shadows on the horizon. "Just be careful."

"Always."

****

"Welcome to our room," Sydney shouted when Brooke knocked on the door. "We're already unpacked."

Brooke glanced around. Clothes littered the floor, phone chargers trailed to wall outlets, and small piles of sand surrounded discarded shoes. All five of them together in one room. She dropped her bag next to a cot. "I need to go for a run."

"It's dark." Mrs. Walton zipped up her empty suitcase and turned to her husband. "Ian, do you think it's a good idea?"

Mr. Walton scratched his chin and peered out the window at the moon. "Just don't go far."

"I'm not being unreasonable." Mrs. Walton angled sideways so Sydney could pass by her. "People go missing. No one ever expects things like that to happen, but they do."

“I’ll stay on the beach, near the resorts.”

Mrs. Walton crossed the room to face her daughter. “How about this—just give me a few minutes and then we can all go for a walk together.”

“Mom, I really need to run. I’ll meet up with you later. I promise.” She hurried into the bathroom and closed the door, ending the conversation. After changing into workout clothes, Brooke examined her reflection in the mirror. Gorgeous and perfectly approachable, if someone had enough confidence. She hoped no one would. She wanted to be alone. She left the bathroom attaching her running belt and slipping her phone into the pouch.

“Okay, I’m going.” Brooke ignored her mother’s frown. Halfway out the door, she turned and dipped her head back inside. “Oh, Dad. I need the car key. I left my cap in the car.”

Mr. Walton tossed the car key. It was the old-fashioned kind, not a fob, but a long piece of etched metal attached to the rental company’s tag. Brooke caught it with one hand and stuck it inside her pouch.

****

Sparkles of light in the flower beds illuminated the path down to the beach. She sprinted toward the breaking waves once her feet hit the sugary sand. Dance music, conversations, and laughter spilled onto the shoreline. She passed a man and woman with their arms wrapped around each other, and another couple holding hands and walking unsteadily. The lights from *Casa de Royale* petered out after a short distance, but another resort picked up where its neighbor left off, casting a glow over the beach.

Brooke ran faster, adrenaline fueling her body and focusing her mind, alert and invincible, like nothing and no one could stop her.

Eventually, she’d run beyond the long string of resorts to an unlit area. Small homes nestled beyond the dunes at the end of meandering walkways. Her phone alarm rang. Forty minutes had passed. Time to turn around. Not exactly the quick run she’d promised her father, but it was necessary. She stopped to stretch, mesmerized by the endless expanse of ocean hiding so much below the surface. She'd always loved the night. She closed her eyes and let her senses succumb to the salty breeze and the rhythmic roar of the ocean.

She opened her eyes when she heard voices. Loud voices. Obnoxious laughter shattered the tranquility as two young men approached.

"Ha, come on, man. No way!"

"I'm not making it up. She was amazing."

"Pff! Right! That's bull and you know it."

Americans. Two of them. Both looking fit and attractive, like they spent a lot of time working out.

Brooke moved farther away from the water, towards a walkway railing and the tall, thick plants covering the dunes. She would wait for whoever they were to move along. They almost walked past, until they spotted her.

"Wait, what's that?" The question came from a young man, early twenties maybe, in a hooded sweatshirt and rolled-up jeans. He stopped walking and craned his neck toward Brooke. "Is she real?"

"Yeah, she's real." His friend snorted with laughter. "What the hell do you think she is? A ghost?"

The guy in the sweatshirt expressed his approval with a long, low whistle. He gaped for a few more seconds before moving toward her. His friend stayed back, the waves lapping around his ankles.

"Hi there. I'm John." He turned his head toward his friend. "And that's Rico." Facing Brooke, he shoved his hand into his front pockets. "What are you doing all alone out here?"

He was more muscular than he appeared at a distance. And cute with his short and spikey blonde hair. "I *was* enjoying the peace and quiet."

"We're headed to a party. Wanna come?"

"No, thanks. But have a good time."

"We'll have a better time if you come with us."

Brooke met his gaze and said nothing.

"I'm worried 'bout you being out here alone." John tilted his head toward the hotels down the beach. "Come on. We'll walk you back to . . . where did you come from? Staying in one of the resorts?"

"Just go on to your party, please."

"Are you sure? We have lots of friends there and plenty of beer." He moved a few feet closer, smiling. The scent of his expensive cologne mixed with the faint smell of beer on his breath. He extended his arm.

"Don't touch me." Brooke stepped backward, the edge of the wooden railing dug into her back.

John's white teeth glowed in the moonlight. "Rico, get over here. We need to convince this pretty little lady she's lucky we found her."

Brooke glanced up and down the deserted beach. She could outrun them, couldn't she? If she got around them. Her muscles tensed, and her heart beat steady yet fast, as if she was already sprinting. Both men had stepped uncomfortably close, inside her personal space. Without warning, John's arm shot out and grabbed hers.

Brooke's eyes grew wide. She struggled to pull her arm out of his grip.

Rico glanced over his shoulder before grabbing her other arm.

"It's all good baby. Just relax. Damn, you're smokin' hot. You really are."

They grinned like crazed clowns. Their large and muscular hands tightened around her upper arms, digging into her biceps when she tried to shake loose.

"This way. Hurry." John pulled Brooke forward.

Brooke dug her feet into the sand and they half-dragged her down the path between the dunes. Her eyes darted around. Still no one in sight. An unfamiliar helpless feeling swarmed through her body, threatening to spiral out of control. Never had she been anyone's victim. Never. The situation seemed surreal. It couldn't be happening. Not to her. More adrenaline flooded her system, swirling up a frenzy of instinct and panic.

No one else on the beach.

No one to hear a scream.

No one to witness what might happen.

Lips pressed tightly together, the corners of her mouth edged up into a slight grin.

Meaty fingers dug deeper into her upper arms, cutting off her circulation. She could barely move her hands, just enough to reach her running pouch. Silently, she slid the zipper open, moved the car key into her palm, and squeezed her fingers shut around it.

The jet-black outline of a cottage loomed closer.

Blood pounded through her temples.

"In here!" They pulled Brooke toward an outdoor shower room, opened the wide creaky wooden door, and shoved her inside. She stumbled forward through sticky strands of a giant spider web and fell against the tall wood-planks in the corner. There was no one staying at the house. No one to see or hear or stop an inevitable crime.

Rico let go of her arm and positioned himself inside the doorway, spreading his legs and blocking the exit. "Why isn't she yelling for help? It's messed up. Don't you think it's messed up?"

"She's into it. Right, baby?" John took rapid, shallow breaths, leering like a predator about to pounce. Brooke recognized the steely determination in his eyes. She could feel his frenzied longing and the surge of power coursing through his muscles and veins. Seeing all of it for the first time in someone else sent chills down her spine like an electric current.

"It might be fun." She lowered her eyes with a sly smile.

"Close the door!" John told Rico.

Anticipation swirled into the heady rush of her already heightened senses as Rico latched the wooden door shut.

Brooke burst forward. She gouged the jagged metal key into his eye, turned it like a corkscrew, and yanked it back out. With a shriek, he collapsed to the ground, gasping, blood streaming down one side of his face. A low guttural moan escaped his lips.

"What the hell?" Rico stared at his friend's grotesque injury and then the chunk of eyeball Brooke flicked off the key. He lurched forward and gagged.

Brooke lunged at Rico. She zigzagged the key, tearing through delicate eye tissue, plunging it into his cheek, and ripping it out through his mouth. His hands flew to his face and he staggered backward into the corner before falling to his knees. "Oh, my God! You demented bitch!" He gurgled through a gush of blood.

"Shut up," she hissed.

One hand pressed over his gaping wound, Rico pulled out his phone. "I'm calling—"

"No, you're not." Brooke bared teeth with her smile. She kicked his phone out of his hand, slamming the heel of her shoe into the raw flesh of his torn cheek. He screamed in agony and turned around to shield his face, rocking forward on his knees.

John stared up at her from the ground, his lips trembling. He lifted a hand into the air as if to say he surrendered. "Get the hell away from me." His voice was shrill and hard to hear over Rico's uncontrollable whimpering.

"I don't think so." She laughed. "We're just getting started."

Quivering with a euphoric high, she glimpsed the ripped suspensory ligaments dangling from John's eye socket. She yearned to touch the bloody, fibrous elements glistening in the moonlight, but not yet . . .

John reached into his back pocket, his hand violently shaking, and pulled out a knife. In a heartbeat, Brooke pounced, tossing the key, and snatching the knife away. A crooked, unnerving smile appeared below her gleaming eyes as the blade sprung open. The pocket knife was nothing compared to the efficient tools she'd left at home, her favorite toys: a scalpel, a razor, and a bone saw, but it would get the job done.

"You're insane, lady! Just leave!"

She shook with laughter at the absurd thought of stopping now. She couldn't if she tried. There wasn't enough willpower in the world. Her heart pounded with excitement.

"Just go! We're not going to hurt you."

Her smile spread. “Oh, I guarantee you aren’t. But you wanted to.” She gazed at the moonlit glint of the blade. Long enough to reach through the thin bones behind their eyes and into their skulls. Long enough to lacerate their brains.

A lightning-fast stab, in and downward, destroyed John’s ability to breathe. Rico met the same fate when Brooke leaped on him from behind as he struggled to leave. In utter fascination, she watched the men choke and gasp for snatches of oxygen, twisting and flailing on the ground until their remaining eyes shone up unseeing at the dark sky. She licked her lips, dragged their bodies together and lined them up side by side. They were big, but lean. Just perfect. Without the layers of fat that so often made dismembering a challenging task.

After removing her clothes, shoes, and running belt, she set them in a neat pile outside the shower. She turned on her phone’s flashlight and propped it up against the shower wall, enhancing the moonlight, and then went to work, savoring the feel of the knife cutting across John’s skull. Unable to stop smiling, she peeled his skin down over his face to reveal the well-developed muscles in his neck.

****

In room 212 at the Casa de Royale, Mr. Walton’s phone pinged with a text. His wife glanced at the screen. “Ian, it’s a message from Brooke.”

“What does she say?”

“She said—I met up with some people my age. I’m having fun. Be back soon. Please don’t worry about me.” Mrs. Walton set down the phone and turned on her side. “Well, what do you think about that?”

“It’s fine.” Mr. Walton slid the phone back off the nightstand, typing. *Okay. Be careful. Don’t trust a stranger. Don’t go to anyone’s hotel room. Text us in half an hour.* He hit send.

“I wish she hadn’t gone.” Mrs. Walton placed her hand on her husband’s arm.

“She’ll text us.” Mr. Walton opened his novel. “She’ll be careful. She’s a smart girl.”

“I know. You’re right.”

“Bottom line, she needs to get out more, not less. She starts that internship as soon as she gets back. Let her have some fun.”

Chapter Two

Brooke dropped a messy armful of John and Rico onto the sand. She scooped up a forearm and hurled it into the ocean, watching it disappear under the churning black water. She chose a foot next, throwing each part as far as she could until the pile disappeared. Behind her, noisy and massive gulls dove into the outdoor shower for a fresh feast, squawking and fighting over choice morsels.

Getting rid of John and Rico would take a few more trips back and forth between the shower and the ocean. Each trip presented a risk. How would she ever explain carrying a bloody mess of body parts? How could anyone? And she'd already been gone much longer than she had planned. Her parents would be waiting up for her, worried. The seagulls and crabs could take care of whatever the sharks didn't. Most likely, the scavengers had already flown away carrying sections of the men's peeled-off faces.

She put her clothes back on, placed her phone behind a large piece of driftwood, and dug a deep hole to bury their wallets. With handfuls of wet sand, she began scrubbing her clothes, her skin, her shoes, and John's pocket knife. She wasn't taking any chances. Fully clothed, she walked into the ocean, through the crashing waves, until the warm water slapped at her chest. She lowered herself so she was fully immersed below the surface. The waves knocked against her, tugging and swirling at her clothes like a giant washing machine. When she could no longer hold her breath, she burst out of the water, closed John's knife, and threw it as far toward the horizon as she could.

Carrying her sopping shoes, she ran back to the resort wearing a grin of satisfaction. No need to worry. There was nothing to connect her to the mess she'd left behind. Those men deserved what happened. They wanted to rape her. She shuddered. Maybe they would have assaulted someone else tomorrow, and someone else the night after. Maybe they had already harmed others. Once a person acquired a taste for *certain things*, and the euphoric surge of energy that accompanied carrying out *those things* there was no stopping them. She, of all people, understood.

I didn't go looking for trouble. I didn't intend to kill them. It wasn't my fault. They all but begged for it.

Others might experience guilt. Like a wave deep in the ocean, it would start to build, surging forward, gaining strength, eventually washing over them, sucking them under. Her body wasn't wired for remorse like a normal person, and she was grateful for that immunity. Who needed it?

When she opened the hotel room door, every member of her pajama-clad family was still awake. Sydney was lying under the covers, iPad in her hands. Amanda was lying on her stomach with her phone. Her father had a book in his lap and her mother had a Kindle.

Amanda rolled over and sat up. "You were gone like practically forever."

Mr. Walton jammed his book mark between the pages and snapped his book shut. "What happened to texting in half an hour?"

"Sorry. My phone battery died."

"You went out like…*that*?" Mrs. Walton frowned, eyeing her daughter's wet hair and clothes.

"Yeah. We were swimming."

"Even your shoes are wet." Amanda pointed to a strand of seaweed stuck to Brooke's shoes.

Brooke grinned sheepishly. "What can I say? It was unexpected fun."

Mrs. Walton sighed. "I know you're an adult and I know you can be out whenever you want when you're at school, but when you're with us, we worry. We can't help it."

Mr. Walton nudged his wife's arm and they exchanged a look.

"Well, you can stop worrying now. I'm back." She grabbed a soft dry T-shirt out of her bag.

"We're glad you had fun." Mr. Walton got up from the bed. "Just put the car key on the dresser. Somehow, we forgot the bag with the sunscreen. I'm going to drive to a store early tomorrow and buy some."

He opened his book, grumbling. "Costs a fortune at a resort. We could have bought three at Walmart for the price of one."

"Okay." Brooke unzipped her pouch. She swept her fingers from left to right.

Nothing.

She turned the pouch inside out.

Empty.

"Oh, no. Oh, no."

"What happened?" Mrs. Walton set her Kindle down.

"I can't find the key."

"You lost it?" Sydney's jaw dropped.

"Yes." Brooke gazed up toward the ceiling. A sick feeling spread from her stomach to her throat.

Mr. Walton stepped over the clothes and shoes strewn across the floor. "Maybe you left it in the car door."

"No. I didn't." Brooke sat down on the cot and dropped her head into her hands.

Amanda raised her eyes from her phone. "If you don't know where you lost it, then how can you know it's not in the car door?"

"It's not in the car door!" Brooke gritted her teeth to keep her body from trembling.

"Calm down. No need to get worked up. It's okay, we'll find it—ow!" Mr. Walton lifted his foot off Amanda's curling iron and kicked it out of the way. "Don't let losing the key ruin the vacation. It's not the end of the world. I'm sure the rental agency has an extra one. They can bring it before we leave. And I can suck it up and pay extra for the sunscreen." He laughed.

"I'll try to look for it tomorrow." Brooke crossed her arms, clutching and kneading her muscles.

"Relax." Mr. Walton put his hand on his daughter's shoulder. "There's nothing we can do about it now. This stuff happens. It's not like someone died."

"Yeah." Amanda's shoulders slouched as she returned her

attention to her phone.

“I hope they don’t charge a bunch to replace it.” Sydney stretched forward, past her toes.

“I’m sure someone will find it.” Mrs. Walton got out of the bed and headed toward the bathroom. “It has numbers on it, it’s coded. So, when they do, it will be easy to call the rental agency and trace it back to us.”

Brooke’s heart was heavy. Worry and fear pulsed in waves through her body, leaving her nerves sharp and raw, and an empty vulnerable feeling in her stomach.

****

If you’re interested in reading more, *The Intern* is available in ebook, paperback, and audio book from Amazon.

JOIN MY READER'S GROUP

Sign up to join my reader's group for special giveaways and perks. You can get advanced review copies of my new books for free. You won't hear from me often, just a few times a year, but when you do, it should be fun! Visit my contact page at Jenruff.com to sign up.

OTHER BOOKS BY JENIFER RUFF

The Brooke Walton Series

Everett

Rothaker

The Intern

The FBI & CDC Series

Only Wrong Once

Only One Cure

The Agent Victoria Heslin Series

The Numbers Killer

Pretty Little Girls

When They Find Us

Ripple of Doubt

Middle Grade Suspense

Lauren's Secret

ACKNOWLEDGEMENTS

While writing *Rothaker*, I received invaluable encouragement from several people. My parents, Blaise and Linda Bisaillon, who have always been there for me. My good friends in Charlotte: CeCe Curran, whose insightful intelligence and enthusiasm was extraordinarily helpful, and Paige Laurie, the queen of positive encouragement, who never allowed me a discouraging word. I am grateful to Susan Brause, MD, who made sure the book was accurate from a medical school perspective, Steve Callahan of Northampton, MA, who read Rothaker with a critical eye, and Tim Bisaillon, DHS Agent, who advised on the military aspects. Of course, my incredibly smart husband, Mike, for being calm in every storm and for repeatedly fixing my computer. And also, my youngest son, Matthew, a voracious reader who helped me to find the right word many times.

COPYRIGHT

Second Edition
ISBN-13: 978-1537293424
ISBN-10: 1537293427
Publisher: Greyt Companion Press
Cover: Kim G Design

Made in the USA
Las Vegas, NV
14 May 2021

23048897R00148